Let's Get Criminal

ALSO BY LEV RAPHAEL

*Hot Rocks*
*Tropic of Murder*
*Burning Down the House*
*Little Miss Evil*
*The Death of a Constant Lover*
*The Edith Wharton Murders*
*Secret Anniversaries of the Heart*
*Writing a Jewish Life*
*The German Money*
*Dancing on Tisha B'Av*
*Edith Wharton's Prisoners of Shame*
*Winter Eyes*
*Journeys & Arrivals*
*My Germany*

# Let's Get Criminal

## A Nick Hoffman Mystery

Lev Raphael

Lethe Press
Maple Shade NJ

ISBN: 1-59021-204-5 / 978-1-59021-204-2

---

Library of Congress Cataloging-in-Publication Data

Raphael, Lev.
   Let's get criminal : a Nick Hoffman mystery / Lev Raphael.
      p. cm.
   Originally published: New York : St. Martin's Press, 1996.
   ISBN 1-59021-204-5 (alk. paper)
   1. Literature teachers--Fiction. 2. College teachers--Fiction. 3. Michigan--Fiction. I. Title.
   PS3568.A5988L4 2009
   813'.54--dc22
                                        2009036716

For Gersh: "one love, one lifetime…"

"… oddity is the natural condition of mankind."

—Anton Chekhov, *Uncle Vanya*
(transl. by Michael Frayn)

# - 1 -

From the beginning—even before the beginning—Stefan had said it was none of our business. He kept saying that, but he meant it was none of my business, because I tend to be too nosey.

Still, I thought that my new office mate, Perry Cross, had something to hide. He had just been hired as an assistant professor of Canadian literature, and everything about the situation was suspicious. For starters, given the terrible state of Michigan's economy and the cutbacks at the State University of Michigan (SUM), where did the money come from for this brand-new position? And why was Canadian Studies suddenly so important at the university? And how come my department (English, American Studies, and Rhetoric), where Cross would be teaching, was filled with so many rumors about this guy and his job? I had not been on the hiring committee (I was too new), but people were saying the whole process had been interfered with at different points by the chair or perhaps the dean of the Humanities College. I also heard rumors that the decision to create the job in the first place and hire *Cross* had come from high up in the administration. There had been no talk about equal opportunity hiring, which was very strange, given that our department (EAR) was top-heavy with white Christian men. It was also strange that the strong "internal" candidate—Serena Fisch, who was already teaching in EAR—had not been seriously considered for the new position.

And I thought it was odd that I hadn't met Perry Cross until a week before the fall semester began. One day I came in and found some cartons stacked on the other side of my office, with a note from Claire, the department chair's secretary, saying they belonged to Perry Cross. Well, I knew he would be sharing my office, so that was no surprise, but I would have thought he'd want to get there early to settle in.

Then there was Perry himself. I wondered about him. I wondered about him *a lot*. I overheard him talking about Ann-Margret too much. It was apparently his little joke, how he'd always had the hots for her, seen all her movies, wanted to give blood when she fell in Vegas—remember, off that thirty-foot platform?—and when Perry was "free" (between marriages), *she* wasn't. Of course he thought she was the best thing ever to happen to Tennessee Williams when she did *Streetcar* on television. I suppose it's like being fourteen and saying, "Boy, if I had *her*" (fill in your own blank), and all your friends leer and shift their legs to give themselves some room. But a man in his thirties, a professor at a big Midwestern state school? It just didn't sound right—it was a cover, and the two marriages were a cover. Perry had to be gay.

"Who cares?" Stefan asked, when I kept bringing it up.

"Material," I said. "It could be material for your writing. Flaubert said that all literature begins as gossip."

"He did not! That's just something you'd tell your freshmen and when they'd write it down, you'd laugh and admit you made it up."

Stefan was right. I *do* have a fondness for inventing quotes, especially faced with thirty or more hands busily filling notebooks with information that is generally useless.

My specialty is Henry James and Edith Wharton, but mostly I teach freshman composition, in the same department as Stefan and Perry Cross—though as the State University of Michigan's writer-in-residence, Stefan is among the elite in the humanities and I'm just a foot soldier.

Most people complain about teaching basic writing courses, but I'm quite good at it. I can help my students revise their work without trying to make them sound like me, and I often connect and help kids see their writing differently, help them discover how to grow, how to find and develop their own voice. I know I sound like one of those Reach Out and Touch Someone ads, but that's how I feel when it works.

It certainly didn't hurt that I also loved living in mid-Michigan and just *being* at SUM. The university is in the state capital, Michiganapolis, an overgrown but unpretentiously pretty college town full of clean and pleasant streets, well-kept homes, nothing very ostentatious or even very old; the gracefulness is of recent vintage, but with all the unassuming charm that I think of as typically Midwestern. Even the golden-domed capitol building and the government offices seem somewhat unobtrusive because they're clustered at the opposite edge of town from the university, walling off the ragged manufacturing suburbs farther west.

While there may be nicer college towns in the country, there can't be a more beautiful college campus. Walking onto the enormous campus from town, which stretches along SUM's northern border, you feel like you're entering a wonderland. Whether the buildings are 1920s hulking pillared limestone, 1950s red brick with turquoise panels under the windows, or 1870s Romanesque sandstone, everything is in scale, with few buildings taller than the trees. It's all bound together by the curving roads and walks, lush flowering trees like cherries, apples, dogwoods, hawthorns, magnolias, redbuds; magnificent old weeping willows, maples, oaks, blue spruce, scotch pine; what seem like acres of lilac and forsythia; gloriously colorful courtyard gardens; brilliant ornamental beds of tulips, hyacinths, irises, gladioli, petunias. The campus is scrupulously maintained and tended, and the loving care the landscaping gets makes you feel you're on a private estate. Heading south away from town and past the river that cuts the campus in half, the trees thin out, buildings get more modern and more spread apart as you encounter wider lawns and greenhouses, and then miles of fields and farmland, stretching off to the horizon, reminding you that the school was originally an agricultural college. Even the sky seems more open over the southern end of campus.

Stefan and I were new to SUM. My cousin Sharon, who's as close as a sister, had asked me if Stefan would be comfortable

living so close to his father, who had just retired from teaching at
the University of Michigan in Ann Arbor, an hour away. It was
a good question, and just like her. But since Stefan's father rarely
called, and Stefan never did, there wasn't much of a problem. The
hour's drive guaranteed that there would be no casual dropping in.
So there was nothing to keep Stefan from enjoying SUM as much
as I did. He had finally come to like teaching, but he didn't like
me rhapsodizing too much about my classes and how happy I was
in Michiganapolis.

And Stefan did not want to hear me theorize about Perry Cross,
or anyone. He may observe people more than I do, but he keeps
what he sees for his novels. I'm the one who loves to speculate aloud,
to make up stories about couples at other tables in restaurants, to
latch onto phrases I've overheard at parties and tantalize myself
with what they might mean. It should be no surprise that my
favorite movie is *Rear Window.*

"Stop worrying about Perry Cross," Stefan said.

I pushed. "Why doesn't he come out?"

"It's not a good time for that."

Well, Stefan stopped me there. In Michigan, the AIDS
epidemic still was a bit unreal and exotic, like the hole in the
ozone layer—newsworthy, but distant. Yet it colored coverage of
gay issues or problems. Like when three arrests had been recently
made on campus, for sexual misconduct in a men's room at the
Union. They were all university employees. Their case had been
lurching from one grim headline to another all over the Midwest,
generating ugly letters in all the local papers. People wrote tirades
about the Devil and sin, filth, sickness, evil and all the rest, as if
the defendants were Jews in the Dark Ages. I was astonished by
the violent rhetoric of people who interlaced their threats with talk
of Christian charity and love—creepy! I found it most depressing
when letters like that appeared in the student newspaper. If that's
how bigoted and unfeeling these kids were *now,* what would they
be like out of school, working, voting, trying to make the world
over in their image? And for every student who wrote that kind of
letter, how many silently cheered when it was printed? How many

of those people were in my classes, hating not just gays but Jews and blacks and women?

As if the arrests and the scandal weren't enough, the outspoken head of the gay students' union had been harassed. It started with threatening letters and crank phone calls at his dorm. One night, the tires of his Escort were punctured and the windshield bashed in when his car was parked on campus near the Union building. The bumper sticker that read *Homophobia Is a Social Disease* had been smeared with dog shit. There had also been a number of openly gay and lesbian students mugged or threatened and chased, usually late at night, when shadows and darkness took over the enormous campus, mocking the feeble lampposts strung along the meandering concrete paths between buildings and along the river. Faculty members who had complained to the president about the "climate" on campus had not been reassured by his vague statement calling for "reestablishing harmony at SUM."

Given the current climate on campus, it was hard for me to disagree with Stefan.

"Okay," I said. "So it's a bad time to come out. But why doesn't Perry come out to *me?*"

"Maybe he doesn't like you."

"Toad."

"Or maybe you're so busy being gay you didn't notice."

"Snake."

Stefan grinned. "If you're so curious, why don't you ask Priscilla Davidoff to check him out? She writes all those mysteries."

"Feh!"

Priscilla Davidoff taught genre fiction in our department—romances, sci-fi, westerns, mysteries—and had the office catty-corner from mine in Parker Hall. She wrote pallid but polemical mysteries in which a murder was always the occasion for turgid debates about an Issue: drug abuse, alcoholism, child support. Her books were as colorless and free of suspense as the Amanda Cross mysteries.

Priscilla's office and mine were sort of off by themselves, given the eccentric way the narrower corridors in our frequently divided and subdivided building spread out from the larger ones. That made for quiet, because nobody passed our offices to get somewhere else, but it was also irritating sharing this little backwater with Priscilla. A few years before, she had written a quietly lethal review of one of Stefan's novels in *The New York Times,* accusing him of writing "egocentric" fiction. She was half-Jewish, so I suspected that she was really responding to the Jewish elements in Stefan's work (though that was certainly a problematic element for him).

"I still can't believe we ended up in the same department as her."

Stefan just shrugged, unfazed, while I muttered and stalked a little, wishing all manner of childish evil on Priscilla, like I usually did when her name came up.

I was trying to rouse him, but Stefan wasn't moved. It didn't even seem to bother Stefan that she was angry that a man—*him*—had been hired as writer-in-residence, instead of a woman.

"How can you be so calm about her?" I asked. "I think she slammed you for being Jewish."

Stefan shook his head, but I really didn't need to ask. Stefan did not viscerally respond to Jewish issues the way I did, and I had to continually remind myself of his past. Until he was seventeen, he had thought he was Catholic, the son of Polish refugees. His parents and the uncle who helped bring him up had all conspired in this fantasy, trying to hide their past as Jews and concentration camp survivors, and, more than anything, hide the terrible weight of death and devastation they had endured. But the secrecy couldn't last, and Stefan's father confessed it all when he was afraid he might be dying. While Stefan had long since stopped having a Christmas tree, he had not entirely switched allegiances. I thought of him as Jewish, but that wasn't exactly how he saw himself. More than twenty years after his father's confession, Stefan had still not entirely come to terms with what had happened in his family. Of course, that was the subject of much of his fiction: the struggle to reconcile disparate identities, to forgive, to speak the truth *clearly.*

"Forget Priscilla," Stefan said to me now. "*Forget her.*"

I was less charitable, and it was very awkward for me running into her in the hallway, though it was dark and deep enough for you to pretend you didn't see people—if you wanted to.

"And leave Perry Cross alone," he added. Stefan was looking at me a little sternly, and I blushed. You see, I had tried *luring* Perry out. I left some novels by Andrew Holleran and Edmund White on my desk in the office Perry and I were sharing, even an issue of *Christopher Street,* but he didn't bite.

By which I mean he didn't pretend not to notice, but what he said was so casual it couldn't seem false. Like Tina Turner sings, I just wanted a little reaction.

Just enough to tip the scales.

Because it wasn't just Perry's being gay that drew me. I confess that another reason he got to me was an obvious one: while he wasn't my type, I sure enjoyed looking at him. He was like one of those tightly knit '30s matinee idols—you wanted to find him a gold cigarette case just to see him take out a Dunhill, tap it once, twice, a gentleman's tap, and stick it into those knife-blade lips.

I started to say something else, but Stefan, he didn't want to hear any more about Perry Cross that evening. "I'll be in my study," he said, and I let it drop, going off to make coffee.

With Stefan's success, I discovered that I *love* being a votary of Literature: screening his calls, brewing his coffee, copyediting, fixing nummy snacks. It's not just a game, because I do believe in his writing. I find his work especially powerful not just compared to other gay writers but to straight writers too. Like the author of an awful fat bestselling book I'd recently read in which, as far as I could tell, the whole point was that a straight white man learned how to cry—after four hundred pages!

Stefan has said in interviews that without me, he wouldn't have made it. And so I felt involved in everything he wrote. When we met ten years ago, Stefan told me that his parents and his uncle Sasha were pushing him to drop "this writing thing" and get a real job. They thought he was wasting money on a degree in writing. Stefan was depressed and wondered if they might be right—after all, he hadn't been able to publish anything *yet.* Somewhat glibly, I told him that the power of parental doubts and prophecies of doom is often in inverse proportion to their accuracy. I was pleased with my formulation, but he just shrugged.

Stefan was even talking about dragging all his stories out of their folders and burning them, just to be free, clarified, to start over—or something.

"Oh, bullshit," I said. "That's just a scene from a cheap movie."

"Actually, writers *have done* that. Gogol, Henry James."

"Sure," I said. "But they were already published. Nobody ever started a career with a bonfire!"

He smiled.

"Are you any good?" I asked. "Well, just keep writing and shut up."

It wasn't a memorable line, but it helped. Like when a friendly old lady on a long bus trip nods and smiles as you reel off your life, your plans, and maybe she's not really following, maybe she's just waiting to talk about her grandchildren, but still it means something, still it feels nice. It helps.

It's not that I've ever been a frustrated writer myself. I've published a lot of academic work, but helping Stefan, I feel like I'm involved with something that will really last, will change people's lives, the way the best fiction does.

Of course, one side effect of Stefan's growing fame is that I get treated in odd and sometimes unpleasant ways. Like when interviewers call me and ask what it's like to live with him, because they want to add a bit of "the personal touch" to their articles. That makes me feel like I'm his housekeeper or something.

I'm always tempted to tearfully say, "What's it like living with him? It's hell!" and hang up, but I generally throw them some vague scraps about his work and bore them enough to make them leave me alone.

Even though I say almost nothing to people who want information about Stefan, the calls keep coming for me. I can't really blame the reporters. If I were an interviewer, I would dig as deeply as I could. Which is what made me so suspicious of Perry Cross. When he'd saunter into our office, he never seemed right as a junior faculty member. There was an air of privilege and masquerade—as if he were serving a strange kind of sentence and would soon be released into a richer, fuller life. Meanwhile, he had to put up with students, secretaries, and people like me who were both insignificant and, more annoyingly, unconvinced that he was as important as he estimated himself to be. With the job market so very bad now, you would have expected him to be grateful to have a tenure-track position at a decent school, maybe even cringe a little. But Perry Cross was too conspicuously confident and detached—and that didn't make sense to me.

Something about him just didn't add up.

# -2-

Being successful, being the new writer-in-residence, there was no way Stefan could avoid the faculty parties, though if possible, he would've sent me by myself since he wasn't fond of chatting. At a party, he often just sat back and observed people, comfortable with his own silence while others usually were not. It had taken me years to get used to his social silences and to stop feeling responsible, as if he were a shy child I had to coax into showing off in front of friends: "Come on, darling, show the Greenbergs your tap dancing." I had long since given up feeling I had to cover for Stefan in case people thought he was being critical, or worse, recording their quirks for a future book. It wasn't my job to make him talk, or to explain to anyone why he was quiet.

Stefan wasn't just quiet because of his personality or even his vocation—a lot of that was simply drawing back from all the foolishness he seemed to elicit as a novelist. Like when people sometimes auditioned for him, offering themselves up as fascinating prospects for fiction: "Wait till I tell you a *real* story!" Even the dreariest academic would fancy himself a Samuel Johnson just waiting for a Boswell, and non-academics often cheerfully told Stefan that they intended to write a book some day—when they had spare time—as if it were a grubby but worthwhile project like cleaning out the garage. To one engineer who said at a party, "They tell me everyone has a novel in them," I had snarled, "You'd be lucky to eke out a haiku," before Stefan dragged me away. But those were occupational hazards for Stefan, just as when I ventured outside of the world of professors and told peopie what I did, they often said, "I better watch my grammar, huh?"

At least at faculty parties, I didn't have to put up with people afraid I'd catch them splitting an infinitive. The anxieties were of a slightly higher order: would a dispute about political correctness erupt, or would someone be raving about a book that other professors hadn't heard of yet, or worse, just have come back from lunch with the author?

For Stefan, all that posturing and pouting was a waste of time. But me, I enjoy the parties, enjoy complaining about students as if we in the department were survivors of some great cataclysmic flood that had swept away all of Western civilization, except for us. Am I exaggerating? Not after four or five drinks. In an odd way, the faculty shared the same view as conservative politicians— that our country was being overrun by Visigoths—only *we* were faced with cultural illiterates, and the politicians feared culture and literacy both.

As usual, the fall semester party was at our chair's house. I did not like Lynn Broadshaw or his house. It started with something very small: feeling odd about his name. Coming from the East Coast, I had never before met a man called Lynn—though that was apparently common in Michigan—and it threw me. Beyond the name, Broadshaw just gave me the creeps. He was a stocky man in his fifties, with a pinched, angry pale face that made you feel even a "good morning" was an imposition. He had only a vestigial sense of humor, and ran department meetings with all the grace and charm of an auctioneer. He was loud, he was unpredictable, he was strange. He had a terrible temper and was often berating the department secretaries. Graffiti in the men's faculty bathroom near our department office said he was taking a correspondence course in Improving Your Interpersonal Relationships. The Remedial Level.

Stefan and I had only been at SUM a year, but Lynn had come in the 1950s when the university was expanding wildly, had always lusted after being chair (we heard), and ended up as chair for reasons no one could exactly make clear to me.

Just before we got to State, he'd had a stroke, and I imagine there were sighs of relief. It was generally assumed, I understood, that this reminder of his mortality was going to make him, if not cuddly, at least less demanding and dictatorial. No way. Fully recovered, he was worse than ever, as if trying to prove that he was alive by taking up far more space than one person needed.

His sprawling U-shaped house in the center of a Michiganapolis faculty neighborhood was rather sinister, an ostentatious series of barren gray and black spaces, with dark polished granite everywhere, and black Italian complicated-looking lamps and chandeliers. Meant to impress, it was balefully chic, an intellectual train station with an enormous cathedral ceiling and spotlighted Matisse drawing over the black marble mantel. But it was a good house for parties, with its enormous living room, dining room, kitchen, and den all open to one another—each room large and public.

Broadshaw greeted me at the door, pumped my hand with a grin as if he was holding himself back. If he really wanted to, the smile and the tight grip said, he could have tossed me over his shoulder like a scarf. He wore a flowing short-sleeved black silk shirt, black slacks, and black loafers. The scrupulously maintained tan made him look like a drug dealer on *Miami Vice.*

"Good to see ya," he growled. Broadshaw seemed to think I was not much more than a jumped-up graduate student, hardly worth his notice or his time, which is why he always shook my hand before Stefan's, I suppose—to get me out of the way.

"Great party," I said, breaking loose.

"Stefan Borowski!" Broadshaw bawled, as if he were announcing the winner of a prize, instead of welcoming a guest. He was always blaring Stefan's name when they met, almost like the way someone superstitious would knock wood, or as if he thought Stefan's growing reputation benefited him personally. He slapped Stefan's shoulders now like a father urging his son to stand up straight.

I tuned out while Stefan was being charming to Broadshaw, talking about some conference.

I saw Perry Cross standing at the unlit fireplace, drinking, holding his glass loose-wristed, elbow on the heavy mantel like someone on Masterpiece Theater. In his modish, wide-shouldered houndstooth suit and long, slicked-back hair, he was stylish enough to be in a Calvin Klein Obsession ad. For a moment, I imagined him dark and shiny, near naked, bisected by clingy white underwear....

Perry really did have what I could only think of as goyish appeal: that dark blond hair brushed straight back, the body whose lines were probably not blurred by hair and thus would seem impersonal, representative. He was in that way more of a statue than a man, and tonight I was surprised that he affected me at all. Usually I could look at a man like that with much more distance and aplomb because I was drawn to Jewish and Italian men, dark and hairy, with rugged open emotional faces, and *yes,* noses that were dramatic.

Perry Cross was surveying the crowd buzzing about the latest publications, the latest bits of rumor, and the looming budget cuts. Back in the early '80s, when the car industry almost collapsed, all the publicly funded universities in Michigan suffered bone-chilling cuts. It was at that time that a number of programs had been axed and faculty ranks were thinned by juicy offers of early retirement. SUM was supposedly in better shape now, but the Big Three automakers seemed to be in trouble again, and there was wild talk at the university of audits, departments being closed, tenured faculty getting laid off. It was a time when old grudges started to simmer again, and given the pettiness of many academic squabbles (bald men fighting for a comb), you could sometimes feel like you had stumbled into a gloomy second-rate opera where banditti were about to brandish long swords and burst into song. The feeling was strangely comic and depressing. I assumed that Stefan and I were safe, but I knew that if massive cuts came again, the turmoil would undermine our confidence and our teaching. It made me think of *Evita:* "... the knives are out."

When Broadshaw turned to someone coming in behind us, I pointed Perry Cross out to Stefan, who said he hadn't talked to him yet, and then I drifted into the stone-walled kitchen that was as big and dreary as a dungeon. I said something innocuous to Broadshaw's wife Maria, a plump and sexy Argentinean who generally laughed at almost any remark, as if she was playing the part of some dim-witted islander in a movie about the South Seas. It was definitely an act because her dark eyes were cold and unyielding. Tonight she was as chic as usual, and her white clingy sheath made her look even younger than her forty years. Supposedly, she "came from money," but no one could tell me how.

Maria had a way with hors d'oeuvres and she was fussing with an elaborate tray: the Rape of the Sabine Women in truffle mousse, I think. From where I stood, admiring the tray, I could see into the enormous living room as far as the stark yawning fireplace. I was a little surprised that Perry and Stefan seemed to be locked in conversation, though I thought Stefan might be trying to figure him out. I didn't want to join them. I nodded at Broadshaw's secretary Claire as she passed. She was a plain, pale, almost owl-faced woman in her fifties, gray-haired, soft-spoken, with a vaguely southern accent that cast even minor interactions in some larger display of good manners and civility.

I headed out into the cavernous and crowded room for some wine. I nodded, waved, wondering who I could pretend to be interested in tonight, wishing the stereo was playing something less endearing and sappy than Mendelssohn. But before I could decide who to chat with, Serena Fisch grabbed my arm.

"Hi, stranger!"

She usually greeted me in a throaty ironic way, as if she felt sorry for me, new in the department, not yet tuned into the various allegiances, not yet fully versed in the complex and overlapping histories that were Balkan *and* Byzantine. I often expected her to chuck me under the chin and murmur how she pitied me—just on general principles.

Serena Fisch made me think of words like "dame," "skirt," "tomato," because she dressed like one of the Lost Andrews Sisters. She wore wide-shouldered suits and clunky shoes like theirs, had her jet black dyed hair elaborately coiled and piled, and strode down a hallway a little uncertainly, as if unsure whether to jitterbug or slink. When I first described her to my cousin Sharon, who was an ex-model, Sharon said, "Oh, she must associate romance with the Forties—that's why she dresses like that."

I'd heard a rumor that Serena Fisch and Broadshaw were lovers, or had been until recently, and that he had pushed for her to have the Canadian Studies position. They were so odd in their different ways that I actually could imagine them in bed.

"Don't you *love* this place?" she asked, her lips curling sarcastically, looking around us. "How would you describe it? Bela Lugosi Moderne?"

"It *is* a little gloomy," I said, as if commenting merely on the wattage of the light bulbs. I was trying to be careful. I didn't want any casual *bon mot* of mine to waft through the department and make its way to Broadshaw.

"Gloomy?" she chortled. "It fits our department to a 't.' Anne Rice could move her vampire novels here. She'd love the way we eat each other alive."

I decided to change the subject because I didn't know her well at all, and I wasn't prepared to dish our host, our *chair*, who could make my life unpleasant for me if he wanted. It could be things like assigning me to more committee work than I could reasonably do, ensuring I had an inconvenient schedule, or something worse, guaranteeing that I never taught a graduate class.

"It's always been bad around here, but ever since Rhetoric was demolished as a department and they dumped all of us into English and American Studies—" She shuddered. "More than a decade later, they still treat us like they're Pat Buchanan and we're illegal aliens!"

"Well, what exactly happened?"

Serena bit her lips. "Budget cutting in the early eighties swept through this school like a firestorm. It was devastating."

That was true, and I lived with the aftereffects, even though I had entered the department well after this shotgun wedding. At department meetings, the animosity was always just about to break, and made me feel like I was watching one of Eugene O'Neill's less peppy plays.

I hadn't heard Serena complain about all this before, and I wanted to hear more. "So how's it difficult for you and the Rhetoric faculty?" I asked.

"We get consistently bad schedules, we have small and crowded offices, and they'll do anything to make us feel insignificant. It's true that some of the former Rhetoric faculty can be a mite prickly at times, but what about the spirit of collegiality?"

I didn't respond to that because at SUM, the Rhetoric Department was widely known as a collection of whining misfits and nowadays had the smothered mournful hysteria of an ancient country that had seen the eclipse of its glory and was now a mere province in some larger empire. Most of them had only Master's degrees, were unenthusiastic about teaching writing and did it poorly, and made no effort to do research that might lead to improving their own skills, or to publishing.

"It's not easy being despised," Serena said darkly.

I wondered if that was really true for *her*, as the former chair of Rhetoric, or whether she was just feeling especially bitter because of Perry Cross getting the Canadian Studies position. Serena was Canadian-born and had published well-received books on Timothy Findley and Mavis Gallant. Though there was sometimes prejudice against hiring an "internal" candidate, she really *was* qualified and the position should have been hers. And the fact that she was a talented woman in a department overloaded with not so talented men should have enhanced her qualifications.

"How are your classes?" I asked.

"Wonderful!" she sighed. "I have so much energy this semester."

"Why's that?"

"Oh, I'm just so inspired by the rich new talent we're bringing into this department."

Now I laughed at her obvious slam on Perry Cross.

"Though I'm sure," she went on, "that Perry Cross will be raided by some finer school very soon because he's so amazingly qualified." She grinned.

EAR had no more nationally known scholars left; they'd been lured away by Stanford, Yale, Columbia, Duke, Brown, given endowed chairs when SUM couldn't scrape together enough cash to endow a footstool.

I confess I liked inciting Serena. I said softly, "I heard Perry's good in class."

"No you haven't," she snapped. "You couldn't have. His students despise him."

"Already? How do you know?"

"They talk. They talk to each other, they talk to me." I recalled hearing that Serena was one of the few faculty members who enjoyed advising students. Serena nodded. "He's arrogant, he talks down to his students—one of them left his office crying!"

I was appalled. I had known a few teachers like that in my lifetime; their whole manner could feel like a cross-examination and you'd end up convicted, hopeless, lost.

Serena lifted her chin regally. "Now I admit I sometimes despair of students who haven't read the syllabus and ask unnecessary questions, or who waste my time trying to be friendly for a better grade, but I do try always to at least be patient and *polite*."

I'd heard from many sources that Serena was more than just polite; she was thorough, professional, helpful, adept. And in all of those ways, she was resolutely unlike the Rhetoric faculty she'd once headed. *Their* reputation for temperament and academic shoddiness still hung in the air, like the dust from a volcanic eruption changing the weather thousands of miles away.

"Perry Cross won't last," Serena added, as if dismissing some tacky fad, like those '70s platform shoes with live goldfish in their plastic heels.

"But how did he get hired if he hasn't published that much?" I was looking for real dirt, for the double-dealing that must have taken place in the search and hiring committees, and beyond.

Serena grinned. "I did wonder at first if some rich relative of Perry Cross's had made a secret large donation to the university. Then I thought, why SUM and not a more prestigious school? Or was that the point? Would a better school have scorned such a deal, no matter how private? Now I think I know the answer."

"And?"

Eyelids lowered as if she were Mata Hari, Serena drawled, "Blow jobs, lots of blow jobs."

I laughed so hard I started coughing and almost spilled my drink.

People turned around, smiling, enjoying my hilarity—or maybe not. Maybe they were enjoying my discomfort—because I sensed that lots of the faculty thought I had gotten the job only because I was Stefan's partner. Despite my publications, my conference papers, terrific student evaluations, despite everything that made my own academic career substantial, I still felt somewhat unwelcome in the department after a year. And then I also wondered how much of it was my being openly gay and proudly Jewish, too, in a department with few Jewish professors and some apparent closet queens.

"Blow jobs," I said. "So that's his secret."

Serena downed her drink. "He won't last," she said again.

"You should have gotten his position."

"You mean, being on my knees? Or his job?"

I gulped. I was not used to Serena talking like this. I looked closely at her, and realized that she was standing up very straight, as if trying not to sway. I had never seen her this close to being drunk.

"His job," I said. I couldn't imagine what it would feel like to be in the same department with someone who was far less qualified than you, far younger, far less experienced, who had bested you as Perry Cross somehow had done.

Serena looked at me as if I were a freshman making the most obvious grammatical error, raising her heavily plucked and redrawn eyebrows.

"What makes you think I *won't* have Perry Cross's position?" She headed away for another drink.

# -3-

Watching Serena Fisch sashay off, I leaned back against a nearby bookcase, thinking about how much unhappiness and dissension there was in the department. Look at Priscilla Davidoff and her animus toward Stefan. It wasn't just obvious in her attitude that she was furious about Stefan winding up as writer-in-residence, she'd even said that to me. We were in the middle of a neutral few lines of conversation at the department mailboxes and she popped out with: "He doesn't deserve it." I was appalled by her rudeness, and wanted to be just as rude and snap, "You're not good enough to be writer-in-residence of an outhouse."

What if Priscilla Davidoff was as determined to get rid of Stefan as Serena was intent on sinking Perry Cross? Was there anything either one of them could *do*?

I scanned the room looking for Priscilla and spotted her off near the kitchen. She was staring at Stefan and Perry, who were now seated halfway up the broad uncarpeted stairs. Stefan seemed unusually attentive, when he wasn't talking.

Priscilla's eyes were nakedly full of hatred. It scared me.

The way Priscilla presented herself to the world was so discordant. She was so hard and angry, but her smiles, her voice, her perfume, and even her clothes were usually very soft. She was quite tall, striking—almost a blond Geena Davis—and given to long velvet dresses with padded shoulders and lacy necklines. She

29

had flowing pre-Raphaelite hair, creamy skin, large brown eyes, long dark lips, and appropriately gentle but dramatic gestures.

Tonight at Broadshaw's party, I wanted to convince her that Stefan really was the right person for writer-in-residence.

I shook my head and moved off to get myself some more wine, some stuffed grape leaves, and torta rustica. And just as I started munching away, I was cornered by Chuck Bayer, the department's chain-smoking, nail-biting fake.

"Nick! Nicky, I want to talk to you! Wait here, I want to get a refill, okay?"

I watched Chuck lope off. He was excruciatingly tall—like Ichabod Crane, with a weird kind of good looks that were highlighted by his shabby-looking blue suits, scuffed oxfords, and bland ties.

I suppose every department like ours has one of these intellectual lounge lizards—oddly magnetic, driven, shallow. They don't do really valuable academic work, but tend to churn out shoddy introductions to insignificant collections or anthologies. Despite the pitiful levels of achievement, they act as if they know everybody in academic publishing and they sprinkle conversations with gossip, talk of contracts, advances, and proposals. They generally don't get tenure, at good schools anyway, because no one's really fooled into taking them seriously.

I did not like it that Chuck kept calling me Nicky, as if we were Hollywood types bantering at poolside. I had tried subtle approaches, and then finally came right out and said, "Nobody calls me Nicky." Chuck had simply nodded, as if remarking on a natural phenomenon he had no control over. I admit that I was jealous that he had done his doctorate at Yale, while I had only gotten into NYU.

Back with his drink, Chuck said, "How about doing a bibliography of Joan Didion with me?"

I knew at once that meant I'd do it and we'd share the authorship. He sounded desperate, and was probably racing a publisher's deadline because he'd talked someone into giving him a contract. "We can do it easy," he kept saying, like a drunk repeating, "I'm all right, I'm all right." And I stared into his slightly cross-eyed, pockmarked, ineffectual face.

As Chuck went on trying to convince me, I knew for sure then that he and reality were not good friends. My Wharton bibliography took me five years of tracking down and reading every single book, article, and review about Wharton and her novels, short stories, poems, and articles in English, French, German, Japanese, Italian from 1897 to the present. *Everything* had to be located, read, sometimes translated, and described in objective tight prose. For those years, Stefan and I lived in a maze of overflowing file cabinets, the stench of Xeroxes, and the nagging fear that something major would get missed or lost or end up incorrect in the finished book, which contained thousands upon thousands of numbers and dates. It's said that Henry James once remarked about someone "with profound stupefaction" that the man was "interested in indexes." By the time I was done with my bibliography, I *was* stupefied. Even Stefan was exhausted, and he said he would never read a word by or about Wharton for the rest of his life.

I had tuned out a little, thinking about Wharton. But Chuck Bayer was still talking about the Didion bibliography as if it were a trip to the mall.

"I don't like Joan Didion," I finally told Chuck. "She's too thin."

"Her prose or her body?"

"Take your pick. Besides, I prefer dead authors—live ones can be so slippery."

"Are you sure you're not interested?"

I nodded.

"I really need your help," he said, his voice lowered, his face—for him—suddenly more open and honest. I could see he was about to reach for my arm, but then he looked a bit frightened and scuttled off. And when I turned, I had no idea who had scared him; there were dozens of faculty members and their spouses in view.

I was startled when I turned back to see Priscilla Davidoff advancing on me, smiling.

"Did Chuck try to get you involved in the Didion bibliography?"

I admit I was surprised. "You, too?"

"What a twerp," she spat. "I don't get him at all. What's the big deal about that Edith Wharton postcard he found? I don't see how that would make anybody's scholarly reputation."

"Postcard! It was a *letter.*" I took a deep breath. "Wharton scholars always call it 'The Letter.'"

Priscilla rolled her eyes.

"No, this was big stuff. You have to remember that until all those love letters Wharton wrote to Morton Fullerton showed up in Paris, people thought of Wharton as stiff and cold. A grande dame out of touch with life. You do remember reading about those letters, don't you?"

"How could I forget?"

Priscilla was sarcastic, but I forged ahead. I was a little drunk, and I proceeded to lecture her about Wharton's love letters, how they had revealed her as a passionate, imperiously demanding, yearning, heartbroken woman—in other words, as a more complete human being. "So it doesn't matter how you see the affair, whether it was a trap or a miracle. It's still powerful stuff—the letters make her come alive in a new way. And they proved that a really intimate diary Wharton kept was actually written about Fullerton, and not Walter Berry. He was a lifelong friend and literary adviser."

"So where does Chuck's letter fit in?"

I almost hugged myself in excitement. "When Walter Berry died, Wharton went to his apartment in Paris and burned all her letters to him. So Chuck found the only one that survived! Berry must have slipped it in a copy of one of her novels, *The Touchstone,* and when his mammoth library got broken up after he died, the book kicked around Paris and ended up in a used bookstore on the Left Bank."

Priscilla frowned. "But why the fuss? What's *in* the letter?"

Here I hesitated. "Well, actually it's kind of ambiguous. Just a few sentences in French." Whether the letter proved Wharton and Berry were lovers, no one could say for sure—but it was still juicy and exciting.

"That's all? And Chucky-lucky found it? How?"

"He was a graduate student on vacation in Paris. He just bought the book and there it was." It pained me to have to tell this part of the story, since I envied the find so deeply. "He wrote an article about it, and he got famous. Among Wharton scholars, anyway."

"How do you know the letter's real? Maybe he forged it!"

I was horrified. "No, it's been authenticated." But then I smiled. "That's the last time Chuck had any success; since then, he's been coasting."

"A lucky break," she said grimly. "Like lots of people in this department." She shook her head. "Like that damned Perry Cross. Can you believe they hired him at fifty thousand dollars?"

"What! I never heard that."

"Sure—nobody's bragging, but that's what he's getting."

"But he's just an assistant professor. *Full* professors get that much."

Priscilla snorted. "If they don't get shafted first." She walked off.

Amazed that Perry was making so much more than I was, I headed for the nearest bathroom, which was down a long, narrow, badly lit hallway. This guest bathroom was pretentious and large, all black and white and chrome—with a tiny stereo system, VCR, and small television. Perhaps the hallway was kept dark so that the gleam and glare of this room would be more surprising and impressive.

On the way out, I passed a bedroom full of light jackets and sweaters. The door was half open and I heard an anguished woman's voice: "You told him? I can't believe you told him! Are you crazy?" And then a quiet reply: "I couldn't help it."

I lingered, pretending to puzzle out the Latin inscription at the bottom of an architectural print of some Roman ruin that was the only thing hung in the dim hallway. But there was silence—perhaps they could sense my presence—and I moved on. As I headed back to the party, I thought someone might have been at the far end of the hallway, beyond the bathroom, because I heard a different door close.

I had recognized the voices: Betty and Bill Malatesta, the Whiz Kids. The two brightest and friendliest graduate students in the department. Both were publishing, going to conferences, smart, likable—a darling couple. Almost too darling. Sometimes meeting them in the department office I expected them to burst into song or announce, "Hey everybody, let's dance!" Betty was slim and sexy, very blond and elegant, given to wearing only black. And Bill was also blond, but more robust—broad-shouldered, over six feet tall.

We often ran into each other at the mailboxes or getting coffee. In the EAR Department, there was an informality between graduate students and professors that had at first seemed warm and relaxing to me, but was actually rigid and ceremonial. As if we were all courtiers vividly aware of varying ranks, but absolutely committed to pretending that the hierarchy didn't exist. It was odd. I had known departments that were honestly unfriendly, and honestly relaxed; this was an uncomfortable mix, in which you could never tell what was real. I sensed that my new colleagues didn't like my spending time talking to graduate students like the Malatestas, but maybe it wasn't so much the time as that I genuinely liked them, or at least didn't think of them as less than human.

I was looking around for Stefan when Bill Malatesta came up to me, a little flushed, to tell me about some article he'd read in *The New Yorker*. Bill had the stance and style of a kickboxer—light on his feet, maybe, but powerful. While he spoke, I wondered if he'd seen it was me outside the bedroom door eavesdropping, and if he were trying to figure out how much I'd heard.

"How many graduate assistants does it take to change a light bulb?" he suddenly asked me.

"I don't know."

"None, because they all asked for incompletes."

I laughed.

"How many linguists does it take?"

"How many?"

"None, because the word is not the thing. How many department chairs?" he went on.

"You tell me."

He smiled. "None—it's easier to stab someone in the back with the lights off."

And instinctively, we both turned to where Lynn Broadshaw was raving across the room about something or other, his lips flecked with spit. Stefan called him "Niagara," because when he got excited, he could spray you from across a conference table.

Bill and I shuddered a little.

"How's your dissertation going?" I asked.

But Bill Malatesta was still looking at our chair. "I need *help*," he said, fixing me with his intense blue eyes as if making me promise something, and then he walked away.

Now that was the second person at this party to ask for my help. What was I, the United Way?

I looked around for Stefan.

Rose Waterman saw me and headed over, slowly pushing her way through the crowded room. She was the provost and so I couldn't escape. At seventy, Rose was nearing retirement; in her many years at SUM she had inexorably risen from assistant professor to professor to chair to dean to her current position, where it was believed she ran the entire university, because our brainless president was all bonhomie and fund-raising. Since she had complete control of SUM's financial affairs, she was of course widely disliked and even feared. She had an excellent memory and was relentless once she had decided on a course of action. It was rumored that she had taken a personal dislike to Stewart Green, chair of the old Journalism Department, and had punished him years back by arranging for the department to be demoted to a program within Communications, depriving Green of power as well as the salary supplement that department chairs earned. When Green committed suicide soon afterwards, his death was unavoidably linked with the way Rose punished him.

I suppose the aura of power was why Rose had so many abusive nicknames like "The Terminator" and "Darth Waterman"—to make people less anxious when they mentioned her. Some people called her Smokey, because she smoked several packs of Marlboros a day (though mostly in private, it seemed) and everything about her stunk of smoke: her curly reddish hair, her small ringless hands, her breath, her clothes, her office, even the memos she signed.

Stefan complained to me that the campus criticism of Rose was sexist, and that if she were a man, we would all applaud her power, her drive, the commitment that most nights kept her working in her office in the Administration Building well past midnight.

Rose greeted me tonight with "How do you like it here at State?"

"It's been a year," I said, puzzled.

"Yes, I know that." She looked as if she could have told me the exact date, even the *hour* of my arrival at SUM. She waited for me to say something. That was another thing about her I disliked: her silences. Somehow Rose Waterman managed to make people feel stupid without saying a word. And while you hesitated, you felt she was gathering information.

So I turned it around: "How do *you* like it here at State?"

She frowned. Junior faculty members obviously did not tease her, and I suddenly felt like Dorothy trembling in the Hall of Oz.

"It's home for some of us," she said sharply. "Others are just passing through." She smiled, revealing her tobacco-stained teeth.

Did that mean me? Stefan had been hired as an associate professor with tenure, but I would have to go up for tenure in a few years, and even though I'd been assured it was pro forma, the thought made me nervous. Was Rose trying to warn me? I knew that's how it was done—nobody said things directly, you were just encouraged not to be hopeful, not to plan to stick around. Was that why she had picked me out tonight to talk to? Usually at parties we just exchanged a few remarks and moved on.

At the best of times, Rose stirred a visceral unease in me that had nothing to do with the way she looked or even her position at the university. It was her accent. Whenever I heard anyone in their sixties or older with a German accent, I imagined they might have been in the Nazi Party. I couldn't help it. Hell, when I saw a dachshund, I wondered what its grandparents had done during the war.

Behind us now, someone agitated was talking about the latest anti-gay incident on campus. A number of bridges had been splattered with painted slogans: "Hitler Was Right—Kill the Queers!"

"Hah!" Rose muttered, looking disgusted. "As if that's important."

"It doesn't bother you?" I asked. "As an administrator it *should.* Homophobia is no different than racism or anti-Semitism—"

"—Why do people say that?" Rose interrupted. "It is *not* the same. Homosexuals are not a minority group like blacks. It's a moral choice, a moral question."

I was flummoxed by her lack of understanding, and that she would reveal it to *me* of all people. Usually Rose Waterman gave nothing away.

"But don't you think the homophobia on campus is connected to the anti-Semitism on campus, the swastikas on Jewish students' dorm doors, the letters in the student newspaper condemning Israel at every opportunity, and the speakers who come to SUM to deny the Holocaust or blame Jews for everything from the slave trade to AIDS?"

"No," she said. "I do not."

"And what about the way black and white students don't socialize here, how they sit separately in classrooms and the dining halls? And the black students getting hassled, abused, even beaten up? The university has to fight all of that at the same time, it has to encourage groups to act together."

Rose had flushed and seemed about to denounce me in some way, but before she could say anything, we all heard a sharp cry and Betty Malatesta came dashing out of the kitchen, her face red.

People were crowding into the kitchen, where Mrs. Broadshaw was looking stunned.

"She burned her hand," somebody said, and first aid was mobilized.

Rose was by her side while the ice was being applied, murmuring something that seemed to calm her down.

Lynn Broadshaw was nowhere in sight, and the noise level rose as if everyone had decided at the same moment to pretend that nothing had happened.

Maybe nothing had.

I found Stefan on the patio, and I realized then that it was late. Everyone out there looked drunk and tired. I was, too.

I waved Stefan over, mouthing, "Let's go."

"I think I should tell you something," he said as we were leaving. "It's about Perry. Perry Cross."

I wasn't really listening. I just followed Stefan out to his Saab, annoyed that he had apparently found Perry so interesting, and all night, too. It was cool and very clear in the sky.

"I know Perry." Stefan sounded stiff, tentative, like someone on a soap opera coming out of amnesia.

"Perry? You *know* him? How?"

"Let's go home." He started the car and we drove away down the maple-lined street.

"Listen," I said. "Just spit it out! Everyone I talked to tonight has been acting like James Bond. Enough! If the Jaguar prowls at midnight, don't make me get my decoder ring, just tell me what it *means!*"

Stefan said, "Wait," but he didn't look at me or take my hand or smile.

## -4-

S tefan insisted on making a fire when we got home even though it wasn't really cold enough.

"Atmosphere?" I asked. "This must be really bad."

Stefan pushed in some more kindling, lit it, and turned to me, still squatting. "No, it's humorous, in a way."

"Remind me to smile at the funny parts."

I sat back in the large leather armchair, put my feet up on the ottoman. Stefan sat crosslegged near the fire, which was catching quickly.

"Okay," Stefan said, as if he were about to take medicine he didn't like. "When I was in my first year as a graduate student at Columbia, Perry was at Yale. But he came down from New Haven to sit in on a writing workshop—that's where we met. He was thinking about switching to our writing program." Stefan shrugged. "And I wanted to get out of it, and switch to the regular graduate program in English." He paused. "Everything started one night when Perry and I went out for drinks after a really degrading class. The professor bashed the stories like piñatas."

"Ouch."

"And there was a girl with us, too, Maggie. She was sweet and pretty and half in love with both of us."

"And confused," I added. "Since you were both gay."

"Well—I wasn't sure back then." He closed his eyes for a moment, then went on. "It was safe," Stefan said. "For all three of us."

They did movies, he explained. Parties, dinners, shows and bookstores, always bookstores—around Columbia, along Fifth Avenue, in the Village. They were happy un-self-conscious refugees, fleeing what they must have thought were the wilds of sex and complication into something purer: friendship. They wound up trapped by their flight. At least Stefan did.

"We were driving," he said. "Up Broadway from Columbus Circle, from a movie. Maggie was sick she didn't go. It was late, very late. Perry put in a Bowie tape, *Aladdin Sane*, and up past Seventy-Second it started raining. All these red reflections, tail lights everywhere, red lights clear uptown. And we stopped, and Bowie's singing, 'Gee it's hot, let's go to bed.' And Perry says to me, "You're gay, aren't you, or at least bisexual?" I felt hooked, I felt ... exposed. How could I lie to him, but it felt wrong to say it. So I just leaned over to kiss him. Perry said, 'You're not what I'm looking for.'"

And the weeks of hiding what he felt from himself and Maggie and Perry were over for Stefan; he was lost, he was stunned. Because he had never been so thoroughly rejected before. He cut his hair, he tried new clothes, read different books, sought in desperate ways to fascinate and compel.

But Perry could have been some ancient absolute ruler, watching with amusement while one of his vassals made himself ever more ridiculously humble to win favor from the unyielding suzerain.

I found all of this amazing. Stefan was a calm and self-possessed man; I couldn't imagine him in a relationship so murky and full of pain, one where he begged with words, with his eyes, with letters and gifts. "Why'd you waste time on him?" I asked. "Was it a challenge? A test?"

Stefan shrugged. "I still don't understand it, completely, it was like an opera or a nightmare. Or bad luck."

"At parties," Stefan went on. "Or in a group, sometimes Perry used to smile at me, but the smile was different, more personal, like he was trying to get my attention, to make me *notice* he was smiling, and make sure I appreciated it, that he was giving me something, finally. And of course I thought it meant more—how could I not get excited, hopeful? And there we would be at some party or restaurant, and he might even touch me, like while he was talking, to make a point, and I'd be ready to explode, and then he'd head off with someone else, a guy, a girl. It didn't matter. He wanted me to see how weak I was, how he could mock me. He made me come on to him when we were in the car that night, and then he used it against me."

They went to bed a few times, inconclusively, when Perry was very drunk, but there was always the sense of a marquise throwing coins to beggars from her carriage—speeding off in a whirl of creaking springs and driving hooves, leaving poverty and bitter gratitude behind.

It dragged on for months, with Maggie struggling to make Stefan give Perry up or convince Perry to love Stefan—*someone* had to be happy if she wasn't. It was even worse when Perry went back to New Haven after deciding he wasn't really interested in Columbia's writing program, and Stefan fired off letters, cards, and called—but Perry wouldn't vouchsafe an audience, or even a reply. Stefan said he kept thinking of what Gudrun said to Gerald in *Women in Love:* "You waste me—and you break me—and it is horrible to me."

"Horrible. Until I met you," Stefan finished. "At the MLA conference."

"What's that mean? Until you met me?"

Stefan hugged himself, eyes down.

"I was the Red Cross after the hurricane? Blankets and hot soup? Great."

I wished then that Stefan had told me all this at the party. I could've gotten drunk and maneuvered Perry over to the grand piano and smashed his head with the lid, or pushed him into a bathroom and drowned him in the tub, or shoved his face into the Cuisinart.

"Then all those times I talked about Perry in my office, you knew exactly who he was!"

Stefan frowned. "I tried changing the subject." Then he added, "When I heard he was one of the applicants for that new position, I said some good things about him. Maybe it helped."

I've always been suspicious of revelation scenes because the truth has seemed sneakier to me, less aggressive.

That night, by the fire with Stefan, I was not just feeling threatened and betrayed, but scared by something new. I'd often worried about death and losing him that way, and though I sometimes got sarcastic if I saw him talking to a striking student of the male persuasion, I did not ever doubt my importance in the life we had created. This was different, unimagined, bizarre.

"You *helped* Perry Cross get the position after the way he treated you? You must be crazy," I said. "No—don't tell me, you thought it would be wrong not to."

Stefan nodded.

"Shit, Stefan! Join the Peace Corps if you want to help people so fucking much! Try Bangladesh!"

"Let's go to bed." Stefan rose and came to my chair. I was too surprised to feel I could let go; I said I would stay up for a bit, with the fire.

"Wake me when you come to bed." Stefan leaned down to kiss me good night. Was I supposed to huffily pull away, or let him kiss me, or what? The whole situation seemed ludicrous, a cliché: The Confession Scene. The Astonished Lover. Maybe Stefan was embarrassed by that, too.

I saw myself sneaking into Parker Hall at night and throwing Perry's books and files out the window onto the lawn. Or I could send him anonymous threatening missives, put some road kill in his mailbox, leave shrunken heads at his door, fly over campus with a broomstick spouting smoky letters that spelled *Surrender Stefan*.

See? The whole mess was partly like a stupid joke to me. I couldn't believe it. And I couldn't believe that when Stefan and I first met, Perry had never come up.

I met Stefan at a Modern Language Association conference in New York, at a session on psychological criticism—at least that's what I thought it was about. But the very first paper destroyed my confidence, because I could not figure out what the hell the speaker was trying to get across. I could pick out nouns, verbs, and occasional transitions that made sense, but mostly it was gobbledygook. And all around me in the room of about a hundred, people were nodding, smiling—at what? Frustrated, I started writing down phrases picked from his talk at random. I got quite a list: "polysemy of manifest meanings," "the hegemony of representationality," "regimentation of reiterative temporality," "locus of contradictoriness," "identitarian metaphysics of presence," "praxis of disposition," "specious centricity."

Behind me a soft and sexy voice murmured, "You left out 'reiterative exchanges and utterances.'" Whoever it was sounded as silky as a radio announcer for a classical station murmuring to you at night.

Then I turned around and was hooked. He looked a lot like the Jewish runner in *Chariots of Fire,* with that same craggy sensual face, and he was smiling so sweetly I said, "Let's get some coffee." Out in the hallway I introduced myself. He was stockier and somewhat shorter than I had guessed, but not unpleasantly so, with a kind of grace that muted his muscularity; under the tan wool blazer I could see a tight but not too bulky torso.

I liked the way he looked at me, openly, and his broad smile. We stood there chatting about the conference, and I took in the intensity of his deep-set brown eyes, the sheen of his thick and wavy hair.

We took the subway down to his studio apartment on Hudson Street, and what I remember of the ride was the Hispanic guy hanging from the strap next to me, his coat and shirt gaping open, revealing one of the fattest, darkest nipples I had ever seen on man or woman. We drank two bottles of something, made love kind of wildly into the night, and then we both passed out. In the morning, we looked as haggard as just-released hostages. What was special the next day, what was remarkable was feeling as if we had slipped into somebody else's comfortable and comforting life.

In the morning we laughed about the awful panel. Though I suppose sitting in on it helped Stefan decide not to switch programs at Columbia, convincing him that regular graduate work in English would be the death of his writing. He needed to be plunged into something *that* alienating to see that his gifts required clearer, more direct expression. And so on our first morning together he seemed to have rediscovered the path that was the right one.

Once he completely committed to writing, everything seemed to change. In my English Ph.D. program at NYU, we had liked to make fun of people doing MFA's anywhere, even Columbia (perhaps especially Columbia). We derided their clothes, their egotism, their romantic chaos, as if they had no claim at all to the peaks of literature *we* had climbed and planted our little flags on. But even my friends at NYU who met Stefan admired him, and went to his readings.

"He's a diamond," a Columbia English professor told me once at a department party in an *Architectural Digest* sort of apartment where the hors d'oeuvres were arranged to look like a Mondrian. "A diamond," he repeated, drunk, confident, as if he were a refugee who had smuggled that gem in his coat lining across an impassable border. I felt momentarily jealous not to have thought of the term myself.

But committing to his writing didn't answer all the questions or ease all of the pain. Stefan's gleam of expectation could not withstand the hundreds of rejections that followed us from New York to small and exclusive Adams College in western Massachusetts where we were lucky enough to get teaching jobs together after he earned his MFA and I earned my Ph.D.

It even hurt Stefan to get the kinder "Send us more" or "Try us again" rejections. By the time we were both teaching at Adams, it was no longer almost funny, no longer a fantasy of "Won't *they* be sorry they rejected you when—" There wasn't any "when." Each manila envelope, each typed label, each trip to the post office was like the part of a painful empty-handed ritual. The man I loved was a prisoner of his dreams.

One day in Massachusetts Stefan got *five* rejections in the mail. Five short story manuscripts came back, and I mistakenly told him that John Gardner had tried for fifteen years before getting his fiction published. Stefan yelled, "John Gardner's *dead!*" and stormed from the kitchen. I heard the closet door and then the front door close.

Stefan disappeared down our dark silent road at the very edge of town, past the condominiums stacked like children's blocks, past the horse farm, trudging with angry hands jammed in his coat pockets. I followed for a bit, to apologize, but his stark striding figure looked so sad I trailed back to our Cape Cod to wait.

Stefan's failure had become like a curse in a fairy tale, a sentence we had no hope of escaping, and I felt almost guilty because I was doing so well. My parents had warned me not to go to graduate school in English because there were no jobs, but I couldn't imagine a more satisfying life than teaching. So, there I was at Adams, enjoying my classes, with half a dozen scholarly articles already published or forthcoming, and a contract to do a secondary bibliography of Edith Wharton's writing. My chairman said that tenure was assured.

I felt terrible.

While Stefan was out, I put everything away, turned on the dishwasher, and settled into the enormous ball-footed leather armchair he'd gotten me for our fifth anniversary, to read the draft of a colleague's article on James Baldwin. In an hour Stefan stood opposite me, red-cheeked, solemn, coat still on.

"I hate it when you're sympathetic," he said.

"Should I make fun of you? Be mean?"

Stefan peeled away his coat and came to sit on the wide chair arm. "In the movies you always see the writer typing, crumbling up the paper, agony, pacing, more typing, a sandwich. Part One. Part Two is the Letter, the phone call, success. We're still stuck in the agony."

His sadness reminded me of a war memorial we'd seen in Stratford, Ontario, the previous summer: a robed woman, head down, shoulders tragically slumped, battered sword at her feet, loss, terrible loss in every line of her face, her robes.

I suggested Stefan go to bed.

"Am I tired?"

While he showered I thought about his work, which he rarely showed me. When he did, it was impossible for me to read anything of his without feeling for the hours he'd sat hunched over his desk, rocking as if to catch a troubling melody, face dark, fingers touching his shoulders, hair, his throat. The nights he worked hardest I wandered through the house, restless, straightening pictures, shuffling magazines, or stalking the evergreen-bordered half-acre behind our house, breathing in the silence and the night, hoping. Hoping he had discovered the words I would someday read in print.

I couldn't *will* his success. I could fill the house with white lilacs in May for his birthday, surprise him with newly published novels he'd forgotten saying he wanted to read, hide jokey little cards under his pillow, cook Julia Child dinners and wear my tux, call him from campus or the mall just to say "Hi!"—but I couldn't fill the emptiness of continual rejection, which was more awful because so many people from the well-known writing programs like Columbia's did get published. I suspected that it wasn't entirely talent, but connections. Every time I opened up another uninspiring collection of stories by someone he might have gone to school with, I ached for Stefan to have that kind of success.

Stefan was asleep as soon as he got to bed. I put some dishes away, cleaned up in the living room, and then found myself watering plants that weren't dry. I was nervous. I felt drawn to his study, which I never entered when he wasn't home.

I slipped down the hall and into the study, turning on the light after I closed the door. It was a small room, painted a glossy forest green, full of file cabinets and books; but not even the peeling library table revealed anything about him. This room without decoration, pictures, and mementos disturbed me for the first time—what was he shutting out besides distraction?

I settled onto the dull green carpeting and slowly pulled open the nearest file drawer. His stories were filed alphabetically by year, and each folder spilled out rejection slips, sometimes dozens. I read those along with ten or so stories and it all began to seem anonymous—the stories no different from the Xeroxed rejection slips.

I had never read so much of his work at one time, and I didn't like it. While I may have enjoyed individual lines, or scenes, or even characters, reading so many stories in a row I was disappointed. His work was clever, I guess, but empty, and I found myself thinking of our favorite movie, *Dark Victory*, of the scene where Bette Davis discovers her medical file in George Brent's office and asks the nurse what the words "prognosis negative" mean. How had I missed this?

I cleaned up, checked the bedroom to see if he was still asleep, and sat at the kitchen table with a shot of Seagram's like my father did when he got bad news—the one drink saying he needed not to forget but to be strong. I was struck by how bland Stefan's people were, and how none were even demonstrably gay or Jewish. His parents had at first wanted to disown him when they found out he was gay. They felt it was a personal attack, a way of hurting them because they had hidden being Jewish, had tried to raise him as a Catholic. His mother even wondered if the Nazis had somehow poisoned her in the concentration camp, changing her genes, and that's why Stefan was gay!

Stranger than the absence of gay characters, none of Stefan's men or women were really Jewish either, which made even less sense. It made me feel invisible, as if he were ignoring that I observed the holidays, lit shabbat candles, and thrived on being with other Jews. I knew that Stefan didn't get much out of the holidays or attending services, but we had been lucky to find a very liberal congregation near Adams with a woman rabbi and a few gay and lesbian couples. When we did attend or get involved, there was no sense of exclusion or embarrassment.

Stefan's fiction was so placid and unemotional; where was his rage at all of them for the years of silence, the years of lies? And because Stefan only found out when he was a teenager that his parents and uncle had been in concentration camps, and that they were Jewish, I was most deeply struck by the absence of any reference to the Holocaust in his fiction. We had certainly talked about it. Just that year we had watched a newly discovered British film of the liberation of Bergen Belsen. In it, British soldiers forced the SS guards to lift and carry corpses, drop, slide, stack them into four or five pits, "as punishment." The film was silent, there was no creak of carts, no engines stirring into life, no shouted commands—just seven days reduced to black and white minutes on film. The civilized-sounding narrator talked of "graves"—which made Stefan furious. "Those aren't graves—they're garbage dumps!" I couldn't believe the SS felt any different, felt repentant while dropping bodies like a gigolo flicking away the useless stump of a cigarette.

"My parents were there," Stefan reminded me. "But they won't tell me about it. First they wouldn't tell me I was Jewish, then they wouldn't tell me what happened to them in the war. I had to read *books* about it, books describing the ghettos, the trains, the killing. Why do they keep shutting me out?"

I tried to imagine the dazed and starved survivors wandering somewhere out of camera range.

I woke up late that night, could feel that Stefan wasn't sleeping.

"They should have thrown the guards in," he said in the dark. "Buried them alive."

"Yes," I said. "I know."

There was absolutely no trace of his anger or pain in Stefan's stories. So much silence in his writing. Why was he censoring himself so heavily?

A motorcycle tore by outside, and I wished then for a galumphing puppy I could scratch and rub and talk to. In all the time Stefan had suffered rejection, I had never doubted his work.

"It's late," Stefan said at the kitchen door, squinting at my drink. His face was creased and red with sleep, his hair flattened. He rubbed his eyes, pulled his robe together, and came to sit by me. "What's wrong?"

"I was reading. In your study."

I expected him to blast me, but he just nodded, leaning back in the captain's chair.

He said, "It's no good."

We had been at this place before, I dousing the flames of his depression with torrents of praise—reminding him of Columbia, his successful fiction readings there, like a court chamberlain comforting his monarch-in-exile. But tonight I couldn't offer anything; there was only silence timidly filled by the humming fridge and vague grunts from the sink pipes. I felt we had come to the end of something and I was afraid. Our first years fragrant with discovery, helping each other finish the graduate degrees, the move to western Massachusetts, the trips to France, England, the Netherlands, renting and decorating this house, all of that seemed one-dimensional now, remote.

Stefan reached for my glass and the bottle, poured himself a shot, and downed it.

"You haven't wanted to see," he said.

"What?"

"To see my work." He looked down. "You want me to be, I don't know, famous, *wonderful.*"

"But isn't that what you want?"

"Not now, now I just want to write something honest. Something *real.*" He stroked my hands. "It's not your fault, it's nobody's fault."

I pulled open the fridge and found some leftover veal stew and half an apple pie to heat up. Fussing at the sink and stove, I was unable to look at him. Stefan came up behind me, gave me a lingering, pleading hug, as if we'd just had some kind of fight.

"I don't have the courage to write about anything that hurts— my parents, finding out I was Jewish, being gay...." He said this to my back.

I felt ashamed then of all the times I'd raved about his writing, gone on and on thinking that I was being helpful, when I was just showing I loved him. It was a subtle form of contempt—I had not treated him as an equal, as an adult, but as a glamorous, talented, demanding child.

"I never have," he said. "Except once. It was something I wrote about my parents and my uncle, their past, their secrets. My secrets. Just a sketch, really, for an English class in college. I was down from Syracuse on spring break and my uncle Sasha found it—well, I left it out where he could. He went nuts. He said I was sick, I was crazy." Stefan held me tighter, still talking to the back of my head.

"What happened to it?"

"He gave it to my mother, she gave it to my father, and I guess he threw it out." Stefan broke away. "Wait, I want to show you something." He went off to his study and returned with a deeply creased single sheet of pale blue stationery that had been crumpled up and then straightened more than once, I thought.

"My father sent this after he read what I wrote."

I read the typed, undated note:

> When we were married your mother said we had to have children because of everything we had lost. I didn't want to have any. Now I know I was right.

"Your *father* sent this to you? What did you say?"

Stefan shook his head, as if unwilling to remember. "I couldn't say anything. I felt ... repudiated."

Feeling suddenly brisk and sensible, I stood up and went to the utility drawer. "Isn't it time for a reply?"

He frowned, not following.

I took the letter and a book of matches to the sink. "Come on."

I held out the matches. Stefan hesitated, came over, took one, lit it slowly as I nodded, and set it to the corner of the letter, dropping it into the sink when it started to flame. Little black specks floated up above us as the letter twisted in on itself, crackling, vanishing into black powder and dust.

Stefan put his hands down in the sink and rubbed them in the ashes, turned on the tap, washing his hands clean.

"Would it change things?" he finally asked, pale, drying his hands.

"Change things if you wrote something real?"

He nodded.

Details in the kitchen suddenly seemed very clear to me: the Boston fern hanging over the sink, the brass cabinet knobs, the Sierra Club calendar near the stove. "I don't know."

He smiled. "Well," he said. "It wouldn't mean I got published, but I'd be honest. Isn't that a start?"

I thought then of my favorite lines from James Baldwin's *Another Country,* lines I had just read in my colleague's article: "You've got to be truthful about the life you *have*—otherwise there's no possibility of achieving the life you *want*."

I said that yes, it would be a start. Stefan grinned and came to hug me.

And I was right. Soon afterwards, Stefan started on something completely different: a novel about secrets, and he gave up short story writing. It was the best possible move. On the strength of just two chapters, he got an agent, a publisher, and a healthy advance.

THERE WERE NO lights on in our mid-Michigan home while I sat remembering all this, about Stefan's haunted family, about our years in western Massachusetts, Perry Cross and the party, thinking about the past, worrying about our future—no lights, just the wavering fire I did nothing to keep going. Watching it, I began to feel like Isabel Archer in *The Portrait of a Lady* when she finally realizes what her husband is like.

I had always thought that Stefan and I were happy together; ten years seemed to have passed with few lasting problems between us. But now I wondered if Perry Cross didn't signify something dark and untameable in Stefan, some fascination with chaos and pain. It was like the wonderful sad passage in a Laurie Colwin story: "Fulfillment leaves an empty space where your old self used to be, the self that pines and broods and reflects."

What if at some level Stefan thought he *had* to suffer, so as not to betray what his parents had gone through? It didn't have to make sense, it just had to fit together.

I grabbed a pen and the *TV Guide* from the coffee table, and in the margins of yet another article on *Friends,* I wrote a list of my options.

(1) I could eat everything in the kitchen.
(2) I could drink until I passed out.
(3) I could drive around aimlessly all night and come back bleary-eyed to haunt and rebuke Stefan.

(4) I could call Perry and curse him out.

(5) I could kill myself.

(6) I could eat everything in *Perry's* kitchen.

(7) I could write a nasty autobiography, *Stefan, Queerest,* go on Jenny Jones, and wow America.

(8) I could hire a hit man to take care of Perry.

(9) I could cry.

I stopped there and put the *TV Guide* down to face the possibility of great pain.

# -5-

I n the morning Stefan told me he'd invited Perry to dinner. We were having breakfast, Stefan dressed for class, me in my bathrobe. I felt vulnerable, unprepared.

Stefan said, "He's had a pretty rough time."

"That's what you talked about at the party *all night?*" I poured myself more coffee. "What is he, the Ancient Mariner?"

Stefan shrugged. "There's a lot to tell. Married twice, divorced, he's got a little girl and his first wife won custody, he can't see her at all, he can't land a tenure track position anywhere, just these one-year, two-year shots, hasn't really published...."

"We're aiding the needy, is that it? Couldn't I just send him some computer paper? A little check, perhaps?"

"It's different imagining him here, and seeing him." Stefan was staring off behind me.

"So it's not over?"

"He's here."

It was a stupid question, I admit that. How could it be over if it'd just begun for me last night?

"Why is he coming to dinner? Why did you help get him the job?"

"I need to find out what I feel." Now he looked straight at me, serious, solemn even.

"Oh shit."

"Listen, people can stop for you but that doesn't mean they end. I have to know."

"But Perry was years ago. And I love you!" It came out angry and inconsequential, an unimportant claim.

"Then you want me to understand this." Stefan sounded reasonable and warm. "If I'm not honest, what'll happen to my writing?"

"Wonderful! Now I'm destroying your career! I hate this! I wish I were dead!"

Quietly, Stefan corrected me. "No, you wish Perry were dead."

His accuracy made me feel as belligerent as if I were drunk. "That's right, and I'm not wild about you either. Go to class!"

The thought of Perry in our wonderful house absolutely sickened me. On a Michiganapolis dead-end street, it's a fairly large center-hall brick Colonial, with pillars on either side of the front door, stone urns full of hydrangeas along the brick path, and a small but exquisite garden in the back that explodes with color from April into the early fall—obviously the work of a gardener far more talented than I would ever be. All the rooms in our house were large and airy, a perfect setting for our comfortable, overstuffed furniture, and I loved coming back there from campus, even from a short trip to the supermarket. Imagining Perry in this haven was like discovering scale on an orchid.

But of course Perry *was* coming to dinner, no matter what I thought. I wasn't just up against him, it was Stefan too, and Stefan's mysterious feelings. After all I'd done for him, been his one-man ticker-tape parade, Stefan didn't know what he felt! I was trapped. I had to be patient, wait this out, help Stefan decide whether he still wanted Perry or not—and what that meant. Can you see Mary Queen of Scots telling the executioner, "Let me help you sharpen the blade"?

I tried calling my cousin Sharon in New York, but her office phone was busy and I didn't feel like leaving a message for her at home. It was always frustrating not being able to get ahold of her, because she was my favorite relative in addition to being sensible and smart. She was also the first person I came out to, and I've confided in her ever since. Sharon was our family's great success, something of a star. As a psychology major at Barnard in the early '70s, she had gotten an unexpected modeling job that continued after college. She ended up doing commercials, print ads, fashion magazine covers, traveling around the world and making a great deal of money until she eventually gave it all up at thirty-five.

Unable to talk to Sharon about Stefan and Perry, I cleaned the house all day in a fury; it would puzzle Mrs. McCormick when she came on Wednesday. Then I cleared out the leaves that had started to collect in the gutters, raked what little had fallen in the yard, got a pile of leaves burning on the driveway, washed my car, and even contemplated reseeding a weedy patch under the kitchen window, but I gave up by the afternoon and settled for doing wash and grading all the papers I could concentrate on.

What made me maddest about the thing with Perry was Stefan framing the whole problem ethically. He was on solid ground, laying everything out like someone setting tiles into a mosaic with a sure, responsible hand. He hadn't gone off to screw Perry, or driven away to be by himself while I stewed and mourned, or manipulated me into blowing up so that he could feel blameless, cool.

He was keeping me *informed*. It would be like having a crisis break on CNN news: I could follow it through each microscopic permutation, all day if I wanted. All night.

I tried Sharon again later that day and got through. I told her all about Perry and Stefan, and that I had been feeling like Isabel Archer in *The Portrait of a Lady*.

"If you want a role model," Sharon said dryly, "why not Alexis on *Dynasty?*"

That intrigued me. "Alexis?"

"Better outfits," she explained.

"Yes! Remember those hats!"

Then I told Sharon that Perry was having dinner with us.

"Why?"

"Stefan invited him."

"This part is a joke, right?"

"It's a nightmare."

"Oh, Nick...."

"And Stefan asked me if I would cook. How could I say no?" There was a long silence on the other end, and I said, "You don't think I need to see a therapist, do you?"

Sharon laughed. "Sweetie, you don't need therapy, you need *revenge.*"

"God, you're right! Dinner should be outrageous, eight courses of Baroque splendor—Truffles on a Tambourine, Pheasant under Tiffany glass."

"No. I'd go the other way. Make macaroni and cheese. Tater Tots, franks."

"What?"

"To show Perry you're not threatened and that Stefan doesn't care what you eat because your love transcends food."

Well, laughing helped, and I hung up a few minutes later feeling much better, but it didn't last.

I saw Perry a few times in our office that week and everything I'd admired in him now aroused my contempt, especially when he said he was "looking forward" to dinner! I almost said, "Why don't you bring Ann-Margret if she's not busy?" But there wasn't much point in sharpening my claws. Not now. Not yet.

Serena Fisch drifted into my office one afternoon, sat on the edge of my desk like a torch singer about to launch into something moody and intense. "So you have a little *cross* to bear now? He's coming over for dinner, I hear."

I flushed, and wondered if she knew about Perry and Stefan. "Who told you about dinner?"

She grinned. "Angel child, I never reveal my sources. So tell me, what are you serving, arsenic and arugala salad? Strychnine soup?"

"Maybe you can lend me your cookbook." And we looked at each other with embarrassing honesty. I realized that I hated Perry as much as she did—and it was frightening, like some conspiratorial moment from a Jacobean play right before a series of gruesome deaths. I certainly had the office for that scene. Parker Hall is one of the older and more dilapidated buildings on campus, an 1880s structure with enormous, inhumanly high ceilings and windows; sagging, heaving floors; exposed piping; more than occasional bats;

and lots of dark and smelly corners. Even though my office had a gorgeous view of two big maples and was hung with bright Matisse posters, it always seemed cold and forbidding, like a hospital room that no amount of flowers and cheery hellos can make relaxed and inviting.

"He is a nasty sonofabitch," Serena said, crossing her legs and swinging one as if she were a gun moll on a gangster's lap.

"But you don't really know him," I said.

"I know enough. I've heard enough. I don't trust him."

I nodded.

When Serena left, I started resentfully thinking about dessert. I make an excellent and attractive cheesecake: the colors and textures always look wonderful up on the glass-topped silver cake dish Sharon gave us on our first anniversary. I would buy a bottle of Baron Philippe Sauternes to go with it, solid but not flashy. Salad would be easy. Stefan loved Brie, so I would make a marinated tomato and Brie salad—the blend of olive oil, garlic, fresh parsley, and basil is almost hypnotic. Braised leeks with a pink peppercorn mayonnaise might be lovely after that, but what about the entree? That evening I picked through our shelves of cookbooks for something new or reliable, I couldn't decide, and Stefan seemed anxious when I hadn't made up my mind by Saturday morning.

"Listen," I said. "*You're* exploring your feelings, *I'm* exploring the menu."

"Let me help."

"Okay. Buy some flowers, tea roses, white, alstroemeria, purple. Clean the bathrooms, wash the guest towels, set the table with Sharon's china. Trim your sideburns."

He didn't have sideburns, but he got to work.

I finally chose pasta shells stuffed with escargots, prosciutto, spinach, cream, parmesan, white wine, garlic, and Pernod. The Pernod decided me—it's so Hemingway in Paris, so slutty and tough. I shopped for an hour and returned with bags of goodies to find Stefan lying on the bed, a hand over his eyes, the window shades down.

"Are you sick?"

"Maybe this dinner is a mistake." He sounded like a medium unsure if she's contacted the other side or not.

"Stefan, if I'm a condemned man, I want my last meal to be a good one."

"Perry, having Perry over."

I asked him to open his eyes: "It's like talking to a tomb effigy."

He didn't open them. "I'm ashamed of myself."

I wanted to shout, Good! You should be! But I just went to unpack the groceries.

Now, I'm a fine cook if I know what I'm doing, if I've made the dish before. Otherwise I get easily panicked, and that whole afternoon I kept rushing to the stove, to the sink or the refrigerator, shouting, "Oh my God! I forgot—"

Stefan would peer in, ask what was wrong as I nervously stirred, poured, mixed, and I'd snap out a sullen "Leave me alone!" or "Shut up." After an hour of that he said, "I'm not going to invite people over if this is what happens."

"How many ex-lovers did you have in mind? Let's do a buffet next time!"

"This would be easier if you weren't so upset."

I was taking shots of Pernod every time Stefan made me mad, or when I even thought about why I was preparing dinner. Each shot I snapped back was like hurling a dart at his face on a wall poster. I began to stop caring how the escargots would turn out; at least the salad and cheesecake were fine. I would just have to keep myself from taking up the baguette and swatting someone.

Stefan stayed out of the kitchen, but he radiated tension and disapproval the way only quiet people can.

Showering, I imagined myself on the Riverwalk in San Antonio, or dancing in Key West rain, or walking the beach at Newport, with those mammoth houses gazing out to sea like the ugly touching monoliths on Easter Island. They were all places Stefan and I had discovered together.

I think of this story as an academic mystery, but since some people with a more limited vision would call it "a gay narrative," now's the time for me to dry myself off in the mirror and admire my rock-hard chest and washboard stomach, bragging about how going to the gym changed my life. No way. Running, weights, aerobics—I can't stand any of it now for more than a few months at a time. Then I stop, my clothes start getting tighter, and Stefan begins watching me intently as if his silence could force me into an aria of confession: "Yes! I gained seven pounds!"

The point is that I hadn't been heaving and grunting for months, and while I didn't look awful, I sure wasn't any slim Jim—and I needed a haircut. Getting dressed, I thought of the *I Love Lucy Show:* if she were faced with her husband's old flame, she'd dress to kill, to *annihilate,* or dress like a hillbilly, blacking out some teeth, to embarrass Ricky.

"You have a comic vision of life," Stefan said to me once, in bed, after chasing me around the house while I went "Mee-meeep" like the Road Runner.

"Is that okay?" I had asked when he didn't go on. "Do you still like me?"

"What're you wearing?" I asked Stefan an hour before Perry was due.

"Socks, underwear, shoes, pants. A shirt. Oh, a belt too."

I didn't smile.

"That was like a joke," he said.

"*Like* a joke, but not an actual joke."

"You win."

"Good, then let's call Perry and cancel."

Stefan ended up wearing the red and blue Alexander Julian outfit—slacks, sweater, shirt—I'd bought him a week before, and he looked too good, too big and inviting, like an athlete turned model.

Stefan hugged me in the kitchen in the large abstract way that sometimes bothers me because it feels like it has little to do with me. It was not the way I wanted to be held with Perry coming in a few minutes. I wanted one of those hugs that fills the world, I wanted everything.

WHEN PERRY KNOCKED and Stefan went out to the front door, I downed another shot of the Pernod, which was starting to taste vile. I was like a fat little kid stuffing donuts into his tear-lined face, thinking, That'll show everybody, choking on hurt and rage.

Perry had brought a bunch of tiger lilies.

Cheerfully, I said in what I thought was an Irish accent, "He's laid out in the other room and don't he look marvelous?"

Perry tried to smile.

Great start, I thought, going off for a vase.

Then I followed them through Stefan's perfunctory house tour, deploring Perry's somber dark blue suit, white shirt, and red tie. He looked like a camera-conscious young senator, handsome, slick, as artificial as floral air spray. We looked out at the garden from the sun room running along the whole back of the house, but I did not want to share a single plant or shrub with Perry, and so I led us back inside.

"This is great," Perry said as we settled down in the living room for caviar.

"Compared to what?" I asked.

Perry smiled again, glancing at Stefan for a sign of complicity, but Stefan just sat back in the blue and sea green tub chair, eyes wide, as if expecting those feelings of his to show up at the door. Perry and I were on the full-armed sofa; I squeezed some lemon onto my caviar-heavy Carr's biscuit and asked, "So what do you think your chances of tenure are, given the budget cuts?"

Perry took that in, sipped his Southern Comfort. I bit into my cracker with all the verve, I thought, of Margo Channing's "Fasten your seat belts." I went on. "*Since* the department is so top-heavy with tenured faculty, I mean."

"I expect to stay here a long time," he drawled, like a shifty claim jumper weighing his gold before it was even mined. "What about you?" Perry asked Stefan.

"Stefan was hired with tenure, of course," I answered before Stefan could. "But he's doing so well, and now his agent has gotten him a contract with Knopf, so we might get better offers. We're talking about someplace warm, where we can tan on the way to class." Well, I had started, and I went on and on through dinner about every one of Stefan's publications, quoting reviews, letters from fans and other writers who'd seen excerpts of his books in *The New Yorker, Paris Review, Vanity Fair*. It was all true. He'd been called "remarkable," "stirring," and even "brilliant." I was cheating there, because almost every other writer reviewed nowadays gets called brilliant by *somebody*, if only in *Entertainment Weekly*.

Stefan and Perry ate quietly while I rhapsodized about Stefan's work, pointing out at least twice that he'd become successful *after* we met, not before. I was as inexorable as a proud grandfather launching his grandchildren's grades, school reports, accomplishments, and personal qualities like a fleet of hot air balloons. I was dizzied by my own praise, the Pernod, and the half bottle of Puligny-Montrachet I downed. They didn't get a chance to talk about the past.

Stefan said almost nothing. What could he say? I'd practically renamed several campus buildings in his honor, established a Stefan Borowski scholarship fund, given him a Pulitzer, an American Book Award, and a Congressional Medal of Honor. Perry nodded, smiled, said, "Wow" or "Neat" or "Really?" when I gave him the chance.

But when I began to feel bloated and sluggish with wine and food, Perry said, "Something odd happened the other day."

Stefan asked what.

"I was in the lot behind Parker," Perry said. "You know there's that long lane that goes straight out to Michigan Avenue? Well, someone driving along there slowly suddenly sped up. I had to jump out of the way. It was—" Perry shrugged, as if embarrassed. "It was almost like he was trying to run me down."

"Who was it?" I asked, wishing the driver hadn't missed. Stefan was so right, I did wish that Perry was dead, and would have happily watched him spontaneously combust or keel over onto the table with terminal hauteur.

"I couldn't really tell. And I didn't really see the car."

"Students," Stefan said. "Probably drunk."

"It could have been fag-bashing," I said.

And now Perry looked offended, as if he could not possibly be perceived by a stranger as queer.

I shrugged. "It's been happening. And you can't tell how much is real, how much is rumors. Like I heard a guy had been mugged in the library, in a men's room, after somebody lured him in, but he was too humiliated to say anything about it."

"I heard that too," Stefan said quietly, not looking at me or Perry. "Everyone says the Campus Police are homophobic, so that would keep anyone from reporting it even if it was true. If you're a gay student and something happens to you, nothing seems to get done about it. The Campus Police are much more interested in damage to university property."

Perry sniffed. "What a snake pit."

"Wait a minute! This is a wonderful place," I shot. "I love living in Michigan—people aren't stuck up here, they're friendly." I cranked up my Chamber of Commerce speech, which aways made Stefan grin because he enjoyed my partisanship, but tonight he was not looking pleased.

Then I told a long and boring anecdote about our seeing the Gay Pride Parade in San Francisco last summer, saying the word "gay" as often as possible, to strike Perry down for ever pretending to be anything else. For *still* pretending about it, or keeping silent. I interrupted myself to toss Perry a hand grenade. I innocently asked, "You don't ever march or anything like that, do you?" and went on before he could answer.

With dessert, I launched into something new: Stefan and me, how happy and productive we were together. I guessed that Perry didn't have any kind of lover at the moment, and I was as cruel as those rebels in the Sudan preventing emergency flights of food into starving enemy-held villages.

"We have a very full life," I said, after talking about our various "travels" and our midsummer trips to the Shakespeare Festival in Stratford, Ontario. "We're very happy. We're thinking of adopting."

Stefan stared at me and put down his fork. Nothing dramatic, no explosion, just that. I thought, It's over, I've gone too far, and Perry's won. I could see that Perry thought so too. He looked like a jackal on one of those nature specials about to dart between two squabbling lions to snatch a piece of the felled zebra.

"It's getting late," Perry said. It was only ten. I managed to ask if anyone wanted more coffee.

"I'm fine." Perry thanked us both and rose from the table like a crown prince waiting for the inevitable news from the king's sick room: gracious, thoughtful, posed. "Dinner was wonderful," he said. "You're a very good cook. And that cheesecake!"

My consolation prize, I suppose.

Perry shook my hand when he left and I turned back to the dining room. Surveying the littered table, I wondered where I would go now and what Stefan would say.

He headed for the kitchen, opened the dishwasher.

When I brought in the first dishes from the table, Stefan said, "You acted like a jerk tonight." I piled the dishes on the counter near the sink. "A real jerk."

"Was dinner okay?"

He turned. "I've never seen you like this."

"I've never been under the gun before! You set the whole thing up like—" But I couldn't finish. I continued ferrying dishes in from the dining room as if each plate passing between us marked the end of our connection. When I pictured myself hurling them all onto the floor, I sat heavily at the kitchen table, wanting him to leave now, to not drag it out anymore.

Stefan knelt by my chair. Here it comes, I thought.

"What's your opinion of Perry?" he asked.

"Perry?" I reached for a napkin to blow my nose. "Perry? *My* opinion? Are we voting? Who breaks the tie?"

Stefan shook his head, that beautiful head full of unexplored feelings. "You know that David Bowie line you like? 'I looked in her eyes, they were blue but nobody home'?"

"Perry's eyes are *brown*."

Stefan pulled a chair close, sat with our knees touching.

"Listen—"

""You said I was a jerk."

"Wait—you were *real*. Okay, a real jerk. But Perry's just the *idea* of a person. Hollywood, you know, perfect stage set, you walk behind it, bare boards propping it up. And he was always like that. Nobody home."

"And I'm a jerk."

He took my hands with the gravity of a nineteenth-century suitor. "Perry can't love, he's too busy watching, seeing what kind of impression he makes. Not like you. I never really understood that about him. I had to *see* it." He shook his head, "I was the jerk. I'm sorry."

"I'm going to torch his file cabinets and take an ax to his desk. Monday morning, I swear."

Stefan hugged me, a real hug, personal, alive.

"You were wonderful tonight," he murmured. "Perry's so bland, really, but you're—you're *various.*"

"Various? Why not call me sundry, too? 'Nick Hoffman, Various and Sundry.'"

"I mean you have shades, you have *depth.*"

Well, I liked the sound of that, but I felt stunned, drained. I slumped in my chair. "So what happens now?" I asked wearily.

"We finish cleaning up, we finish the Sauternes, we make love, we live happily ever after. How's that?"

"Then I want to go to sleep and pretend this never happened."

He smiled. "Whatever you say."

In bed, lying spooned against me with my right arm around his chest, Stefan said, "It's an old story, isn't it? The Triumph of True Love."

"We'll do *tableaux vivants* some other time." I had been thinking about the whole bizarre evening with unexpected relief. Stefan had *enjoyed* my bizarre performance, found me delightful.

"I'm glad you didn't try poisoning Perry's wine or anything," he said through a yawn, on the very edge of sleep.

"Hey—there's still plenty of time to kill Perry Cross."

# -6-

I had some pretty strange dreams, and woke up once feeling almost drowned in nauseating and confusing events, with scenes and figures shifting and gluing together. At first I wasn't entirely sure that I was awake—it might just have been a more normal-seeming part of my dream. But then I heard the throaty hooting and roar of the train that cuts through town every morning at two o'clock. It's a warm and comforting sound, to me anyway, as it fills the night. I reached over for Stefan, but he wasn't in bed. I looked up and through the open doorway, but there was no light on in the bathroom. I wondered if he was having trouble sleeping and had gone to work in his study—at least I think that's what went through my mind. Because before I could get up to check, I was out cold again.

There was no mistaking what truly ended my night's sleep. The clock radio got us up with local news at eight o'clock on the public radio station. The unctuous voice said, "An SUM professor was found dead on campus early this morning. He has been identified as Professor Perry Cross of the English, American Studies, and Rhetoric Department. Campus Police have released no other details."

As the announcer went on to some item about the state legislature, I rolled over to find Stefan staring at me.

I stared back. "How can he be *dead?*"

Stefan frowned, shook his head as if he hadn't really heard me and wasn't even sure he was awake.

"He was just here at dinner last night!" I shook my head. "And now he's dead?" I sat up, leaned back against the headboard. "It *was* Perry, wasn't it? You heard it too? I'm not dreaming this, am I?"

"We're awake," Stefan said, and reached back to shut off the radio.

I didn't know what to say. Just before falling asleep, I'd joked about killing Perry; I felt disgusted to have said it.

My mind was full of flickering images of people in movies and on TV finding out about a death: they were usually shocked, they screamed, cried, rushed around, stuffed fists into their mouths, stumbled backwards into a chair, quivering—did things that seemed extreme, no matter how limited the compass. But I was just dumbfounded.

I guess Stefan was too.

Suddenly, last night's dinner felt retrospectively eerie, a portent of even worse things to come.

We had been eating dinner with a corpse. That's what it felt like here in bed this morning. I felt deeply ashamed of how upset I'd been to have Perry over—that seemed trivial now when weighed against his death.

"I guess I don't have to share my office anymore," I brought out. "Or not for a while."

Stefan grinned a little strangely, and I realized that joking was definitely not the right tack.

We got up. We showered and ate breakfast without saying much at all. I felt as if I'd taken too many antihistamines: my vision, my hearing, my thinking were all clouded and dull.

Stefan had an early class and left before me. Luckily I didn't have to teach that morning. I only had a long stretch of office hours, and it was somewhat too early in the semester for students to have questions, problems, or even feel like coming in to chat.

Usually, I went to the department office first to check my mail, say hi to the secretaries and whoever was there, plugging in to the prevailing current. But today I headed right up to the third floor of Parker. I didn't want people reminding me that I'd seen Perry the night he died, had made dinner for him. It seemed embarrassing and grotesque to talk about him at all, especially since he wasn't a friend. How could I mention his name without some of my antagonism leaking through? I could imagine Serena Fisch's smile when she met me. It wasn't that long ago that we had acknowledged how much we despised Perry.

I felt guilty somehow, as if saying good night to Perry Cross had sent him off to death. It was weird that I was so affected, but perhaps I was responding to Stefan's heavy silence.

If you've lived with an introvert, then you know that they can have many different levels and kinds of silence. You become expert at tuning in, listening, interpreting. Or sometimes ignoring. But I didn't know what to make of Stefan's silence at breakfast, and felt sucked into my own.

Unlocking my scarred office door, I shuddered at the two cheap black and white plastic nameplates, mine and Perry's. Someone would have to remove his, I thought. And I pictured his mailbox right above mine in the department office.

Inside, at my desk, with the office door open just a crack, I was glad that Perry's desk and file cabinets were not in my immediate sight line but behind my back, where I could ignore them. I would have to make an effort to either inspect what was on his desk or to take in the still life his death had left behind.

I knew the student newspaper was downstairs and wondered if there was an article in there yet—or was it too soon? "Found dead on campus"—what did that mean? Where did it happen? Who found him, and when? How did he die? Was he wounded? Were there witnesses?

I sat at my desk, unable to take out any papers to grade, unable to push my thoughts in some productive direction.

I hadn't liked him even before I knew what he had done to Stefan, so I wasn't *sorry* Perry Cross was dead, but I wasn't relieved. His dying so soon after dinner even made me feel cheated, a little. Lying in bed with Stefan last night, I'd imagined many scenes of quiet but vindictive triumph in our office. Like heading off up north to our cabin on Lake Michigan for a weekend. Or coming back from an opera in Chicago. I'd be casual as I shared information about our good times with Perry, a nasty kid holding a scrap out of his hungry dog's reach, waving it back and forth hypnotically.

I was also ashamed of myself for being so vindictive. Perry was dead; nothing that I felt, nothing that had happened really made a difference now.

Perry's death was bound to create confusion in our department, and not just because of the need for someone to cover his classes. Broadshaw would probably take Perry's death personally, and storm around kicking desks and shouting. I dreaded the chaos our chair would make. I'd seen him enraged last year by a snowstorm that kept some faculty members at home in their rural towns. I felt sorry for everyone who'd have to put up with Broadshaw, which of course included me.

There was a knock and Stefan came in. I checked my desk clock; he had another hour before his next class. He was pale and more out of it than he had been at home. Today his clothes looked incongruously good on him—they fit so well that the dark green and black checked shirt and black slacks only heightened how miserable he was.

He sunk into the comfy chair I had bought for my students (since I couldn't requisition anything from university Stores that was acceptable). Students are usually nervous enough talking to a professor, and watching them twitch and stretch in a stiff-backed unsteady chair would have been distracting for me.

"They found him in the river," Stefan said.

"The *river?* How? What the hell was he doing?"

Stefan shook his head absently, like a parent staying connected to his child with vague murmurs and smiles, but not really listening. "It's just what the secretaries told me. In the river, by the Administration Building bridge."

The narrow, shallow Michigan River runs through the center of campus and widens a little right by the Roman Revival-ish Administration Building with its gorgeous Corinthian pillars looming nearby like the calm classical backdrop for a bloated opera. There's a four-foot drop in the river's depth at that spot, and a row of artfully planted boulders makes what passes for rapids on our flat campus in the flattest part of Michigan. Three sets of wide granite steps descended on the southern side to a spreading terrace low enough for you to sit and dangle your feet in the water. It's one of the loveliest spots on campus, the setting as ordered and restful as an ornamental pond in a formal garden, and it draws ducks and students all year round.

"But what happened to him?" I asked. "How did he die?"

"Nobody really knows."

"What do you mean? This isn't New York, this is Michiganapolis. We don't have dead bodies turning up all over the place, like in dumpsters. How can they *not* know what happened?"

"All that takes time, I guess. They just found him this morning." Stefan cleared his throat. "Why do you think he was over by the bridge?"

I wondered why we weren't saying Perry's name. Was it superstition, fear that naming him would call him back in some way, or make the death seem more terrible?

"I don't know. And how'd he end up in the river?"

"An accident?"

"What kind of accident?" I asked.

"Heart attack? Stroke?" I must have looked dubious, because Stefan said almost defensively, "It can happen to someone his age."

"He was healthy. He looked it, anyway."

Stefan frowned, trying to puzzle it out. "Okay," he said. "What if he was walking on a path by the river, and a biker zoomed by and knocked him over. You know how reckless they are even during the day."

"And he fell and rolled down the bank into the river?"

Stefan nodded thoughtfully. "And there're all those rocks there by the bridge. If that's where it happened."

"But which side of the bridge—the rocks are to the west of the bridge."

"Maybe he fell in somewhere else, and drifted."

"Drifted? Is that possible?" I asked. "Is the river deep enough? Is there much of a current?"

Stefan shrugged.

"I guess you could fall somehow and knock yourself out, get a concussion or whatever. If that's what happened." I found the picture rather unlikely. "But what time was it? We heard the news at eight o'clock. Was it just before that—or a lot earlier? And what would anybody be doing on the bridge that early? And wouldn't there be witnesses?"

"Do you think it was suicide?" Stefan asked.

"Please! If you wanted to kill yourself by drowning, you wouldn't do it in the Michigan River. And if you wanted to jump from someplace on *campus,* you'd throw yourself off a building or something, wouldn't you? If you were serious?"

"You think he couldn't have jumped off the bridge?"

"But it's not that high up, is it?" I thought then that I had to get to the bridge and check out the scene for myself.

Stefan frowned. "If it wasn't an accident, and it wasn't suicide—"

I nodded. "I can imagine wanting to kill Perry."

Stefan grimaced. "No—that's not what I meant. It could've been a robbery, or a gay-bashing, or something like that."

"Who'd attack a professor? I don't buy it. Listen, Stefan, I just met him, and I hated him. There must be lots of people who know him better who feel the same way—like everyone at all the other schools where he ever taught at before."

"Hate him enough to come out to Michiganapolis and kill him?" Stefan shook his head.

"I'd believe that before I'd believe he was robbed. Murders are almost always committed by someone who knows the victim well—that's what the papers always say. Didn't you tell me he had two ex-wives? Maybe he was stiffing them for alimony or child support."

"And one of them murdered him?"

"She could have hired somebody to do it," I pointed out, warming to the possibility.

"Kill him and stop the money completely?" Stefan shook his head.

"Why are you so dubious?" I asked. "Didn't you ever wish he was dead? I did."

Stefan's eyes hardened. "But I would never do it—and you wouldn't either."

I shrugged. "You're right. We don't even know how he died or what kind of wounds he had. Was he stabbed, or strangled, or shot? He could have been bludgeoned to death...."

Stefan looked pale. "This is gruesome."

"Professor Hoffman?" someone said at the door, pushing it open without knocking.

I looked up.

"Detective Valley. I'm with the Campus Police Squad. I'm investigating the death of Perry Cross."

I stared. Detective Valley was a gangling, freckled man with curly red hair and an incongruous Vandyke; he was wearing a dark pinstripe suit, maroon print tie and blue buttoned-down shirt, shiny black oxfords. He looked less like a detective than a salesman at a "Going Out of Business" furniture outlet.

"Why do you want to talk to *me?*"

As if speaking to someone a little dense, he said carefully, "I've seen the chair already, and you're next on the list. This was Professor Cross's office, and you shared it with him."

I snorted. "I thought all you guys did was hand out parking tickets. How come the Michiganapolis police aren't investigating?"

Valley walked on in and handed me a business card with his name, address, and phone number on it under a shield logo with CPS in the middle. Across the top, the card read: "Serving the SUM Community."

Valley said, "The Michiganapolis police don't have jurisdiction on campus."

I didn't stand or move forward to shake the detective's hand, and he didn't seem to expect it. I disliked his dry supercilious voice, his knowing eyes.

I glanced at Stefan, who didn't seem to be paying attention.

Valley said to Stefan, "And you are—? Stefan Borowski? Good—you're on my list, too. I'd like you to stay." The detective gestured to the small chair near Perry's desk, said, "May I?" and pulled it over before I could say anything. "I want to ask you some questions, Professor Hoffman."

I asked, "Where's your notepad?"

He smiled as if at the antics of a puppy chewing on a rug. "I've got a good memory," he said.

Stefan just sat there like a patient waiting for the doctor to give him bad news.

I asked Valley, "How did Perry Cross die?"

Suddenly Valley was warmer, more expansive, leaning back comfortably. "Well, right now it looks like he fell from the bridge, struck his head on a submerged log, and drowned while unconscious."

"He fell from the bridge? How do you know that?"

Valley shrugged off my question.

"And the river's too shallow to drown in," I said. "Isn't it?"

"Not really. Water in your lungs is water in your lungs."

There was a creepy kind of enthusiasm to Valley now that made me feel like I was in some movie with Vincent Price playing the mad scientist delightfully sharing his forays into darkness.

"How long have you known Professor Cross?" Valley asked me.

"Professor Cross" sounded strange to me, distancing. "A couple of—no, since just before the semester started."

Valley nodded, crossing his long thin legs. He waited, but I didn't add anything.

"Was he happy here?"

"I don't really know."

"Was he unstable? Nervous? Hysterical?"

"What are you talking about?"

"Wasn't he a homosexual?" The clipped dispassionate way he said it made it sound like he was using a word he was as disgusted by as terrorist, pervert, kidnapper—but trying to deaden his feelings for the sake of law and order. I realized then that this man might be the one in charge of responding to the incidents on campus like the gay student leader's car being trashed.

"What's your point?"

"It was a question, not a statement."

"You think he might have killed himself because he's a queer, because all queers are miserable and sick, and that's how they end up, that's how they *should* end up?"

"I just asked if he was a homosexual. It's part of the whole picture."

"Well, *I'm* gay, and so is Stefan."

Valley surveyed us coolly. "Yeah," he said. "But you're not dead."

I willed myself to calm down. I looked at Stefan, who wasn't offering any help.

"Perry wasn't 'unstable.' He was—arrogant."

"You didn't like him."

"No."

"Even though you shared an office?"

"It wasn't my choice."

Valley nodded. "When's the last time you saw Professor Cross?"

I hesitated. "Yesterday."

"And what time was that?"

"Dinner."

"Who else was there?"

"Just Stefan and me."

Valley turned to Stefan. "And where was this?"

"Our house," Stefan brought out quietly. "Nick and I live together."

Valley smiled. "Professor Cross was your *dinner guest*. When did he arrive—when did he leave?"

"Seven o'clock," I said. "And he was gone by ten."

"What did you talk about?

I shrugged helplessly. How was I supposed to answer that one? Stefan did: "We talked about the university, about our careers."

Valley asked Stefan, "How would you describe his mood?"

Stefan and I looked at each other, looked back at Valley. "That's hard to do," I said.

"But you're an English professor, right? Words are your business."

His eyes seemed alive with malice. The silence dragged on until Valley abruptly broke it himself with "What was the occasion? Nothing special? Have you had dinner with him before for no special reason? What else have you done together?"

I felt like an idiot, and a liar.

Valley was not gloating, exactly, but he seemed delighted to be making us squirm. He leaned back in his chair. "How would you describe your relationship with the deceased?"

Stefan said, "He was a colleague."

"Who neither one of you seemed to like, but invited to dinner anyway."

Stefan bristled. "Detective Valley, if you only had dinner with people you liked, wouldn't you spend a lot of time alone?"

Valley shrugged. "Maybe. Maybe not." Looking at me very intently, Valley said, "Tell me about his mood. Was he depressed? Was he taking any medication, did he drink, anything like that?"

"I don't know. We weren't living together, just sharing an office."

And now Valley smiled. "*Did* you like Professor Cross?" he asked Stefan.

"Not really, no."

I was afraid to look at Stefan or the detective because Stefan's answer was so, well, incomplete.

"Did you know him well?"

Stefan sighed. "Not exactly."

"Do you know his friends, any of his family, anything about him?"

Stefan shrugged. "Why should I?"

I had to stop this, so I asked the detective, "Do you really think Perry Cross might have killed himself?"

Valley scowled at me, but then he said, "It's a possibility. That's why I want to know if he was happy here."

"Well, he wasn't," I said. "He hasn't had much of a career until now, and there's no guarantee he would get tenure at State. With jobs drying up all over, he was *doomed*."

I felt Stefan stir uncomfortably while I spoke, and he coughed when I stopped.

"Doomed," Valley said. "Interesting. But he couldn't know how things would turn out at SUM." Valley went on, as if trying to catch me in a lie. "Not so soon."

"Well...." I was beginning to wonder if Perry had realized after dinner that he hadn't really scored any points against me, that it was hopeless trying to cause trouble. But could he have been that astute, that sensitive to realize what I didn't even understand until Stefan told me how he felt? And was knowing that Stefan didn't want him enough to make Perry kill himself in however unlikely a way?

"What did you find at his apartment?" I asked.

Valley frowned.

"I assume you did some kind of search, right? That's what always happens on TV, anyway."

"He was working on grading papers last night," Valley said grudgingly.

"That explains everything! There were too many punctuation problems and he flipped out."

I grinned at Stefan, who looked at me wide-eyed.

Valley nodded now, kept nodding, as if something were beginning to make sense to him. "What time did Professor Cross leave your house?" He fixed my eyes as if daring me to blink.

"We told you—around ten o'clock."

"Was he drunk?"

"I don't think so. Why?"

"And where were you early this morning, from approximately two o'clock to four o'clock? Both of you?"

"Is that when he died?" I asked eagerly.

Valley seemed to hesitate, and then shook his head. I wasn't sure if he was answering the question or what, exactly.

"Where were you?" Valley repeated. "From two o'clock to four o'clock."

"At home," I said. "In bed. We live together—-but then you know that already."

Valley didn't smile. "In bed. Asleep?"

I didn't look at Stefan as I said, "Actually, we were wide awake, if you get what I mean." I smiled. "If you want more details, I'd be happy to supply them."

"And you knew what time it was? You turned on the lights? The clock dial glows in the dark?"

"A freight train comes through town right around two every morning. I'm sure you've noticed."

"And—"

"Are you trying to find out if one of us *killed* him? You think he was murdered? Why? Were there any signs of a struggle? Was he wounded?"

Valley ignored those questions and asked one of his own. "Did he have any enemies?"

I couldn't really answer without revealing that Stefan had lied about how well he knew Perry Cross.

"He wasn't very popular around here," Stefan said a little awkwardly.

And in the silence, I thought it was a remark that would sound suspicious to anyone: after all, Perry Cross had only been in the department for a month.

Valley nodded and rose. "Thank you for your time," he said. "I'll be back if I have more questions, or I'll call you."

I stalked to the doorway, watched the detective head down the hall to the exit. I closed the door.

Stefan was up and staring out the window.

"Why did you lie about Perry?" I asked.

Stefan didn't turn around. "He's dead, what does it matter? It's nobody's business how well I know him." After a moment, he added, "Knew him. And wait a minute! *You* told him the truth? What was that stuff about us being 'wide awake' in the middle of the night? Were you trying to antagonize him? What for?"

"Stefan, he was a *creep,* a fag-hater."

"Right."

I felt we were on the edge of a terrible argument, and I didn't understand why or what exactly it was about. I sat down, not letting myself say anything nasty, and just took a few deep breaths.

"Why did you lie about Perry?"

"I don't want people to know. It's one thing being out, it's another having people gossip about you."

"But it's not a secret that Perry was at our place for dinner."

Stefan shut down, the way he does when he thinks talking to me is hopeless.

"I'll see you later, back home," he said, walking out.

And he was gone before I could ask him what he'd been doing when I woke up at two o'clock and found myself alone in bed.

# -7-

I sat in my office as if the whole weight of Parker Hall had descended on me. The building was a sad, featureless, ramshackle heap of brick and sandstone that looked like an abandoned nineteenth-century mental institution. It had badly worn staircases, sagging floors, and flaking ceilings. The bathrooms were all moldy and marred by leaking pipes. Right now, I felt just as decrepit.

Like many universities, SUM had a history of cruelly underfunding the Humanities compared to the lavish sums it threw at the Medical School, Business, and Engineering (in our case, add Agricultural Economics). The salaries were lower, budgets tighter, support staffs smaller, even supplies far less plentiful. The disparities were especially obvious when you looked at the different buildings. The privileged departments and colleges either had gleaming new air-conditioned facilities and offices bristling with computers, or older buildings that had been as lovingly restored and updated as if they were smack in the middle of a rapidly gentrifying city neighborhood.

Parker was a dump.

From out in the hall I suddenly heard a cheerful "Hi, Professor Hoffman."

At the door was a former student of mine, Angela Sandoval.

"I was just dropping a paper off for Professor Davidoff," Angela said, turning to go. She looked so bright and pretty she was completely out of place in this dim setting.

Then something hit me. "Angela! Are you still a Criminal Justice major?"

Angela nodded.

"Do you have a few minutes?"

"Sure." She came in and sat right down, as relaxed and easygoing as she'd been last semester, the kind of student who smiles encouragingly at professors throughout class, but not because she's witless or angling for a grade. Angela just showed her enjoyment and comprehension; every class should have at least one student like that.

"Angela, do you know anything about the Campus Police?"

"A shitload!" She blushed. "Sorry. I know a lot—I wrote a whole paper about them last year."

"Perfect. What are they—are they real cops?"

"Definitely. Fully authorized by the state—just like police in a town. SUM is their jurisdiction. If you call 911 on campus, that's who responds. The phone system is set up that way."

"Can they arrest people?"

"Oh, for sure!" She squinted a little, as if trying to visualize the paper she'd written. "I think there's about sixty of them all together, but some of those are administrators. They're all armed, though. Most of them served in other police forces around the state first—this is considered a great job. Some of them have Master's degrees, or law."

"What kind of crimes do they deal with?"

"Everything! Rape, assault, burglary. Mostly 'malicious destruction of property'—you know, drunk students trashing a dorm or knocking over a parking meter."

"How about murder?"

Her brown eyes went wide. "Was somebody murdered? Wait! That professor in the river—him? Was he murdered? You think he was murdered?"

"I don't know. But if *they* thought it was murder, would they contact anybody, like the Michiganapolis police?"

"No way. They'd investigate it themselves. Why do you ask?"

"The man in the river? He was my office mate."

"Wow!" Angela stared over at Perry Cross's desk as if it were a shrine and she were a supplicant.

I went on. "So what does that mean when they... investigate?"

She considered it a moment. "Well. First they'd secure the scene and gather all the evidence, examine the body to see its condition and if anything was missing. Like a wallet, watch, whatever. They contact the Medical Examiner—the ME—and the County Prosecutor. Then they send the body to the morgue at Robbins Hospital in town for the autopsy. That can take a while unless they're in a hurry."

"What else?"

She bit her lip. "Umm.... They'd find out who the last person was to see him, call his family, check medical records, interview friends, look for his car, go to his house, see if he was on any medication. All of that stuff." Suddenly she seemed to see me more clearly. "When's the last time *you* saw him?"

It was so unexpected I blurted out the answer: "Last night."

"Oh, wow! Are you a suspect? This is *way* cool!"

I managed to say, "There aren't any suspects yet. At least I don't think so."

"Well, my cousin's a great lawyer, if you need one. He's right here in town."

"How would they know if it was murder?"

"You mean instead of an accident, or suicide? They'd look for signs of a struggle—cuts, abrasions, like that. The nature of the wounds would tell you a lot—" She broke off. "Hey, are you investigating this? Like Jessica Fletcher or something?" She seemed beside herself with excitement. "Because if you are, remember that cool guy Neil Case in my class last year? His mom is the County ME. You should call her."

Angela suddenly checked her watch. "Shit!" She blushed again, then faked smacking her cheek. "Sorry. I have to get to the library!"

I thanked her and she rushed off leaving me even more depressed than when she'd said hello in the hallway. It was a big mistake for me not to take Detective Valley seriously—he was the real thing.

I headed downstairs for my mail. The department of English, American Studies, and Rhetoric was clearly one of SUM's stepchildren. You saw that in the main office, which was pitiful and depressing. The grimy linoleum floor was cracked, the windows rattled in the winter and the walls hadn't been painted in years; they were still some kind of green: Nile, bile, or vile. As if that wasn't grim enough, when you walked in the one door to the main office, you almost bumped right into a high, forbidding, linoleum-topped counter that kept people as far as possible from the secretaries and the chair's office somewhere beyond all the looming file cabinets.

It was not a welcoming place.

There was very little room to congregate and chat in front of the counter, but today it was as crowded as during registration when frantic frustrated students broke against the counter like waves of dirty surf. Faculty members were standing around holding their mail, pretending to be involved in it, but chatting about Perry Cross. I had heard his name from out in the hallway.

Their faces were all awash in eagerness, as if some televangelist had been found committing bizarre but laughable peccadillos in a trailer park. Larry Rich, the battered ex-hippie who taught Renaissance drama and poetry, was there; and Martin Wardell, the Victorian specialist who never returned student papers on time; Alec Wade, the oily fashionplate Colonialist; Les "Jock" Peterman, the rangy '60s expert, who was always injuring himself at pick-up games of basketball with students.

Everyone stopped talking now when I walked into the office. Alec Wade drew back as if I was contagious and Martin Wardell looked away. Larry Rich cleared his throat. "They're asking about you," he said.

"What?"

"The Campus Police are asking people about you and Stefan. About last night."

"But we didn't *do* anything! We just had Perry to dinner!"

Everyone's eyes were on me now as if I had just confessed my guilt. Oh, God—what if no one else had seen him last night after dinner?

Then from inside the chair's office came what sounded like a book being hurled at a wall and a smothered but audible "God damn it!" Broadshaw rocketed out of his office over to a file cabinet, almost knocking one of the secretaries over en route (that was why people called him "Broadside" behind his back).

While they all turned to stare at the chair, I grabbed my mail and left.

But just outside the office door I was stopped by Serena Fisch, who glided over from the coffee room. She was grinning and waved me to the battered bench against the wall under a bulletin board jammed with notices about conferences, special theme issues of scholarly journals, and new publications. Swathed in black with touches of white, she looked like a chic ex-nun today.

"So you and Stefan got to give Perry his farewell dinner."

Her malice was infectious; despite myself, I smiled.

She was apparently waiting for more, but I didn't say anything.

"I don't care what people are insinuating. I don't believe you and Stefan would have gone to all the trouble of making dinner for someone you wanted to kill. So do you think it was drugs?" she asked. I must have registered confusion, because she went on, "Was it a drug deal that went sour? Can't you see some muscled tough with a ponytail holding his head under water?"

"You read too many thrillers." But I wondered. There had been a number of shooting deaths in Michiganapolis and some suburbs over the last year, and the police almost always classified them as "drug-related." Was that true, or just a catch-all phrase that attempted to make violence seem rational in some way, and thus less threatening, even invisible?

"What a way to go," she said, "in the river. Drowning in duck shit." Serena wriggled her shoulders and I thought of the German word for delighting in someone else's misery, *Schadenfreude*. But this went even further.

"How do you know he drowned? I thought nobody was sure yet what happened."

Serena ignored my question. "Maybe Perry was cruising," she said languorously, as if talking about a trip in the Caribbean rather than hunting for sex.

So she knew he was gay, knew for sure, hadn't just wondered or assumed. Had *everyone* known? "Cruising at the Administration bridge?" I asked. "In the middle of the night?"

She shrugged it off, as if the place and time were inconsequential kinks of Perry's.

"Who the hell is out that late?" I asked, and then remembered my conversation with Stefan about someone biking near the river. I could answer my own question; people ran at night on campus, some workaholics like Rose Waterman stewed in their offices, and maybe someone from town was trying to break into a building or steal a bike or something. But if you were looking for sex, wouldn't you do it indoors and at a more reasonable hour? Unless the weirdness and publicity of the bridge was the whole point.... Like rest-stop sex. I hadn't been at SUM long enough to know where they were, but I imagined that like any school, SUM had tearooms and cruising spots. Why not by the river on that pretty terrace? Couples brought wine there early in the evening, publicly romantic—so maybe later, when campus was deserted, something less romantic took over.

Serena tapped my knee. "I'm going to cover Perry's Canadian Lit survey and the Margaret Atwood seminar."

"But that's a major overload!"

"Lynn's giving me a reduced load spring semester and the following fall off. He's arranged it with the dean."

That meant Serena would be off from the university from mid-May to mid-January. I thought of all those months away from teaching. I was envious; even if you like to teach, the time off is heavenly. No grades to agonize over, no exams to write, and best of all, no papers to read. That assault of other people's voices, that constant *noise* in your head, ceases for a while, and you feel like you're no longer living in an airport, intermittently deafened and stunned.

Just then, the department office door slammed open and Lynn Broadshaw charged out, cursing under his breath, heading down the hall to the men's room.

Serena shook her head, smiling. "He's terrific," she said.

"Terrific?"

"Wouldn't it be funny if it was all just an act?"

"An act," I said, not following.

Now she squinted at me, as if disappointed. "Nobody could be that frazzled all the time and not be putting it on a little. It's camouflage," she said, nodding. "Protective coloring. He makes so much noise you can't take him seriously, and so you eventually tune him out."

"But he did have a stroke."

"Yes, he did, didn't he?"

I couldn't figure out what she meant by that. "When you say camouflage, you think he's hiding something?"

Serena drew back and grimaced as if I'd eaten too many onions. "That goes without saying. We've all got something to hide, even bores. And then *really* interesting people, well—" She smiled expansively. "Like you and Stefan. I'm sure you have loads of secrets." Then she added, in a different voice. "And Perry...."

She lifted her head as if hearing triumphal music. "I can't wait to see what our esteemed chair says at the memorial service."

"Memorial service?" It struck me that I must sound like an idiot to her, repeating everything she said.

"You don't think Lynn would miss the chance to boss people around and give a speech no matter how inane, do you?"

"But Perry just got here. It's not like he was a professor emeritus or anything."

"It's got to be done. Everything has to be tied up neatly."

I was still struck by all the time off she had coming. "Will you do some writing?" I asked. "When you're on leave?"

"*First* I want to write a thank-you note to whoever bumped that bastard off."

Her expression didn't change, so I couldn't tell how much of a joke it was to her. I decided to play along a little, and asked her, "Why are you so sure he was bumped off?"

Serena did something with her eyes that made her look both coy and goofy. Quite a combination. "Honestly, Nick, do you think Perry Cross could kill himself? He was far too conceited."

"It could have been an accident."

She shook her head. "That man was much too careful. At least he tried to be."

The way she said it made her sound as if she'd known him before he got to SUM, or at least knew him better than I would have imagined.

I tried not to look suspicious. "Careful how?"

She crossed her legs like a movie queen chatting with one of her fans, utterly in charge and center stage.

"We'll all be better off now that he's gone," Serena said, ignoring my question. "I'm sure *you're* pleased."

I knew she didn't mean that I was probably glad to have a whole office to myself again, even a small one.

She said, "The way Stefan looked at him!"

"Huh?"

"At the party. It was obvious."

"*What* was obvious?"

"Stefan and Perry went way back. How could anyone miss it? There was *history* in the way they sat there talking, talking...."

My first thought was what would happen if she told that to Detective Valley. Would Valley be asking her questions? Had he done so already? Shit!

"Don't be alarmed," she said, and I cursed myself for letting anything show. "He's out of your hair. It's all over."

"How do you know it *wasn't* an accident?"

"It certainly looks like one, and isn't that enough?" Serena rose and headed into the department office.

Right then a gaggle of Rhetoric staff people came chattering out of an office down the hall. Their shabby quirkiness made them all blur together for me; it was a group worth the satirical eyes of

Rowlandson or Daumier. They stopped when they saw me, fell silent, and stared.

I rushed back to my office, feeling branded, accused.

Was I a victim of too many episodes of *Columbo* and *Murder, She Wrote?* I had actually sat there in the hallway with someone I didn't really know or especially trust, and chatted, yes, *chatted* about a death. It was one thing to raise the question of murder with Stefan, but with Serena Fisch? And the more I talked about Perry's death, the less real it seemed. But it was also talking to Serena Fisch; something about her made me feel silenced, drawn in, diminished. Was it suspicion? Fear? Look at all the dumb questions I asked her; anyone listening would have thought I was a high school student conducting a lousy interview for the school newspaper!

Now I sat turned from my desk, deliberately taking in Perry's side of our office. His desk was neutrally covered with stacks of student papers, with a row of reference books between two green alabaster bookends along the back edge where it met the wall. Above it hung an elaborately matted and framed print of Fragonard's *The Bolt,* which he had mentioned buying at the Louvre. It was a studied display of heterosexuality, I think—but the true message was in the taut satin-covered buttocks of the man almost on tiptoe, bolting the door to keep his fainting mistress trapped. That's what I'm sure had attracted Perry, what drew him into the picture. Overall, though, Perry's was not a very revealing desk, which made me suddenly want to start pulling open the drawers.

I mean, what did I know about Perry except for his impact on Stefan, and what little I'd observed of Perry in the office and watching him with other people? He had been phony, arrogant, high-handed, superficial—a *type* as much as a person, and quite at home in an academic setting. And even his role in Stefan's life—Heartbreaker—was nothing original. So who was the man behind these banal characteristics?

And why was he dead now, so soon after I'd found out who he really was and why he'd come to our house for dinner?

Jesus, I thought. If somebody did kill him, maybe they would try to frame me and Stefan. Weren't *we* the ideal suspects?

I was just about to roll my chair over toward Perry's desk when someone knocked.

I looked up and gulped. It was Rose Waterman. Because she always wore red, like her suit today, I sometimes thought of Rose as the Red Death in Poe's story.

"Hello, Nick. I was in the building. Talking to your chair."

The way she said "your chair" was like somebody's mother saying "your father." It was both intimate and vaguely threatening, as if they had been consulting about my punishment for not doing my chores on time. And with her German accent, it sounded particularly ominous.

Rose walked in without my asking or getting up. She stood close enough for me to smell her lush perfume and underneath it the cigarette smoke. She leaned against one of Perry's gray file cabinets possessively, like a hunter displaying his dead buck for a photograph.

"I was wondering how you were doing," Rose said.

"What do you mean?"

She shrugged lightly, looking very European in her sleek pants suit, as if Marlene Dietrich were her standard of posture, poise, beauty. She said, "The Campus Police are stirring everyone up—and it can be very disturbing when death comes so close."

Rose made it sound so personal that it was all I could do not to crane my neck and see if Death were waiting out there in the hallway for me.

"I'm okay," I brought out, thinking that Stefan would *never* believe this conversation. Rose Waterman had come to my office to see how I was doing! It was grotesque.

"Were you talking to Lynn about the memorial service for Perry Cross?" I asked, trying with a question to make myself feel a little more present and in control. Even though it was my office, I felt cornered.

Rose shook her head. "There won't be one. The publicity is bad enough already, what with the governor—Well, you know all about that."

I assumed she meant the governor's last public address, in which he had not only threatened deep and bone-crushing budget cuts at all Michigan universities, but was urging them to cut whole departments and thus eliminate low-level administrators, clerical staff, and tenured faculty.

"But how is this bad publicity? It was an accident, right?"

Rose breathed in slowly, as if annoyed. I was not used to asking her so many questions, but her pause actually made me feel a little better. She wasn't sure how to answer me, and Rose Waterman being unsure was a very comforting sight.

"It looks bad," she said. "What was he doing there? How did it happen? Why did it happen?"

I thought of Oscar Wilde's Lady Bracknell loonily telling Jack that "to lose one parent ... may be regarded as a misfortune; to lose both looks like carelessness."

"If you're worried about PR, doesn't it look worse when we ignore somebody's death?"

Rose glanced around the office a little proprietorially; she could have been a future occupant casing it, imagining the changes and improvements she would make.

"I don't agree," she finally said, and then wished me a good morning.

When she was gone, I sat there thinking that it was very doubtful I'd get any work done at all today, what with people parading into my office—first Stefan, then the detective, now Rose Waterman. Where were all my damned students? Why couldn't someone have had a problem with a paper, a question about one of the essays? I would have leapt at the chance to be busy and involved, too busy to talk to anyone except my students.

But then I thought of the alternatives to Rose coming up to see me. I doubted that being summoned to her office would have been pleasant, and even getting a phone call from her would have worried and unnerved me. I just did not like or trust Rose. Her type of person always had an agenda, so I could not remotely believe that she had come by just to find out how I was doing. Why the hell would she care?

Or did she for some reason think I was so unstable that I actually might be falling apart over the news of Perry's death? Had Rose worried that there might be *another* campus crisis to deal with, another "problem" with a faculty member? Was that it? She certainly couldn't have imagined I was Perry's lover or anything, and distraught. I just didn't understand.

And what did she mean about the campus cops stirring things up?

While I sat there mulling over our exchange, the phone rang. I hoped it was a student to see if I was still there, but it was Stefan.

"I'm sorry," he said. "Walking out like I did before was very rude."

I'm a sucker for his apologies, especially when they come with self-blame, so I think I just cooed a little into the phone. "Oh, honey...."

"Let's go out for lunch," he said. "I have an hour."

"Great! I'll come down to your office."

I checked my watch. I had only fifteen minutes left in my office hours. I left a note saying I wouldn't be back today, hurriedly grabbed my mail, and headed for the door.

Locking it, I saw Priscilla Davidoff striding down the hall to her office. She glanced away as if she hadn't seen me and, irrationally, that made me mad. I called out to her as she neared the turn in the hallway leading to her office: "Strange news about Perry, huh?"

Without turning, she kept on toward her office. Taking out her key, she said, "He got what he deserved. He should never have come here." She was inside with the door closed before I could think of a reply.


STEFAN AND I had lunch at the small, charming Vietnamese restaurant right across from campus on Michigan Avenue, Michiganapolis's main street. It was vaguely country French inside, with pretty rose and green cafe curtains and wallpaper. We both ordered *bun*—lemongrass, cucumbers, tomatoes, and chicken over noodles, artfully arrayed in a deep wide bowl and quite tasty.

I especially enjoyed eating there because of our favorite waiter, a slim Vietnamese young man with a spectacularly bright smile and gorgeous thick dark hair. He always beamed when Stefan and

I held hands on the table, and that made me feel deeply welcomed and comfortable.

I told Stefan about my talk with Rose Waterman first.

"Can you believe they would think about finding Perry in the river as a public relations problem?"

Stefan expertly scooped up some chicken with his chopsticks. Chewing, he said, "Don't be so outraged. You know what universities are like."

That was certainly true. When you hear complaints about colleges not being the real world, believe me, they're more accurate than you can imagine. Universities function as holding tanks for people—the academics—who just couldn't make it in business of any kind. Professors are hardly answerable to anyone, have little contact with reality, see people consistently for very few hours a week. It may keep them off the streets, but their lunacy has plenty of room to grow and spread when they're supervised so damned little. What might just be an eccentricity could become something monstrous, given enough time and disappointment. Most academics have an inflated view of the importance of their work and the range and depth of their talent, and they tend to be habitually disappointed, waiting for the glorious trumpet fanfares of recognition. What they usually get is not much more than the fart of a balloon losing air.

"But why would Rose Waterman bother talking to *me?*"

"It's obvious," Stefan said, putting down his French iced coffee. "She's obsessed with details. She wants to know everything."

If it weren't daylight, I might have shuddered a little. There was something nasty and Gothic about Stefan's assessment.

"Maybe she's nosing around to help the Campus Police," I said. "Maybe she already knows Perry's death was suspicious. They'd probably tell the President first, and she's so tight with him."

"Maybe she came by because she likes you," Stefan said thoughtfully.

"Likes me!"

Silence spread out from our table as people stopped eating and talking, and looked at us. I flushed.

"Sure, likes you. I don't mean sexually. But I don't think someone like Rose would really be able to be friendly. I think she antagonizes everyone more or less, even when she might not want to."

The careful way he said that made me ask, "Are you using Rose for a character in your next book?"

He grinned. "Somewhat."

Now I was pleased. I liked the way Stefan pieced together his characters from different people we knew: using a tic from one, the stance of another, the history of a third. All of it was doubly transformed, of course. First by the new combination, and then in whatever way Stefan decided to disguise the original source. So he might be basing a character on Rose Waterman who could end up to be her opposite—which still left Rose the inspiration. I couldn't wait to see what Stefan made of her.

Then I told him about chatting (or whatever it was) with Serena Fisch. "Is she playing with a full deck?"

Stefan nodded. "She's just very angry."

"Tell me about it! Couldn't you see her in a dungeon strapping somebody down, tightening the cords?" But then I remembered Larry Rich and said, "The Campus Police think we're involved, somehow, in what happened. We're obvious suspects—at least *I* am. God, what if they arrest me! It could be like one of those movies where they frame somebody. I'm *sure* Valley hates queers—and he'd probably get a promotion for nailing me."

Stefan frowned. "That's ridiculous."

"No it isn't," I said, trying to keep my voice low. "If Perry Cross was murdered, who are the suspects around here?"

Stefan didn't answer.

"It's just me. Can't you see what it would look like? A Gay Love Triangle Gone Bad."

"What about Serena?" he said. "Perry got the position she wanted."

"Serena wouldn't kill anyone—she'd just poison their *reputation*. I'm the most logical suspect."

"Nick, you need to calm down."

I breathed in deeply. "I need sex," I murmured, my lips barely moving. "*That's* what I need." Stefan smiled until my comment led me to ask a natural question: "What were you doing last night? When I woke up and you weren't in bed?"

He looked down and shrugged. "Writing. In my study."

"So late?"

"It was hard to sleep." He looked at his watch and called over our waiter for the check. Once again, I felt shut out, dismissed.

Driving home a little while later, I thought that Stefan must have been writing about Perry and was too ashamed to admit it.

# -8-

When I got home, there was a message on my tape to call Chuck Bayer. I groaned. Was he going to be hassling me about helping him on the Didion bibliography again? Didn't he listen to me at Broadshaw's party? I wasn't interested in working with him on *anything*.

I called Chuck right away to get it over with quickly, and stood at my desk while his number rang as if to distance myself from the phone, from Chuck, from my annoyance.

"Terrible about Perry, huh?" was the first thing he said.

I muttered something that might pass for sympathy. I was already sick of Perry, but he seemed to be haunting my every move now. That's what I got for wishing he was dead!

"Did you know if Perry was working on something?" Chuck asked me, and I hesitated, because I didn't know what he meant right off. Chuck explained: "Any manuscripts? A book, maybe?"

Then I got it, and I was disgusted: Chuck was a vulture, hoping to profit by Perry's death. Chuck wanted to know if there was something unfinished of Perry's that he could finish and take credit for, research and work that he would benefit by. Finishing a dead man's work would be easier than tackling a project of his own, and would bring him certain praise—as if it were some kind of charitable endeavor.

I almost slammed down the phone, but told Chuck that I really didn't know what Perry had been working on, if anything.

There was a silence, and somehow I felt accused by it, as if Chuck suspected me of stealing a manuscript or hoarding information.

"He was in Canadian Studies," I pointed out softly. And Chuck wasn't.

But Chuck laughed. "Scholarship is scholarship."

I felt strongly tempted to tell Chuck that he was a moron.

"Well, Nicky, just let me know if you find anything, okay?"

I told him I had work to do and hung up. How was I going to find anything? What did he think I was planning? A raid on Perry's files? Then I flushed, remembering how I'd wanted to look through his desk. Didn't that make me as intrusive and obnoxious as Chuck Bayer? Yuck.

I was reminded of the first time an archivist at a rich southern university contacted Stefan to ask him what he planned to do with his "papers." Would he consider loaning them until he made a definite arrangement? Would he consider donating or selling anything yet?

We had laughed about it, until the reality sunk in. There were boxes and boxes in the basement and his study: diaries, journals, manuscripts, corrected galleys, correspondence with editors and interviewers, fan mail, and correspondence with other writers, some of them quite well known. My cousin Sharon was currently an archivist in Special Collections at Columbia University (having gone back to school at thirty-five to earn a degree in library science) and she was quick to explain to us how it was all potentially quite valuable. The money didn't affect me as much as thinking that one day Stefan would be dead, and his papers exposed to the eyes of people who had never known or loved him.

"You wouldn't let anyone see my letters to you?" I had asked Stefan nervously. "Would you?"

"I don't know."

I was as chilled by Stefan's uncertainty then as I was today thinking about Chuck's hunger to know about whatever Perry Cross might have left behind. I made myself a pot of very strong coffee, brooding about death. I had always thought of it with terror, because I imagined my own pain and agony, fighting to stay alive in some hospital bed, hysterically unable to leave Stefan behind.

Or I'd imagined my parents' death, but always in the context of a terrible family scene of grief and hysteria.

But this was different, this was Perry's death, not my own or anyone else's close to me. Had he died alone? Did he know it was happening? I had no idea how he had felt, but I was certainly getting to study the impact of his death on people around him. Like our furious chair, who seemed to think it was an inconvenience; gloating Serena Fisch; image-conscious Rose Waterman; and greedy Chuck Bayer, hoping for an advantage of some kind.

And Stefan—stunned, peculiar. I remembered then some years back at a party in Massachusetts, when Stefan, quite drunk, raised his glass for a loud toast: "To former lovers." Everyone in the room smiled at his generosity, at his rising above circumstance, jealousy, and spite. Then he added: "May they all *drop* where they stand," and there was embarrassed laughter, some frowns. A few people just turned away; his anger and contempt were nakedly inappropriate, and so unlike him.

I thought of what Stefan had said to me before Perry came to dinner, that just because an affair ended didn't mean it was over. Even when Stefan felt he had chosen between us, had seen Perry revealed as empty, Perry was still part of his life. We had happily and drunkenly made love after dinner, but something kept him awake, something made him get up to write.

I would probably be seeing Perry in Stefan's writing for years, like an atmosphere, a presence, a chill. Perry's death was too ugly and unexpected not to scar Stefan in new and disturbing ways.

I couldn't help thinking of poor Kate Croy in Henry James's *The Wings of the Dove* crying out to her lover at the end of the novel, "We shall never again be as we were."

That was Stefan and me, irrevocably changed by someone—but someone we both hated. No. I hated Perry; what Stefan felt for him was a mystery.

The phone rang and I monitored the caller leaving a message. It was a resonant, excited voice and every sentence seemed to end up in the air like a question.

"Professor Hoffman? Your chair suggested I call you? My name is Mike Brewster, with Channel Nine? I'd like to talk to you, to get some information about Perry Cross?" He went on to leave an office number and a home number. I didn't bother replaying the message, just erased it. Channel Nine was the best local TV news station, but I didn't think much of their reporters or news anchors. All were pretty and on edge, like college seniors wearing their interview clothes, desperate to make a good impression. Watching Nine's broadcasts, I often had the sense that they were little kids playing a schoolyard game of News.

The phone rang again, but it was Sharon this time. I snatched up the receiver as soon as I heard her start to leave a message. "Sharon, I'm so glad you called!"

"How was dinner?" she asked warmly.

"Terrible! Perry's dead."

"He's *dead?* Oh, my God—was it food poisoning? Are you guys all right?"

"I'm fine. No, I'm not fine." I filled her in on everything that had happened. "Don't you think it's suspicious he was found in the river?"

"Possibly. Listen, do you want to come out to New York and stay with me?" she asked. "You sound terrible."

"I can't. I've got my classes—there's the investigation—and if he was murdered, I'm the chief suspect because he came here for dinner and I hated him. You should see the way people in my department are looking at me and they don't even know the truth."

"Maybe you're just feeling a little paranoid, Nick. I know I would."

"It's not paranoia. They think I'm guilty of *something.*"

"If you're so freaked out, then you should try to find out what happened to Perry, find out how he died. At least it'll put your mind at ease if you know the details, won't it?"

"How do I do that?"

It was so overwhelming a prospect I tuned out the rest of the conversation, and when she said she had to go, I hung up in a fog.

I took a cup of coffee out onto the deck. In Michigan—as in Massachusetts—they like to say, "Wait an hour if you don't like the weather." It had been cool and cloudy before, but now the sky was clearing and it was warm and clear enough to get some sun.

I had come outside to lose myself, to escape my thoughts, but it wasn't working. I kept picturing Perry at dinner just last night: smug at first, then puzzled, finally looking triumphant and ready. He left our house probably expecting that Stefan and I would have a furious brawl and Stefan would move out, or kick me out, and Perry could move right in. I felt sorry for him, driving off into the night, not knowing it would be his last night alive.

Stefan had often accused me of being melodramatic, and he was right. I did have a tendency to turn a hangnail into a whole *film noir* (though Perry's burst into and exit out of my life was not exactly trivial).

And I lived with a *writer,* for God's sake. I wasn't just lecturing about fiction in the classroom, it was the air I breathed; how could I not see everything around me in dramatic terms?

But that dramatic sense was also driving me crazy, and I knew Sharon was right. The only way I could stop feeling powerless was to start finding answers on my own, and not wait for people like Valley to dole out the explanations.

I TRIED TO focus on the garden now to unwind a little. Late September, the range of colors was narrow, but it still looked pretty. There were purple and pink wild asters, silvery artemisia, red-leaved plumbago with its sharply blue little flowers. Everything blended together well.

I had come to love gardening after nurturing an ailing little soulangeana magnolia behind our rented house back in western Massachusetts. It had produced only two blossoms the first spring we were there, and I turned to gardening books with curiosity. I quickly discovered that the soil needed to be acidified, and for months afterwards I gave the magnolia regular feedings.

"How can you spend so much time on that thing?" Stefan had asked.

"It's not a thing, it's a tree. Well, it can *be* a tree if we help."

One night Stefan found me out there in the moonlight, gently holding two pathetic branches, murmuring.

"Don't tell me," he said. "You're converting, you're a Druid."

"I was just sending it love. It needs love."

I battled magnolia scale, I battled mites, and the tree grew more than a foot a year, bursting into dozens of lavish white and pink blossoms each spring—when the weather didn't change and kill them off overnight, that is. I developed a more sustained interest in planting, adding foundation plants to our rented house, since the landscaping was rather sparse: interesting little slow-growing evergreens, mugho pines, some variegated dogwoods, viburnums, flowering quinces, and lots more myrtle for ground cover. The landlord certainly appreciated my efforts.

Whenever I'd be out there, though, with the knees of my jeans brown and moist from the soil, sweating, smiling, Stefan would come outside and eye me as if about to say something sarcastic; but he never did. Perhaps he thought it was ridiculous that a born and bred New Yorker like me could take to gardening.

"I'm a shrub queen," I told him. "You'll just have to live with it."

But the garden in our Michiganapolis house was so well designed—with its gazebo, herb garden edged with miniature roses, and brick walks—I hadn't fussed with it much at all, had simply weeded and protected what had been passed on to me. I wasn't yet prepared to make major changes; I wanted to live with it for a few years, to study it, which was actually a soothing prospect. It was like the house itself. When we moved in, there was nothing that needed immediate attention, and we didn't even have to buy rugs or curtains or redo wallpaper because we liked the colors that were there and everything was in pristine condition.

I closed my eyes now, sipping the strong coffee, enjoying the rustle of leaves, the muffled sound of cars, the mourning doves up in the shagbark hickory at the back.

Something Angela had said to me before suddenly floated back to me now. After she'd asked if I was investigating Perry's death on my own, she suggested I contact the Medical Examiner, who was Neil Case's mother. I could do that easily, since Neil—bright and hardworking—had aced my course last year and wouldn't have had any reason to gripe about me. I was about to go back into the house to get the Michiganapolis directory when the doorbell rang.

I called out, "Back here!" Someone came down the side path and opened the gate. It was Bill Malatesta as I'd never seen him. He was sweaty, bare-chested, with a light blue T-shirt stuffed into the back of his soaked-through blue running shorts. His sneakers looked very dirty.

"Are you busy?" he asked.

I shook my head. "Do you want some water?" When he came over and sat on the Saratoga chair opposite me, I went in and brought back a large plastic tumbler of spring water, well filled with ice.

He gulped from it, and we talked running for a while. That is, he did. He told me his favorite routes in town and on campus, and about running marathons, training for them. I was barely paying attention to what he said, I was too struck by his body, which I had never seen so uncovered before. Usually I don't find blond or hairless men attractive—they always seem undernourished, even a little anemic. Bill struck me differently. He was very big, but incredibly lean, with body fat so low that his veins, his muscles, seemed not just alive but glowing. The tan helped, as did the sheen of sweat. Watching him, I felt like I was in the opening sequence of a porn movie—me the stuffy professor, him the student hunk who happened to drop by. Or he could be a pool boy, someone delivering pizza, whatever. He crossed and uncrossed his legs. He could have been framing and reframing the still life gathered at the center of his barely adequate shorts; I thought of a Cezanne bowl of fruit, the refracted echoing shapes gravely, heavily beautiful.

And I wished Stefan was there, so I wouldn't feel so much like a voyeur. With Stefan on the deck, it would seem less *tacky* to find Bill appealing—we would be sharing the moment as if it were a field trip.

Suddenly I was snapped out of my reverie by the sound of the name that had been vibrating around me the whole damned day.

"Did you know Perry Cross well?" Bill asked me, and I was instantly sure that this was why he had come by. He had told me that it was a spur of the moment decision: he was running, he needed a break, he realized our house was nearby. But I didn't believe a word of it now. He could have splashed himself with water and simply come right over; after all, the SUM married students' housing complex wasn't all that far away. I sat up a little straighter.

"Why do you ask?"

He smiled. "Well, he's dead."

"And?"

Bill's smile stiffened. Evidently he had not expected me to bristle. And I *was* a professor, not his best friend. I did nothing to soften my reaction, and I could see the uncertainty hitting him, but he went on.

"We're all talking about it," he said. "The graduate students." He shrugged. "It's pretty typical. You know, somebody dies, people want to know whatever they can find out, people gossip, somebody says, 'Last time I saw him—.' That kind of thing. He was at the party. And not that many grad students knew him or were in his classes. So suddenly you're important if you know something about him, or if he said something to you, or—" He grinned helplessly, shrugging at his growing incoherence.

"You want a colorful anecdote?" I asked.

Bill flushed. "Nothing like that! I just … I just wondered, that's all."

And I wondered, too. Was Bill asking questions for somebody else—like Detective Valley? First Rose spying on me, now Bill! No, that was paranoid and silly. But why *was* he asking?

"You and Perry weren't good friends, then?"

Bill was certainly persistent.

"No, not at all," I said.

"So he wouldn't have confided in you about—?"

"I can't picture Perry Cross confiding in anyone."

Bill seemed startled by my vehemence, which only drew me out further. "I don't know why you're interested in him, but he wasn't an interesting person." I was lying, of course, so I hurried on. "And anyway, I think that you should spend your time on your dissertation and teaching your classes, instead of wasting it on—"

But here I didn't know what to say. What the hell was he wasting his time on, exactly? Why was he so curious about Perry Cross?

Then it clicked for me. I recalled overhearing Bill and his wife at Lynn Broadshaw's party, Betty angry that Bill had let something out, Bill apologetic, helpless. He had said, "I couldn't help it."

"Did you tell Perry Cross something about you and Betty?" I asked. "Did you ask him for advice?" It was a ludicrous notion, but then Perry might have seemed more like a contemporary to Bill, given his low rank in the department, wiser than another graduate student but not unreachable.

"What? No, of course not! Why would I ask him anything like that?"

"Then what *did* you ask Perry? What did he know about you?"

Bill stood up, practically slamming the tumbler on the small glass table. "Nothing," he said. "Not a god-damned thing!" And even in the middle of this strange scene, I found myself admiring his tight and concave abdomen, which was tensed as if he expected an assault.

"I should go," Bill said. "Sorry," he threw off over his shoulder as he headed down the side of the house to the street.

Not a typical conversation between a graduate student and a professor. And not the way your typical porn sequence ended, I thought wryly, already unhooked enough to imagine describing it to Stefan with appropriate embellishments. That was a quirk we joked about—the way I occasionally told stories. I could never be counted on to describe an event accurately; I was almost always shaping and editing. I punched up colorful details, or added them if necessary, conflated comments, and left out whatever didn't quite fit my angle of vision the particular time I told the story.

And I frequently backtracked, filling my description with elaborate parentheses.

"Listening to you sometimes is like watching an anthill," Stefan once said.

I beamed. "You mean I'm industrious and productive?"

He glumly disagreed. "No, there's all this commotion that's hard to figure out."

"Not true! I make sense, eventually."

Stefan was not convinced, perhaps because he, the fiction writer, felt obliged to be careful, even scrupulous describing real events.

When Stefan got back from campus an hour later and we brought a nicely chilled bottle of Vouvray out onto the deck, I was disappointed that Stefan didn't let me get a full head of steam going about Bill Malatesta's visit.

Stefan asked, "What makes you so sure Bill wasn't telling the truth?"

"When he said he stopped here in the middle of a run? Because he was too curious about Perry. And he softened me up first—lounging there like he was Dolf Lundgren or I don't know who! He *knew* I was checking him out. And all that boring talk about running. Then bang, suddenly we're on Perry Cross. You know, they might as well offer an elective course in that creep with everybody so fucking interested in him all of a sudden."

Stefan smiled sweetly. "Who'd teach it?"

"Not me!"

"Was Bill nervous?"

"When?"

Stefan waved his hands. "Anytime while he was here."

I thought about it, sipped from my glass, enjoying the cool sweet wine. "Not really. It's more like he was on a mission."

Stefan frowned.

"No, *seriously*. He wanted to find something out, he wanted to pump me." And then we both started laughing. "Maybe he does," I groaned.

"He is hot."

"He always wears those loose chinos, but today!"

"Let's call his wife and ask if he's curious."

"Are you kidding?"

Stefan raised his eyebrows. "Am I?"

Sitting near him, I felt as drawn to Stefan as if we'd just met, as if everything about his body, his smells, his textures, the different shades of skin, the curves and whorls and bulk, as if all of it were intoxicating and unknown.

"Let's do it," I said.

He quoted my favorite line from *Prizzi's Honor:* "Right here on the oriental?"

I laughed and led him inside.

LATER, WELL AFTER dinner and a second trip to the bedroom, we lolled in bed with the TV on more for noise than anything else.

Suddenly I remembered that I hadn't even looked at my mail. This was a sore point with Stefan. Perhaps after all the years of rejection slips, now that his career was established and secure, he was quite greedy for mail. He had preternaturally good hearing, and when he was working at home, he could tell when the mail carrier's little jeep was a few houses away. He could hear it start up and pull to a stop, could hear mailbox doors clank shut. If he wasn't dressed then, he'd hurriedly throw some clothes on and get ready to rush down the driveway to the mailbox as if he were a retiree expecting a sweepstakes win. Stefan's eagerness to pounce on the mail and rip it open was amusing to me; just as he was frustrated that I could actually enjoy using a letter opener to calmly, neatly get into whatever had come for me.

Now he seemed amazed. "Your mail at the department? You haven't looked at it yet?"

"It's just one of my little ways," I said. "You've had ten years to get used to it."

He shook his head as I padded off to my study, turning on lights as I went. While I waded through the pile of boring letters and brochures about conferences, new publications, department memos about nothing significant, and requests from Wharton scholars around the country for information and help, I thought it all could have waited until the morning. But then I found a note on a piece of plain white Xerox paper that was folded not very neatly in thirds and stuffed into an unsealed envelope.

It read, "Please forget what we talked about." It was signed "Bill."

I felt momentarily disoriented, and somehow imagined that Bill Malatesta had left this for me after our talk on the deck.

But how had he gotten into the house? I had left the front door unlocked when I got home; surely I would have heard him sneak into the house and enter my study?

I bore the note back to Stefan, who read it as if expecting a message in disappearing ink to suddenly pop up between the lines.

"This is strange," he brought out, looking from me to the note and back.

I crawled in next to him and he took my hand, squeezed it. "I don't get it, unless—"

"Unless what?"

"Well, at the department party, we were just bullshitting some, and then he said he needed my help. Could that be it? But it's not like he actually said anything specific that I could forget about."

Stefan shrugged, peering at the note.

I said, "Don't you think everyone's acting a little crazy today? Maybe it's more than Perry's death. Maybe it's sunspots, or a change in barometric pressure."

"It could be global warming," Stefan suggested.

"The war in Bosnia?"

"Anxiety about the national debt?"

We went on like that for a while, amusing ourselves.

# -9-

The next morning there was a front-page story on Perry Cross's death in the *Michiganapolis Tribune*. There was the suggestion that he might have been drunk, but nothing about an autopsy.

"He didn't drink that much at our house," I said to Stefan, who agreed. If anyone was likely to get in an accident, it was me that night: all the Pernod, then the wine. I was lucky I hadn't passed out or tripped in the bathroom and knocked myself unconscious.

If Perry wasn't drunk when he left our house, but was drunk when he drowned, it would have been afterwards, I thought, feeling guilty. He could have gone out drinking, or gotten drunk at home. I had poured it on at dinner, bragging to destroy Perry's confidence, and look what had happened.

I could see the news from Rose Waterman's perspective. It *did* look bad. People would be reading the newspaper and thinking, Those SUM professors—that's all they do is drink and get themselves in trouble or dead. Whether it was true or not, just the suggestion was bad publicity at a time when more budget cuts were looming once again in a state that claimed to support higher education but often seemed quite hostile to those who provided it.

Stefan sat next to me at the kitchen table, reading aloud as I drifted off. He quoted the county prosecutor, who was reported as saying, "The injuries Dr. Cross sustained were not inconsistent with an accidental death." Pressed, the prosecutor also said Cross could

107

have fallen from the bridge. There would not be an inquest, and the article didn't mention a memorial service one way or the other. Clearly the reporter hadn't done much thinking on this article. There was a quote from Lynn Broadshaw: "Perry Cross was a fine addition to a substantial department. Unfortunately we will never get to see the full flower of his teaching, research, and service."

"Oh God," I moaned. "The land grant troika!" Not just speeches but casual remarks by administrators at SUM almost always used the three terms—teaching, research, service—that summed up the university's mission as a land grant institution, that is, a university built on land originally granted by the federal government. The incantation had a dry and perfunctory feel—the way ancient veterans in wheelchairs were given places of honor at Memorial Day parades, their shriveled little smiles, their fragile waves empty footnotes to history.

As often as not, the university was touted as being larger than the *sum* of its parts, because of teaching, etc. The consistent punning on SUM/sum had of course led our in-state rival, the University of Michigan in Ann Arbor, to call us SCUM and DUM(B) and so on. The abuse appeared on T-shirts and bumper stickers all over the state. I actually found the nastiness a relief from the high-toned ponderous blather we suffered at the hands of our president and his minions.

"Not much of an article," Stefan concluded.

"Did Perry deserve more?"

Stefan shook his head.

"Don't you love Broadshaw about Perry flowering? The guy was a stink weed, nothing would have flowered—and do not give me any Baudelaire shit about Flowers of Evil."

Stefan smiled a bit guiltily—I had obviously headed him off. Then his expression changed, and he pushed away his coffee. "Will you talk to Bill Malatesta about the note?"

"I have to, don't I? I don't understand what's going on. And if there's something he doesn't want me to talk about, I should at least know what that is, right?"

"You really think he snuck back into the house after he talked to you?"

I wasn't sure.

Stefan left before I did, and I didn't tell him about Sharon's suggestion to start looking into Perry's death myself. I knew it would make him angry because he'd insist it wasn't my business, but I couldn't let this thing drop.

I looked up the number of the Medical Examiner—Dr. Margaret Case—and was surprised at how readily her secretary put me through. I'd expected having to explain myself in detail, but apparently my name and saying I was a faculty member at SUM was enough.

"Professor Hoffman, this is a treat. Neil loved your class—he said you were the best teacher he had all year. He talked about you a lot."

I flushed with pleasure and mumbled something about her son's writing.

"How can I help you?"

I told her I'd like to see her in a professional capacity, as soon as possible.

"What about?"

I was afraid she'd say no, so I hedged. "Actually, I'd prefer talking about it in person."

There was a hesitation on the line, but I heard her shuffling some papers. "I have a free half hour just before lunch—at eleven-thirty."

I took it. She gave me directions to the office downtown and I raced over there. The building surprised me. Her office was in the Department of Health and Social Services; the squat beige brick building was teeming with mothers and children, and filled with light from huge windows and skylights. Maybe because of the children, everything inside was splashed in primary colors. It was bright and a little disappointing. I'd expected someplace dark and full of tension, filled with nervous bureaucrats racing around from one crisis to another. The only racing I saw was the toddlers hurtling off to grab or investigate something shiny or pretty, with anxious mothers charging after them.

I found the Medical Examiner's office down half a dozen corridors. Her secretary was so cheerful I wondered if it was an act.

Dr. Case came out as soon as she was buzzed, to usher me into her office. She had the same no-nonsense air as Attorney General Janet Reno, and was almost as large and imposing. But the resemblance stopped there: she wasn't dowdily dressed, had no glasses, and her hair was curly and dark blond. And she didn't look at all like her son, Neil, who was short and dark.

The office was jammed with books and files and mugs from scenic spots all around Michigan. Except for the cheerful colors, it could have been any office back on campus.

The ME smiled broadly, waiting for me to begin.

"This must be exciting work," I said.

She laughed. "Not really."

"But going to a crime scene, or whatever—"

"Oh, the police usually don't like me around, getting in their hair. I generally meet the body at the morgue. And it's really not what you see on television—it's all pretty cut and dried." She frowned. "Not the best choice of words, I suppose."

Neil's mother was so relaxed and welcoming that I was about to tell her why I'd come. Before I could, though, she asked me, "Are you doing some sort of research about death investigation for a book?"

"No. I came because of the man who was found dead on campus yesterday morning. Perry Cross. He was my office mate."

She nodded. "I wondered if that was it."

That startled me. "Why?"

Dr. Case shrugged. "He was a professor, you're a professor. It seemed obvious. I suppose this has been a shock to you."

I nodded, trying to look mournful as opposed to overly curious. "How did he die? Do you know yet?"

"I shouldn't tell you before the information is public, but it'll be in tomorrow's paper."

When she paused, I said, "I don't know anything about medicine."

"Fine, then I'll keep it simple. According to the pathologist's report, in layman's terms it was massive head injury, hemorrhaging."

"What happened?"

"There were wood splinters in the wound, and mud, so all that's consistent with his having sustained the damage through falling from the bridge and striking a half-buried log in the river. Apparently the Campus Police on the scene made a similar assumption, and they were right."

"He didn't drown?"

"Well, when you find a body in the water, it's always harder to determine the cause and manner of death. And there aren't any witnesses. There was water in his lungs, but he may have been dead before most of it got in."

"You said they found wood splinters. How do you know that wasn't from a—from a baseball bat or something?"

It must have been a very naive question, because she seemed to make an effort at keeping a straight face. "Processed wood is very different."

"Oh. But was it ... an accident?"

Now she frowned. "Honestly? If someone pushed him," and here she shoved out her hand as if in someone's back, "we couldn't know. But given how much alcohol was in his system, I'm ruling it an accidental death. I go by the preponderance of evidence—that's my standard." Her eyes narrowed. "Do you know anything that would change that?"

"Not at all!" I cursed myself for being too vehement. I went on more calmly: "It's just that the whole thing surprised me...."

She nodded a bit suspiciously, but then seemed to remember me as her son's professor. I thanked her for her time and we chatted briefly about Neil's current classes on my way out.

Her secretary was on the phone, apparently reading from some report. I heard "facial fractures and cranial contusions" before the office door closed behind me. Outside, the knots of mothers and children made my little interview seem more unreal. I'd been talking about death and injury but everything I saw shouted of life.

Now I knew more about Perry's death, but it wasn't enough. I had to go to the Administration bridge and check out where they found his body. That was an obvious step that might make the next steps clearer.

But first there was Bill Malatesta. I knew Bill taught on the same days that I did, so I called from home to leave a message for him at the EAR office to call me or come to my office in the half hour I had between my first and second class. Surely that would be enough time to figure this thing out.

I have often taught some of my best classes on cruise control, and my first class was terrific. Even though I was full of curiosity about Bill's note, and wondering about Perry and how Stefan was dealing with all this, I managed to say all the right things when we discussed a set of student essays. I could feel the approval, the admiration, the understanding. I managed to be clear and helpful without being at all authoritarian or intrusive. When I came back into the classroom after the five-minute break, the noise level was high, as it gets only when students are excited and pleased because they're *learning* something.

How was I doing so well?

Of course, it wasn't just me. They were my favorite group of students this semester: a good relaxed group, self-motivated, with more than half a dozen people who liked to talk and had something valuable to say (not a typical combination). It certainly helped that our shabby high-ceilinged room with the scarred seminar tables and gauged wooden chairs was such a strong contrast to most campus classrooms where the seats were nailed to the floor and everything looked sterile, mass-produced. Somehow the barriers between us all were lower, helped along by sitting around the four grouped tables and having to face each other when we talked.

I was soon back upstairs in my office, glowing.

Even Bill's sour face when he knocked and came in didn't faze me. He looked so different in loafers, blue broadcloth shirt, chinos, and black V-neck sweater: like someone auditioning for a role he wasn't sure he wanted.

He wouldn't look right at me, as if I were a headmaster who had found his young pupil cheating on an exam.

I waved to the seat by my desk, and Bill came to sit there reluctantly, poised as if to charge off. I brought out the note and handed it to him.

"What's this about?" I asked.

He tried to smile but must have known he looked sick and unconvincing.

"It's your note, right? What's it about?"

"You've gone through his stuff already?"

"What? Whose stuff?"

"Perry's."

"I don't get it. This is for *Perry?* Then why was it in with my department mail?"

"Shit!" he hissed, smacking a palm to his forehead, cursing himself: "Asshole, asshole, asshole."

"The note was for Perry," I said as if trying out the words. Perry's mailbox was right above mine, and occasionally mail of his had been popped into my mailbox by mistake. But nothing like this. No wonder I'd been confused.

I suddenly felt like a trespasser. What was I supposed to say now? Should I ask Bill to leave? Yet he didn't seem outraged as he had yesterday afternoon at my house; just defeated, drained.

He breathed in deeply, nodded a few times. "You try to keep things quiet, but it never works, does it?" Now he looked at me and I felt our connection was finally back. We were friends again, or—given the difference in rank and power—at least friendly. Bill laid the note face down on my desk.

"I'm not surprised you weren't Dr. Cross's best bud or anything. I don't think he was that great a guy. His students didn't like him. Even when you figured he was new here, trying himself out, even when you gave him that, he still was kind of—"

"He was a schmuck," I said briskly, and Bill nodded, grateful.

Abusing even a dead professor doesn't come easily to a graduate student; just disagreeing can be tricky enough. Many graduate students live in fear of making a mistake in a seminar, or idly saying something that could be misinterpreted and then ending up having earned a professor's enmity without really understanding why. I'd heard that in our department the attrition rate of Ph.D. candidates was very high: two out of three never got degrees.

"I was working on a paper in the library one night, just before closing," Bill said, "And Dr. Cross—"

"Let's call him Perry, it sounds more natural."

"Okay. Perry. Perry walks by and we start chatting. He sounded really interested in my research. And then he asked if I wanted to have a drink in town. So we headed out, and had a couple of drinks, at Jimbo's."

It was a loud student hangout in town that I usually avoided.

"And then he said—right in the middle of something completely ordinary—that I looked kind of haunted, and was somebody in the department hassling me." Bill sighed as if recounting a terrible accident he'd seen. "He asked me if somebody had been *sexually* harassing me."

That was Perry, I thought, rude and prying. And on the mark.

"I was so surprised I said yes."

"How did he know to ask?"

Bill gave a big Italian shrug that was as beautiful as it was helpless. And I thought of the way Perry had made Stefan come out to him that night in New York. It was all about power.

Now Bill hesitated. Up to this point, he had been on somewhat safe ground talking about a professor who had died. But going further could be dangerous to him. I *knew* that. I had seen other schools where accusations of sexual harassment had been covered up, denied, squelched, or brutally controverted. Nobody came out of it with their head up, nobody, even those on the fringes— because it could poison whole departments with people taking sides, slandering each other, threatening lawsuits, acting like Stalinists.

Merely to listen to Bill's story was to be involved.

But I couldn't tell him to stop. It would be wrong, and I was curious.

"I said yes," he repeated, shaking his head in amazement. "I was so surprised Perry asked me, I couldn't pretend. It was a shock."

"I know."

He frowned, but I just gestured for him to go on.

"It happened last year. I was going to that conference on Hemingway and Sherwood Anderson in St. Louis, not to do a paper, just to go. But you know it's not cheap, so when I heard Lynn Broadshaw was going to the conference and wanted to share a room to save some money, I thought it would be great. I was nervous, of course. I mean, he's the chair. But I also figured it couldn't hurt to socialize with him some. You know what I mean?"

I nodded.

"So we drove down there together and basically he told me his life story—the Merchant Marine, grad school, teaching ..." Bill shrugged a little, as if unsure how dismissive to be, so I said, "Boring?"

"Oh yeah! I mean, he just talked and talked like he thought he was being interviewed, like he thought he was important, like he thought he had something to say, like—"

"I get it, Bill."

He flushed and settled back into his narrative.

"We were just there over two nights. It was great being introduced to all these people I knew from their books, their articles, and listening to their opinions, you know."

I figured "opinions" was a polite way to say gossip, and I remembered what a hollow thrill it had been for me as a graduate student to associate with professors, imagining I was one of them when really they were demonstrating how relaxed and kind they could be, a sort of dreary academic noblesse oblige.

"I was pretty drunk by the time I went up to bed the second night, and I must have passed out. It was late, I think, when I heard the door open, and I was groggy. I heard him changing, hanging up clothes, washing up in the john. Then there was more light, and he came out of the john in...."

I forced myself to wait and not say anything lurid.

"He was wearing bikini shorts," Bill said with his head high as if willing himself not to laugh. But then he added, "Tiger print."

I was glad the door was closed because I must have sounded like Cher in *Moonstruck:* "Animal!"

Bill grinned now, but held a hand up to his mouth as if he were a little boy who had just tried out saying a bad word for the first time. "It's not that he looked all that terrible without his clothes—well, actually he did. And he's kind of old for bikini underwear." Then Bill's face changed and he dropped his hand. "He sat on the edge of the bed, talking about the conference, the papers we had heard, just talking, but looking at me like every word meant something different. I think he even put his hand on my knee—on the covers, I mean. I kept yawning and finally said I had to sleep 'cause I was wiped out. He looked at me real sharply and went over to his bed, got in, and that was it. In the morning I wasn't sure I was right—I mean, right that he was making a pass. But he acted weird, wouldn't look me in the eye, and we just listened to the radio on the whole drive home. It was miserable. I didn't know what to say, because I wasn't really sure what happened."

Wonderingly, I said, "Lynn Broadshaw is bisexual."

"We don't know that!"

"Forget what you call it. He wanted to sleep with you, right?"

Eyes down, Bill said, "Probably."

"So what happened after that?"

"God, it's been terrible. He told me he didn't think Betty was worthy of me when he heard we were getting married."

"He *what?*"

"That's what he said. I couldn't believe it either. I mean, he's not my father, he's not my adviser, he's just the chair, he has no business telling people who they should marry, come on!"

I felt I should say something nice about Betty, but I didn't really know her and I didn't want to sound phony. Besides, I was still marveling at the picture of Battling Broadshaw on the make with another man, a *student.*

"And I should have known it would be bad news for Betty to take one of his classes, because he's been really critical about her papers. She's gotten A's from *everyone* else in the department till now, but he's giving her B's."

That was a disgraceful grade for graduate students—anything lower meant the course couldn't count toward their degree. B's were rock-bottom and embarrassing.

Bill leaned forward. "He always gave me A's, and so I wrote one of Betty's papers for her, just to see what would happen when she turned it in."

"He bombed it, I bet."

Bill nodded. "But that also made me wonder about how I did in his classes before the conference. Maybe he only treated me well and said I was 'a scholar with promise' because he wanted to get me into bed. I mean, you should see the letters he's written in my file, for scholarships and stuff! But what if that's all just bullshit?"

I could see that this potential blow to Bill's confidence was as upsetting as, maybe more upsetting than, the fear of being sexually victimized by Broadshaw. And I felt ashamed of my fantasy yesterday afternoon on the deck, ashamed of basking in Bill's sexual allure.

"You told all that to Perry?"

"I did. It was good to get it out, and—I don't know—maybe I thought he could help me somehow. But there isn't anything to do."

"You could file a complaint."

"Yeah, right! Tell a committee of Broadshaw's colleagues and friends that he sat on my bed in his underwear. I'm sure that would really sound terrible." He shook his head almost violently. "It's hopeless. I can't risk not getting my degree, or a job. I mean, he told me I should forget using him as a reference. But what if he does more than that? He could really screw me over. Jobs are too tight now, I have to keep quiet, I have to not make him mad at me."

"Like Anita Hill," I said quietly.

"Exactly."

"So you tried to leave Perry a note to keep things quiet?"

"Yes. I was afraid it would get around the department and hurt me, hurt Betty, too. Lynn could make sure we never get academic jobs. What if I've interviewed really well somewhere, and the choice is down to me and one other person and they call SUM to talk to someone who 'knows' me, huh? Broadshaw wouldn't have to say a whole lot to fuck up my chances."

I could imagine just such a scene, Lynn Broadshaw making veiled references to having "heard something" about a problem with drinking, or unreliability with getting papers back to students, any number of damning little remarks that would say very subtly but very clearly: Don't hire the man.

It was ugly. "Is that the whole story?" I asked. "There's nothing more between you and Lynn?"

"Nothing."

"You're sure?"

He bit his lower lip and breathed in once, twice. "Well, there was this time before the conference, I had to drop a paper over at his house, at night...."

"And?"

Eyes closed, head drooping, Bill went on: "And he came to the door in a towel. He'd been in his hot tub out back, and he asked if I wanted to join him."

It was hard for me not to sound suspicious. "And did you?"

"He's the chair! When he asks you to do something, you can't say no. Once he called me to take over another grad student's class, which meant I was teaching three classes *and* taking three—nobody ever does that. I got bronchitis that semester I was so tired, but I had to say yes. He's the chair."

"Did he offer you a bathing suit or"— I paused—"or did he blithely say it didn't matter?"

Now Bill's cheeks were bright red. "I just went in nude. But *nothing* happened!"

I nodded, taking it all in. How could Bill complain to anyone? He had sat in a hot tub with Lynn Broadshaw nude, not at a health club but at his home, and then shared a hotel room with him at a conference. Who'd believe that he didn't know what was going on, who would resist blaming *him?* Even I was beginning to feel suspicious.

"I left after he had another glass of wine. He was pretty looped."

*Another* glass of wine, I thought, but kept silent.

"Okay, it was stupid to share the hotel room, but I didn't know how to tell him I couldn't. I mean, I was planning on going to the conference, how could I back out all of a sudden without making him mad?"

Bill sounded like he was trying to convince himself more than me, and failing. I felt sure this was not the first time.

"So when you came to my house yesterday, what was the sweaty stud routine about? You wanted to distract me?"

"No!"

But I stared at him, held his eyes until he looked away, ashamed.

"Yes," he said softly. "I didn't want it to be obvious what I wanted."

"And you blew it, kiddo. Asking me about Perry was a mistake." But then so was slipping the note in my box instead of Perry's. Bill was not careful, he was too rattled. Why? Was there something else he wasn't talking about?

"I had to know if Perry told you anything. I have to get a job, Betty has to get a job, we have to keep this quiet."

There was no need for me to tell Bill that his chances were slim, given the economy, and given that he and Betty were both in an incredibly over-saturated area: modern American fiction.

"It's okay," I assured him. "Perry's—" I was going to say Perry's dead, but I realized how cold and awful it would sound. I glanced at my watch and cursed. I was going to be late for my next class. "I have to go," I said, standing.

Bill rose and reached out to shake my hand. "Thanks," he said. "I know I can trust you."

He left, and grabbing my briefcase to head for my class, I couldn't help wondering if I could trust Bill.


AFTER CLASS I headed for the gray steel and concrete Administration Building bridge, which seemed to be about twenty feet above the river. I wasn't the only gawker. Dozens of people were on the bridge and at opposite ends pointing at a spot on the bank that looked as if it had been trampled by lots of feet. There wasn't any yellow Police Line tape up anywhere, so you couldn't really tell exactly where the body had been found.

I mingled with the crowd, looking for something that could explain what had happened—but it was impossible to concentrate. I wandered back a little off the bridge and sat on an empty bench, relaxing despite myself.

The terrace and banks right next to it formed one of the most popular areas on campus. For some people—like me—the river was a wonderful place to sit or nap by, a channel for dreams and canoeing, a quick and easy reminder that classes and exams and student loans and job hunting and promotions were ephemeral and even ugly. For others, I suppose it was a mirage of sorts, a false escape from the inevitable judgments, deadlines, pressures, fears that hung over every building on campus with the thickness and weight of the battered-looking weeping willows lining the riverbanks.

That place was sometimes a strange mix of the peaceful and violent. Students, faculty, alumni, parents, townspeople, came here on sunny days, on weekends, to watch and feed the ducks, to watch each other. You almost always found delighted toddlers not much bigger than the ducks they waved their arms at, chased, loved, possibly feared. People went through whole bags of stale bread, ripping and tossing. It was like a *National Geographic* special—intimate, exciting, a bit unnerving.

With just one piece of bread, you could wreak mayhem on the water, sending the fat glossy dark ducks into furies of diving and stealing. The flapping of wings, the splashing and quacking spiraled as more bread flew and sank, and some ducks were pecked, nearly trampled down into the water, while other smaller ones fled to quieter spots on the river, or waddled up the grassy sloping bank on the north side to lurk hopefully by picnic blankets. The softly besieged picnickers usually took pity until duck radar spread the alert that there was a new outpost for food, and the noisy demanding cloud shifted. It was sometimes funny, sometimes disquieting and cruel. So much commotion, so much transient violence, so much apparent hunger—though even the ducks found there in the height of winter when most of the river was frozen over never looked underfed.

Occasionally you saw pop cans, condoms, even SUM notebooks in the river.

I thought that Perry's was probably the first body.

I was about to leave when a student hurrying by stopped and hissed my name: "Dr. Hoffman!"

It was Chad, who was on the SUM wrestling team. He had surprised me last semester by writing so maturely; his prose was as lean and powerful as he was.

He sidled over, looking uncustomarily furtive. "Can I talk to you?"

"Sure. What's up?"

He sat down and shook some of his thick Hugh Grant hair out of his face.

"I'm the one who called the police." He gestured discreetly back at the bridge.

"*You* found the body?"

He nodded. "I was jogging before six, that morning." He kept his voice as low as if he were a spy. "I always come across the bridge. And I heard all these ducks quacking like crazy, really *loud*. So I stopped and looked over the rail."

"And?"

"It was like hunting dogs that corner a fox, you know? They were all around it. Him, I mean. His arms and legs were snagged in some rocks or something, I think. He wasn't completely under the water, and the current was pushing at him. It was almost like he was trembling from the cold."

Chad blinked rapidly as if to fight off the scene he was describing. I felt breathless.

"He was soaked through," Chad went on. "His suit looked black from all the water."

"Did you try to see if he was—?"

"Oh, man, the dude was dead. You could just tell. Nobody could be alive lying there like that with their head mostly under water." He gulped. "He looked *stiff*."

I nodded. "Why wasn't there any mention of you finding the body in the newspaper?"

He lowered his voice even more. "Because I called the Campus Police from a public phone and didn't give them my name. I can't risk getting involved in anything like this—I might get thrown off the team, then I'd lose my scholarship and have to drop out."

"Wow," was all I could manage.

"But I had to tell somebody—it's just eating me up. And I trust you." Before I could say anything else, Chad darted off.

Bill trusted me, Chad trusted me—or so they said. What was going on here?

STEFAN MADE DINNER, and while he prepared the sole meuniere, I had a vermouth cassis and filled him in on my conversations with Bill Malatesta and Chad. I had considered not telling him everything, or editing the stories somehow, because I didn't want to feel more deeply involved. But after ten years together, I was once again struck by how unreal events could be until I told them to Stefan, shared and relived them. Did that make me codependent?

"You don't seem surprised about Lynn coming on to Bill," I said. "Or whatever it was."

Stefan carefully coated another piece of sole in flour and put it in the hot buttered fry pan. I enjoyed cooking, but I liked watching *him* cook even more. Without turning, he said, "People go to conferences to get laid. They expect it."

Maybe so, but I didn't expect Stefan's cynicism. "So you think it's Bill's fault?"

"Not at all. But he made some mistakes. You said that too."

I was waiting for outrage, surprise, disgust—*some* intense reaction from Stefan. But then, maybe that was because I wasn't really sure how I felt about Bill's story myself. Was it true? If so, should he have known better after the hot tub incident? Or was Bill deliberately using his good looks with Broadshaw for some advantage, just as he had when he talked to me on our deck, lounging, shirtless, sweaty.

And I wondered what Lynn Broadshaw's version of the story would be.

"Well," I said, as Stefan turned down the heat under the sole. "What should we do?"

Stefan muttered, "Nothing."

When Stefan cooked, everything always looked good. His eye for detail always delighted me, like tonight. The sauteed red and yellow peppers went beautifully in their curved slices with the golden brown sole sprinkled with freshly chopped parsley. I tended to be less artistic, and could sometimes mistakenly serve a meal in which everything was the same color—as if I were stocking a school cafeteria line.

Over dinner, Stefan showed me his copy of the campus newspaper, which I had somehow forgotten to get for myself. The article about Perry Cross there wasn't substantial either, though you rarely expected that with student coverage anyway. But a professor's death—surely that warranted more attention?

"No memorial service," I said to Stefan. "Short articles. Serena almost bragging at the party that Perry won't last here, and she's already assigned to teach his classes. Rose Waterman saying it's bad PR."

Stefan forked some of the sauteed peppers and brought them up to his mouth, raising his eyebrows. "And?"

"Don't you feel like we're *supposed* to forget about this as quickly as possible?"

Chewing, he said, "Maybe."

"And what about Chad? Should I tell him he has to come forward? Does keeping quiet about what he told me make me some kind of accomplice?"

"Accomplice to what? We don't know that anything happened."

Later that evening we sat on the living-room couch with the stereo playing Bach's soothing *Goldberg Variations*. We sat side by side, shoulders touching. Stefan was reading a set of student papers and I was trying to do the same thing, but finding it difficult to concentrate.

Did *he* want me to forget about Perry too? Why? What was Stefan hiding? I didn't think I *could* forget, and I didn't think Stefan could either.

"Where did you talk to Chad?" he asked me suddenly.

I hesitated, and he had no trouble guessing. "At the bridge? I can't believe you went there like some kind of tourist! Or were you trying to be Sam Spade? You should stay out of this."

"Stefan, I'm in it, whether I like it or not. And so are you."

We didn't talk to each other again that night.

# -10-

In the morning we heard more news on the radio about Perry. The report said that Perry's blood alcohol level was three times the level established for drunk drivers, and the death was ruled accidental.

Having met with the Medical Examiner, I didn't bother reading the Michiganapolis newspaper for a fuller version of the story.

"It's over," I said to Stefan, more to test his response than anything else. I didn't feel finished with Perry's death, but rather *more* burdened, now that I knew for sure that Perry was drunk when he died.

"I guess it's over," I said, suddenly possessed by the image of Perry stumbling around campus, bombed, desolate, maybe leaning over the Administration Building bridge to puke or cry, losing his balance, falling. It was as pathetic in its own way as William Holden's drunken death, banging his head on a bed table. What a way to go, even for someone like Perry Cross.

And I wondered, gruesomely, if Perry had died instantly or had struggled against it, called for help or tried to. What would that have been like, lying there in the river with your life draining away, desperate for help, knowing no one would save you?

The thought made me shiver.

But it annoyed me that I was feeling more and more sorry for Perry. The hostility I'd enjoyed before he came to dinner, and all during dinner, was fading. In just a few days he was being absorbed into history, into the past, into my imagination. The process was new to me and disorienting. I wanted to still hate Perry, but it seemed pointless. If anything, it was now his influence on Stefan, his emotional residue, that was the problem. How could you combat that?

Stefan was sitting at the breakfast table, staring at the cabinets opposite him. He looked dazed and forlorn, like someone who had no idea where he was. And he cast quite a pall on what was on most mornings a lovely large warm room: with oak cabinets whose golden stain had streaks of blue in it, sky blue and gold counter tiles and kitchen carpeting, and wonderfully framed and matted Vermeer prints. I liked the prints especially because they were a less than typical choice for a kitchen, and for the way they each opened up to a serenely ordered and peaceful scene.

But Stefan was more like El Greco today.

I was tempted to shove his elbow to get his attention. But I just waited, because I knew he had heard me, it was just taking a while for the stone I dropped into his well to reach the bottom and splash.

"Wh … What?" He focused on me now, but with not more recognition than he gave his cereal.

"It's all over now." And then my phone rang.

Claire, Lynn Broadshaw's secretary, told me that the chair wondered if I wouldn't mind packing up Perry Cross's "things" in the office. I was so surprised and grossed out by the idea that I agreed and quickly hung up.

"If you don't want to do it, why'd you say yes?" Stefan asked me after I went on to gripe for a while. He was fully attentive now.

"Because I didn't know what else to say. I wasn't thinking!"

He nodded, and I found his silence insulting.

"Don't agree with me!" I snapped. "Help me."

"Just call back and say you changed your mind. What's the big deal?"

I thought of Bill Malatesta telling me how impossible he had found it to say no to Broadshaw. Wasn't I just as powerless in my own way? I *felt* trapped. Broadshaw was not the kind of man who forgot what he thought was a slight, and changing my mind like this would surely displease him. I'd once heard Broadshaw enraged by a graduate student who had contradicted something he said in a meeting: "Who the *hell* does he think he is! In my day—" And he went on and on about people needing to "know their place." It was a fiery and depressing litany, and Broadshaw stomped around the department office for days. In case anyone wondered whether it mattered, the graduate student Broadshaw was mad at left the Ph.D. program, whether from fear or failure (or both) I didn't really know. That's how things worked in most graduate programs—students who couldn't cut it, or who for some reason were unpopular, or made someone angry enough, tended to get squeezed out. They disappeared, and usually the circumstances were vague enough to strike terror into the hearts of the other students, who would be eager to show themselves off as superior, dutiful, accomplished in the wake of this disappearance. I suppose it was like the way police states used to operate when Eastern Europe was Communist. The stakes might not have been as high, but the feelings were the same, as were the parties: the captives, the bosses, the collaborators, the onlookers.

"I don't want to go over there. I feel like somebody's picked me to negotiate with terrorists."

"Oh, Nick." Stefan smiled. "*Que vous êtes romanesque—vous voyez des drames partout.*"

"Did you just call me an arch? A Romanesque arch?"

"No, that's from Cocteau's *La Machine Infernale*. It means," and he paused to translate, "'You're so romantic, you see everything as a drama.'"

That kind of exchange is an occupational hazard of living with a writer, but I was still annoyed. "Stefan, please don't quote French to me at a time like this. It's pretentious and your accent is far too good."


Driving over to campus, I could not stop feeling intensely uneasy about going through Perry's "effects."

Broadshaw's secretary, Claire, helped calm me down a little. That was her great gift. She could make you feel like you were the most fascinating guest at her party. And Claire never raised her voice, never lost a file or forgot to do something she said she would do. That conspicuous competence and breeding threw Broadshaw's bluster into high and unpleasant relief.

I found her in her office adjoining the chair's. It was something of an oasis in that bleak building—painted a sunflower yellow with a matching new-looking carpet. The room was hung with brightly colored samplers with dour admonitions, a large antique-looking Michigan map, and what I took to be her young grandchildren's stick figure drawings. These were always changing, always exuberant and cheerful.

Today she was wearing a very stylish dark green suit, pearls, and a white blouse with flowing jabot; the subdued tones made her look not just serious but important, investing each line of her face with significance. She might have been a senator or a successful entrepreneur, and on a day like this she fitted my fantasy about her—that she was actually rich, and serving out some kind of private penance by working for an extraordinarily difficult man like Broadshaw.

"Thanks so much for your help," she said. "I left some boxes for you in your office, Professor Hoffman." She smiled up at me from behind her desk. It was teeming with dozens of family pictures in shiny gold and silver frames and tiny weird-looking cactus plants that didn't look real.

"Who are they for? Has anyone been contacted?"

"Well, I don't really know. We haven't heard from anyone." The statement was softly regretful. "So we'll just leave everything boxed until we know just what to do."

"Isn't there always someone listed in the personnel file to contact in emergencies? What about his ex-wives? Doesn't he have a daughter?"

Claire smiled gently and said, "Well, I don't really know about that."

Which struck me as peculiar, because I doubted there was a thing in the department that Claire didn't know. She'd been around for nearly two decades, had keys to every office, knew all the files.

But Claire didn't say anything more, just kept smiling, which I took as my cue to leave. I had one more question, though.

"How about his course materials?"

"Oh, Professor Fisch already has everything. The grade book, the class lists, his notes, student papers."

"Everything," I repeated. Serena hadn't wasted a minute! I pictured her triumphantly going through Perry's desk and file drawers, scooping up what she needed as if she were on a shopping spree.

"She's very dedicated," Claire said with finality, as if arranging the last flower for a centerpiece, smoothing down her skirt to await her guests.

Out in the hallway, I ran into Chuck Bayer, who came up to me with his usual driven smile.

"Need any help cleaning out Perry Cross's stuff?" he asked.

I was still thinking about Serena Fisch in Perry's office, well, in *my* office, so it took a while for me to register Chuck's question. Then I focused on his wrinkled cheap dark blue suit and bland tie, his vague blue eyes, his carefully combed thin blond hair, as if he were on *Star Trek* and had suddenly beamed down to my planet.

"How'd you know that?"

He shrugged. "How do people know anything around here?"

"Well, it wasn't in any department memo!"

"Hey, Nicky," he said, sounding like a druggie. "Chill out."

I just walked away, annoyed that I had to get advice from him of all people, and wondering why the hell he was so anxious about Perry Cross's "stuff." This was the second time he had mentioned Perry to me. I didn't like it.

Upstairs, I saw that Perry's nameplate had already been removed from the office door. I had not expected it to happen so quickly. I unlocked the door with hesitation, as if Perry himself might pop up from behind something, sneering, pointing his finger: "You thought I was dead! Surprise!"

There was a neat stack of liquor boxes at the side of Perry's desk, and it looked incongruous, because I associated them with moving, with change and excitement. But I would be using them to clean up, to erase; each item that went into them further eliminated traces of Perry Cross from the world.

That should have made me happy, but instead I was creeped out.

I sat at Perry's desk, wondering how and where to start. A line of reference books ran along the back of his desk between alabaster bookends, further held in place at one end by a very pretty clock, and at the other by what I'd thought was a tacky eight-inch bust of Michelangelo's *David* on a square base I had taken to be marble. Looking closer, I wondered if the head weren't carved out of ivory. When I reached for it, steadying the books, I realized the base was malachite, and that this was not some cheap Pier 1 type purchase. The little statue was surprisingly heavy. The base reminded me of a fabulous store in New York opposite the Plaza Hotel: A La Vieille Russie, whose windows were always filled with czarist *objets*—like enormous porcelain vases with gold handles and trim, extravagant mantel clocks crowned by lolling gilt gods and goddesses, Faberge eggs, and often, that czarist favorite, malachite, whether in tables, lamps, vases, torcheres.

I got up to set the *David* head on my desk, where there was no chance I could break it. And I moved the silver clock too, whose face was marked "Tiffany & Co." I had seen clocks like that advertised in *The New York Times*—they cost several hundred dollars. The clock and the *David* seemed expensive *tchotchkes* to keep in your office.

Perry's reference books were nothing unusual: several dictionaries in English, French, and German; usage guides; dictionaries of literary terms; Oxford Companions to British Literature, American Literature, Classical Literature; various handbooks on etymology; an encyclopedia of poetry and poetics. It was almost too representative, too typical, I thought. But there were some odd exceptions: William Shirer's *The Rise and Fall of the Third Reich;* a book about the Nazis and the German press; one on Vichy France; and a large German-English dictionary. What were they doing here? I leafed through all three books, looking for underlined passages or marginal notes. All I found was a series of three dates in 1944 written on the back inside cover of Shirer's tome, but I had no idea what they could mean.

I hoped Perry didn't have some gross fascination with concentration camps or something like that.

But then I figured I would find something to criticize in whatever I went through of his, so I piled the books neatly into a Seagram's box, tightly closed the flaps, feeling oddly virtuous.

There. I had filled one whole box. I was making progress.

I wasn't sure what to do with his blotter, pen cup, letter tray. They were all burgundy leather, I saw, stroking the grain, and I didn't want to mess them up. I guess I could ask Claire for some newspaper or something to wrap and protect them with. Then there was the framed and matted Fragonard print over the desk; but that could wait until the end, I thought. I studied the print, remembering its power when Stefan and I had come across it in one of the vast, stifling red velvet and gilt galleries of the Louvre. I liked the painting's energy, the way your eyes were swept across the disordered draperies of the bed to the swooning, struggling woman and up, up to the young man's hand bolting the door, and then down (for me) to his taut, tensed buttocks and legs. It was phallic and a bit chilling.

Now it was time to open the desk, and I pushed back in his chair to make it easier, but I couldn't. I felt awful. Why was I doing this—for Perry? Wasn't there anyone else in the world who cared for him? Surely someone had been deluded enough to think he was a good man.

"Having fun?"

I jerked around to see Priscilla Davidoff peering at me from just outside the open door. She was obviously not teaching today because her hair was pulled back and she had on an oversized SUM sweatshirt and jeans tucked into fancy brown cowboy boots. She looked kind of sexy, I thought, a little disconcerted as always when I responded to a woman *as* a woman.

"I'm surprised they didn't cart his desk away in the middle of the night," she observed.

I realized then that we were on the same wavelength. "Right, like he never existed," I added. "And we'd all wonder—"

"*The Lady Vanishes,*" Priscilla said, nodding, and we both smiled, sharing our enjoyment of the Hitchcock movie.

I was not used to such a pleasant interaction with Priscilla, so I wasn't sure how to go on. I hated what she had written about Stefan, but I think I would have preferred being able to chat with her like this, without rancor, instead of enduring our typical frosty exchanges.

"I was thinking of the way Communist countries used to be," I said.

"Oh, I know what you mean! My grandfather was a Bolshevik and for a while he was in the Soviet encyclopedia, but he eventually got written out."

That was Perry. He was being written out, expunged.

"Broadshaw wants me to do this," I said, waving at the boxes.

"Better you than me," she said, drawing back, and we smiled awkward good-byes. She edged off and then clomped over to her office.

Wait till I tell Stefan that Priscilla and I made nice a little, I thought, picturing how honestly pleased he'd be. He enjoyed the drama of my anger, my grudges, but I knew that he sometimes thought the emotional brouhaha was a waste of his time.

Perry's desk itself was just like mine across the office: a hulking, scarred, battleship gray affair with no character at all. I pulled open the middle desk drawer, where I found neat trays and tray-lets filled with rubber bands, paperclips, pencils, pens, etc. It was almost a parody of order. Post-it pads were aligned by size—and even by color!

Nothing like my desk drawers here and at home, which were always sticking, since things crept to the back and got caught, mostly because each drawer was chaotically stuffed with more letters, envelopes, business cards, and just plain junk than was ever reasonable.

I reached over to the pile of boxes for a small one and started packing it with the contents of this drawer, trying for some kind of orderly arrangement, but failing. It seemed disrespectful to make such a mess, but I couldn't help it.

I was almost done unloading the drawer of its contents when I found something underneath a fresh white legal pad. It was a piece of yellow legal pad paper scrawled over in red. It was face up, and when I read what was written on it, I decided that I'd had enough of sorting through Perry's things for now, maybe forever.

It didn't take much convincing to get Stefan to cancel his office hours for the next day and drive up north with me to our cottage on Lake Michigan for a long weekend. It was a relief just to be heading away from Michiganapolis, from the university, from everything that had happened in the last week.

The four-hour drive gets more and more scenic and relaxing as you leave the flat area around the state capital, and north of Mount Pleasant you find yourself in what travel brochures would call "gently rolling" farmland. Then as you head northwest to Lake Michigan there are more and more lakes, the woods are denser, and you begin to feel transported, free.

Which was exactly what I needed, and why I loved the cabin that Stefan's stepmother had given us when we moved to Michigan. Off a three-mile dirt road near Norwood just south of Charlevoix, it was right on the lake, with over two hundred feet of beach on a deep half-acre site that was well screened and canopied with poplars, white pine, hemlocks—and privacy fencing that did not let our neighbors on either side participate in the nude sun-bathing we liked to do on the tiny deck. Well insulated and winterized, with reliable forced-air heat and a wood-burning stove as back-up (and decoration), our cabin was really a gem. We never had people up there because there were just two rooms: the larger one taking up two-thirds of the space was the open kitchen and living room; a cozy bedroom and a bath with a sunken whirlpool tub took up the remaining third of the cabin. Heavenly for two, and even in the summer we never stayed there long enough to get on each other's nerves.

I also liked it in contrast to the summer home Stefan's father and stepmother had south of us on Glen Lake. They had completely renovated a Victorian home, giving themselves all the comforts of this century with the style and swank of the last. Though I got along well with Stefan's father and stepmother, their house intimidated me, and I never truly enjoyed staying there. Not that we ever had much chance. Stefan was still angry at his father for waiting until he was seventeen to tell him he was really Jewish. That was the reason we generally avoided going to Ann Arbor for *anything*. It was there, midwinter almost twenty years ago, that Stefan's father had blurted out the terrible secret, and Stefan also heard that his parents and Uncle Sasha had been in concentration camps in Poland—the Poland Stefan had grown up loving and longing for because he thought it was his parents' home.

Like so many other things, it wasn't just the revelation but the way it came.

"Nick, I was *seventeen*. Why'd they wait so long! The only reason Dad stopped hiding it was he thought he might be dying. He felt sorry for himself, he felt guilty." Stefan helplessly held up his hands in a gesture that was just like his father's—but I would never say that.

Stefan wasn't quite as angry at his mother or his uncle about being lied to all his life, which made me wonder if he hadn't dumped it all on his father in an act of emotional economy. Demonizing one parent was easier, somewhat less destructive, perhaps. But he was distant from all of them, a distance I didn't challenge, but didn't actively support, either. I hoped he'd eventually be reconciled with his family.

Stefan and I unpacked as soon as we got to the cottage, and I turned up the heat we kept at low while we were away. It was 50 to 60 during the day at this point in the fall, but could go down into the 20's or 30's at night, and the west wind off the lake could be fierce.

I had brought up the shabbat candles and a challah so we could make shabbat there. Lighting the candles, blessing the wine, the bread, and saying the short version of the after-meal blessings (*Birkat ha-mazon*) were rituals that Stefan had at first felt awkward about, then grudgingly observed, and now participated in without resistance. He had come a long way in our ten years together, but sometimes he had the air of a badly injured man whose accident still beclouds his successful physical rehabilitation. He can walk, but he remembers a time when it was impossible. Stefan could join me in the blessings, and a mild bit of Jewish observance, but he was still haunted by all those years his parents and uncle pretended they weren't Jewish, worse, pretended they were *Catholic*, but ambivalently so.

We always left the freezer and cupboards in the cabin well stocked, so dinner that Friday night was easy. I started putting together my favorite chili: meatless and fast, which we ate with a red pepper and cucumber salad. We killed a whole bottle of Médoc before Stefan said, "So what did you find in Perry's stuff that scared the shit out of you?"

I set down my glass, trying hard to glare, to be stern, but I giggled instead, as much drunk as feeling ridiculously exposed.

"It was that obvious?"

"You come home half an hour after you left, looking like Medea, make me eat an enormous lunch, tell me we should pack up and go to the cabin for 'a change.'" He shrugged. "You'd never make a good spy."

I took his hand across the table. "How could you wait all this time to ask me?" I knew the answer, though: he was patient, he was kind. He knew I wanted to escape, so he let me. But now I suppose we had to face whatever I was running from.

I reached into my pants pocket and brought out the note, unfolded it, passed it over.

"STOP WHAT YOU'RE DOING OR I'LL KILL YOU," Stefan read, without inflection. The air around us, fragrant with cumin and coriander, oregano and garlic, was like a shroud, muffling the ugliness of those words.

Stefan held the note and gazed down at it with puzzled regret as if it were a mirror and he were a faded actor wondering where his youthful face had disappeared to.

"This is a joke," I said. "I can't believe any of this is happening."

"Stop what," Stefan said slowly. "And who's this for?"

"It must be for Perry. I found it in his desk. I was right that people hated him. Maybe he's dead because he didn't stop—"

"Stop what?"

I shook my head. "God, I don't know. But I don't think it was just an accident him winding up in the river like that—even if he was drunk. What if somebody *got* him drunk?"

"And then killed him? Who? A mystery figure from his past?"

"Somebody from the present. I'm not the only one around here who hated him. Look at Serena Fisch—she's ecstatic now that he's out of the picture. She's got the courses she wanted, and I'm sure she'll get his position officially."

Stefan looked disgusted. "So she killed him for that?"

"What's so unbelievable about it? We don't know anything about her."

"Okay, then what about Priscilla Davidoff? You said she was really hostile about Perry. And she writes mysteries, doesn't she?"

"They're awful—"

"But somebody always *dies* in her books, right? So she thinks about murder, she imagines it—why couldn't she do it?"

"What's her motive?"

Stefan shrugged. "We don't know anything about her, either. Maybe she just hates male academics."

"Great. Now you sound like Rush Limbaugh complaining about feminazis." But I thought that writing about murder did seem a possible path to committing it. "And there's also Bill Malatesta," I said quietly. "He could've done it because he panicked after he told Perry that Broadshaw came on to him. If it got out, Bill would probably never get his degree."

"And what about Chad—your student who said he found the body? Why wouldn't he talk to the Campus Police? What's he got to hide?"

"You really think he could have done it? Perry was so much bigger." I answered my own question: "But Chad's a wrestler, and Perry was drunk." When I looked up, Stefan was smirking.

"You've been making fun of me," I said.

"Once you start looking for suspects, everybody looks guilty. And what if *Perry* wrote the note?"

"You mean he was going to give it to someone?"

Stefan nodded thoughtfully.

"But if that's true," I said, "that's just as much reason for murder. If he threatened someone with murder, then—"

Stefan shook himself. "I hate this. Let's wash up and take a walk."

I was glad for the break, for the release into habitual activity, and enjoyed washing and stacking the dishes as much as if I were in someone else's kitchen helping out after a party.

"Now why *is* it that other people's mess isn't so offensive?" I asked Stefan, when the last plate was done. "Maybe that's because you know you're not trapped there."

He said, "Any more questions you want to ask and then answer yourself?"

I grinned. "What if we just crawl into bed now? We've already missed the sunset. We can take a walk tomorrow."

"Getting horizontal sounds great."

"I hope we can get vertical too."

Stefan followed me to the bedroom.

WE SLEPT VERY late, took a long bath before breakfast, which was really lunch, cooked and ate far too much food: creamy scrambled eggs, peppered bacon, French toast *and* buckwheat pancakes doused with real maple syrup. It was as if we were in training for some ordeal. We ate greedily, enjoying every bite, making quite a mess of our faces and hands.

We finally heaved ourselves up to get the dishes to the sink. We washed up without talking, moving around each other with the easy grace of years together. Once we had started sharing a house in Massachusetts, I discovered something I had never known: the simple joy of quiet and undramatic moments together. It's hard to talk about it without sounding like a Hallmark card, but I still sometimes marvel at how much fun it can be to do work around the house with Stefan, set a table, watch TV. And to touch each other casually, as a sort of low-key emotional punctuation. Sharing a life is what I mean—since most of life is not dramatic, is even routine, but the routine can be beautiful. I'm not trying to glorify domesticity, just give it a little dignity, I guess.

With the dishwasher churning away, we headed out to the lake. I always enjoyed walking along the curving wild beach, especially where the sand turned rocky, and beyond to the low cliffs with tangled slabs and steps of gray shale at their feet. The shale looked black and shiny when the waves broke over it, and there was something monumental and sad about it—like the remains of some ancient palace. I usually felt like a little boy on the beach, wanted a shovel and pail, and could almost always get Stefan to join me in stomping and jumping in any puddle we found. Today, though, he seemed much less inclined to be silly.

We ended up sitting side by side on shale ledges well back from the waterline for a long time, staring out at the enormity of Lake Michigan, making inane comments now and then about the colors, the size, the smell. It heartened me that even a writer could be overwhelmed, deprived of originality in the face of something so beautiful. We were both used to the roaring salty Atlantic besieged by sunbathers, ships, gulls; but here was what felt like our own private ocean, no matter how many sailboats or swimmers we ever came across. Today the lake was very quiet, almost absurdly picturesque.

Often when I feel very close to him, I also am amazed that Stefan and I had grown up not that many miles apart in Manhattan—him in Washington Heights, me on the Upper West Side—but had never met until we were in graduate school.

"Did you ever think you'd end up in Michigan?" I asked.

"*We'd* end up in Michigan?"

"I never even thought of Michigan. I always figured I'd live in New York. Have a terrific apartment on Riverside Drive." He closed his eyes as if picturing himself unlocking his fantasy front door.

"In the low Seventies?" That was not too far from where I'd grown up, though on the less impressive West End Avenue.

Stefan nodded, smiling at his old dream.

"Well I wanted Park Avenue—"

"And somebody playing Cole Porter at your parties?"

"Yes! And me as slinky and smart as Myrna Loy." Suddenly I pictured her and William Powell in *The Thin Man.* Stefan seemed to catch the change in my mood.

"You think someone killed Perry for sure," he said, not looking at me. "That he was doing something worth being killed for."

"Yes, I do. I mean, there are a lot of loony people around at the university, but I can't imagine someone writing a threatening note like that who was just *kidding.* It doesn't feel like a joke."

"What are you going to do?" Stefan asked me, face blank.

Did I have to do anything? So what if I'd found the note in Perry's desk? It wasn't as if anyone had asked me to report on his things. What if the note was from a crazy student, or something personal that had nothing to do with his death, and nothing to do with me and Stefan? How could we even tell that the note had been written here in Michigan? Maybe it was some bizarre kind of souvenir or talisman. Some people kept old photographs; Perry liked to keep his favorite threatening notes....

I was really clutching at straws, desperate to believe the note wasn't important, when of course it was.

"God, I'm hungry," I said. And we headed back to broil some two-inch-thick steaks, which we ate with French-fried yams and a bottle of Cahors. We played the radio very loud during dinner and our conversation was episodic and strained, as if we were soldiers back from the front unwilling to talk about the horrors they had survived, but too clouded and distracted to pretend everything was fine.

We eventually staggered to bed, as surly and uncommunicative as if being together in this cabin were an accident, not a plan.

# -11-

Stefan drove us home very early on Monday morning because he had two afternoon classes back to back. There wasn't much traffic until we got closer to Michiganapolis. I slept most of the way, waking up sweaty and uncomfortable now and then, asking where we were, peering woozily out the window, with the receding towns like pages torn from a calendar in a movie to economically show the passage of time. We were home sooner than I expected, and I brought in the mail and started the wash while Stefan showered again. On his way to his office hours before class, he pawed through the mail, but didn't have time to open much.

"You'll sort everything, right?"

"Of course."

I always did; he always asked. I suppose most couples have these ritual little interactions that are the equivalent of chimps grooming each other—a sign of closeness that might seem strange to outsiders.

After he was gone, I wandered through the house a little. Usually I feel released and happy to be back no matter where we've been—up north, San Francisco, Paris. But today I couldn't relish being home because of the note I'd found in Perry's desk.

I checked the campus directory, made a quick phone call, and drove over to my office in Parker.

Detective Valley showed up five minutes later, wearing the same suit as before. It must have been a *Columbo* raincoat touch,

I thought, something to make people more relaxed and more voluble.

"Thanks for meeting me here," I said, nodding for him to take my students' chair. He closed the door behind him and sat down. I passed him the note.

He read it without a change of expression, put it down on the desk, and just looked at me.

"That was in Perry Cross's desk."

Nonchalantly, he asked, "How'd you find it?"

"Lynn—the chair—asked me to pack up Perry's things in boxes." I turned and waved to the mess on Perry's desk.

Valley's eyes seemed to flicker with doubt.

"Well, actually, it was his secretary who asked me *for* him. Claire. She said he wanted me to do it. You can check with her. She's in charge of all this."

"I'll ask her," Valley said quietly. "When did you find the note?"

"Friday. I was—"

"Friday? Today's Monday," he said sharply. "Why did you wait three days to call me?"

"I went up north—Stefan and I went up north to our cottage. I needed to get away." As soon as those last words were out, I felt like an idiot. Valley just waited for me to go on.

"I guess I could have called you on Friday. I just wasn't thinking straight."

Valley glanced over at Perry's things. "Why didn't you finish clearing up?"

"I found the note and had to leave."

"Just like that." Valley didn't sound convinced, but why should he be?

"Listen, the note really freaked me out, and all this has been really hard for me," I said.

"But you didn't especially like Perry Cross."

"I'm not a monster! He was my office mate and he was killed. It would shake anybody up."

"That's it, huh?" He nodded, cool eyes on me.

I didn't look away.

"Killed?" he asked. "You said killed—but the Medical Examiner's report says it was an accident. Why do you think he was killed?"

"Look at the note."

"It could be just a threat—it could mean anything. A practical joke." He shrugged. "We'll examine it. Not that it'll tell us much since you've been carting it around the state."

"Hey!"

"Who else saw you find the note? Nobody?" He nodded grimly.

Oh great, I thought. I was digging myself in deeper.

"Has anyone else seen the note?"

"Stefan," I said sullenly.

Valley pressed on. "And he didn't bring it to my attention either."

"We were up north!"

"Without a phone?"

I didn't answer that one.

"Why are you so sure Professor Cross was killed?"

I went on the offensive. "The physical evidence doesn't rule out that somebody pushed him."

"How do you know that?"

"I just do."

Valley shook his head. "Are you telling me that Perry Cross had real enemies at this university? You said he wasn't popular. Did people hate him enough to kill him?"

I shook my head, feeling sweaty and dizzy.

"Did *you* hate him? Did you kill him and then fake this note to make it look like someone else did it? And you're the hero who cracks the case?"

I wanted to get the hell out of there and keep going, but I forced myself not to bolt.

"Did you hate Perry Cross enough to kill him? Did you?"

I closed my eyes. "Yes, I hated him." It was out—now I could meet his stare. "But not enough to kill him, and if I did, why would I show you this note *after* they rule his death is an accident? That's not very swift, is it?"

"I've been here fifteen years and professors do lots of stupid things."

Despite myself, I wanted to ask him what he meant by that.

"What did you have against Perry Cross?" Valley brought out.

I stammered, "Nothing."

"But you just said you hated him. Why? What did he do to you?"

"Not a thing—I hated the kind of person he was." It sounded so lame I wasn't surprised when Valley chuckled.

"I get it," he said. "Generic hatred."

"What's it matter anyway?" I asked. "Since you're convinced it was an accident, who cares why I hated Perry Cross?"

Valley let the question hang in the air, his silence answering me. I felt exposed, hung out to dry—and it was my own fault. I was the one who called *him*.

He stood up and smiled, obviously pleased he'd gotten me to blurt out what I really felt about Perry. And I thought he enjoyed my general discomfort—it probably amused him to torment faculty members, or maybe he just saved that for queers.

"We'll get back to you about the note," he said. "If we need to." At the door he turned and added softly, "Now, is there anything else you're not telling me, any other surprises?"

"Nothing!" I snapped, feeling my face turn red, thinking about when Chad had told me he was the one who had found Perry's body.

Valley nodded, eyeing me suspiciously, opened the door, and slipped out of my office, as cool and controlled as when he'd come in.

Dragging myself home, I wished I had just destroyed the damned note and saved myself the inquisition.

Dispiritedly, I moved the wash along to the drier and started another load. While the washer chugged away in the laundry room off the kitchen, I made a pot of coffee. When I poured myself a cup, I sat down to go through the mail. It had to be done, and I figured it might calm me.

Bills went into one pile, circulars and requests for money into another, mail from Stefan's publisher and personal letters in another. There wasn't much for me, so I picked at his mail a little jealously. There was always more mail for Stefan, just as there were always more messages on his answering machine than on mine.

One letter puzzled me. It was a thick white business-sized envelope, with the return address of a law firm in town. I recognized the name because this firm often underwrote local public radio and television broadcasts.

But it wasn't our law firm. I hefted the envelope, as if I could do Johnny Carson's Mighty Karnak and come out with the set-up for some snappy joke.

There wasn't any Ed McMahon to egg me on, but I opened it anyway, since Stefan had long ago given me permission to open anything I thought was "interesting."

It was a very short letter addressed to Professor Stefan Borowski, incongruously short, given the complicated masthead listing all the partners and associates of the firm. It was paperclipped to another smaller envelope inside.

The letter read: "Our client, Professor Perry Cross, requested that in the event of his demise we forward the enclosed communication to you."

And the smaller envelope, also white, was simply addressed "To Stefan," in what I assumed was Perry's handwriting.

I dropped it onto the table. Going through Perry's desk drawer at the university had not seemed as personal as holding this letter, a letter he had addressed to Stefan.

A letter he had addressed to Stefan *in the event of his demise.*

What kind of planning ahead was this?

I got up to phone Stefan, hoping to catch him at his office, but no one answered, and the department number was busy.

I started to redial, then put the phone down and sat at the table again.

Perry had written something for Stefan. When? Why? Something that required lawyers, but what for?

I tried the department again, and got through. I left Stefan a message to call me, but there was no way he could call me soon enough. I knew that. I stalked through the house carrying Perry's letter—or whatever it was—from room to room, waving it as if it were a swagger stick or a fan.

Was I being a little kid, hoping it would magically fly open and reveal its secrets?

Perry had written something for Stefan, thinking about his own death. What could he possibly have to say to Stefan at a time like that?

I gave up waiting for a phone call. I took the letter into my study, as if sheathing uranium in lead. I sat at what Stefan called my Napoleon desk, because it was vaguely Empire in style, and reminded us of furniture we'd seen at Malmaison, Napoleon's favorite palace outside Paris. I loved this room with its floor-to-ceiling bookcases. The maroon drapes and thick rug muffled sounds from outside and made me feel protected, cocooned. I was especially fond of the overstuffed armchair and ottoman, covered in a tapestry print of slate blue and maroon: something out of Watteau with shepherdesses and shepherds. It was just this side of being tacky, but it too reminded me of all those endless tapestries we'd seen in France, chateau after chateau filled with the damned things.

I used a letter opener, imagining the blade sliding into Perry's flesh.

Another short note, but this one was more mysterious than the lawyer's.

> Dear Stefan: If you get this, something's happened to me. Expect something else.

It wasn't even signed!

I sat there reading it over and over as if I were a stubborn archeologist confronted with maddeningly half-familiar hieroglyphics. What the hell could it mean? Was it a joke?

I cursed aloud, wishing Stefan had an answering machine at his office so that he wouldn't just have a memo slip waiting for him in his department mailbox, but my voice, immediate, demanding, real.

Perry Cross, Perry Cross. I was surrounded by him. It was like suddenly being struck with an illness that changed the configuration of every aspect of your life.

Despite myself, I smiled. I imagined the next time someone asked me how I was, I could say, "I'm not feeling well, I've got *perrycross*." As if it were bronchitis, or a skin disease. Well, now *that* was more appropriate, because the son of a bitch certainly had made my skin crawl.

I called the EAR Department again, but hung up before I got an answer. There was no point in leaving a second message for Stefan. I knew where he was teaching. Couldn't I just go to campus, lurk outside his classroom, and catch him at the inevitable break? Or why bother waiting? I had every right to march up to the door, knock, and ask to talk to him.

But I'd never done that before, for any reason. How could I do it now without getting him upset and then nervous? Seeing me, he'd assume there was an accident, that someone was ill. And what the hell could Stefan say that would make me feel better?

I had already poisoned the day by opening the two envelopes— nothing could change that. Nothing.

The washer chugged to a stop, and I was soon switching things to the drier and starting another small load. It was a small and stuffy room, apparently carved out of the kitchen at some point after the house was built. Stefan and I had idly talked about bringing the kitchen back to its original shape and size and moving the washer and drier to the half-basement, but every time I did laundry I thought about what a pain it would be to haul baskets of wash up and down stairs. Besides, basements made me nervous, and I never went down to this one alone. I suppose it was growing up in apartment buildings where basements were public and alien space.

"And you're afraid of ax murderers, too, I bet," was Stefan's take one time.

I could only nod, a little ashamed. Too many horror movies, or maybe just not enough childhood trips to suburbia where basements were an insignificant fact of life. I kept the door locked during the day and checked it every night before I went to bed, and even whenever I left the house—though there was no way to get to it from outside, no windows, no door.

Folding the wash, I ran everything through my mind. I was absolutely sure now that someone had killed Perry Cross, and that he had known he was in danger. Why else had he planned ahead for his death? The letter from the law firm said "in the event of his demise." He was obviously afraid someone was after him.

He wasn't drunk when he left our house, but was stinking drunk when he wound up in the Michigan River some time early in the morning. Where did he go after dinner? Was he alone or drinking with someone else? How did he *get* to the river? Why was he there? Was he meeting someone? Or was someone chasing him? Maybe that's how he wound up in the water.

But why hadn't anyone found him sooner? Students are up all through the night—didn't anyone see his body before Chad did?

I felt overwhelmed by the letters, by the chill conviction that Perry had been murdered, and by my own inadequacy. How was I going to figure any of this stuff out?

With the wash taken care of, I suddenly panicked. In my rush to leave town, I hadn't brought any schoolwork with me, and now I realized I wasn't ready for Tuesday's classes. I spent the next few hours immersed in catching up, which I guess was good for my state of mind. Now and then I wondered when Stefan would call, but not enough to go to the phone or even stop work.

Finished with grading papers and done with my reading, I was hungry, and anxious again. When I called, the department number was busy. Stefan was done teaching, so why hadn't he returned my call? Or didn't he bother getting his messages?

Then I felt like an idiot, or more so than I had until that point. On the ride home from the cottage, Stefan had reminded me that he would be having dinner with some creative-writing students who wanted to talk to him before his reading that night. His reading! I'd completely forgotten that too. As the writer-in-residence, it was expected that he give at least one public reading at the university each semester, and tonight he'd be doing that after dinner in town.

Of course he'd told me all this more than once, even offered to write it down in my datebook, but I had bristled—as usual—at the implication I could forget.

"I'm not being rude," he'd said last week. "I just know how busy you are…."

I had glared at him, ready to pounce on the least hint of sarcasm. He wasn't being critical, though. He never was when he suggested ways to help me remember something important—like where I'd jotted down a colleague's phone number, which would almost always be on the back of a receipt or inside a magazine rather than in my phone book.

I often complained, "How come *I'm* the one with the artistic temperament, how come I'm so dizzy, when *you're* the writer?"

I made myself a cheese omelette and a small caesar salad, with the radio tuned to the local classical station, and ate my meal in the kitchen feeling somewhat calmer. I was looking forward to Stefan's reading, which would be at the one good used bookstore in town: Ferguson's. It was a large, long, theatrical-looking, thickly carpeted store that felt like someone's movie set study, with what seemed like acres of dark bristling bookcases, curious antique prints massed on the worn flocked wallpaper, busts and statuettes peering down from elaborately carved little ornamental shelves. You expected Ferguson's to be musty-smelling, but it never was.

Stefan found it a bit too Bombay Company-ish, but liked the light, because it was warm and diffused, perfect for a reading. And that was important, because the setting he read in could sometimes throw him off—make him feel tired if the lights were glaring, or the store was too warm or too noisy. I liked Ferguson's because it wasn't as sterile as most bookstores, and because the readings were always held after hours, with the cash register closed. Stefan didn't seem to mind the ringing bell and slamming cash drawer at some bookstores, but I was always irked by that, and by the customers wandering past, looking at him curiously, stopping for a bit and then moving on as if he were selling hot dogs on a street corner and they were trying to decide if they were hungry. Readings were special events, not just a piece of a store's commerce, and they deserved attention and respect.

Especially for a writer like Stefan, who read his own work so well.

Most writers don't, you know. They're too shy, or too arrogant, or can't project, or can't feel connected to their audiences, or treat the whole thing as an obligation and not an honor, not a chance to connect with their readers. Readings are performances, and Stefan understood that implicitly. He was almost always relaxed, smooth, engaging, and never made you feel it wasn't important for him to be there.

He wasn't acting all that, he simply was more himself than usual.

"I used to fantasize people listening to what I had to say," he told me after his first book tour. "Really listening. Wanting to. And now it's happened." He smiled and shook his head. Perhaps that was the essence of his success on the road—he didn't take it for granted. Even after several books, he was still pleased, still excited.

It had certainly helped that I came along on many of his readings, sat in front and smiled, but also kept an accurate count of how many people were there, and watched for their responses. When Stefan was at his best, sailing along as if every second had been rehearsed, he was both aware of his audience and not aware—building on their responses instinctively. And so he needed me to replay the whole evening afterwards. And when he was not at his best, he needed me to remind him of the larger picture, to soothe and amuse him.

Showering, I was suddenly cheerful, imagining the pleasure of bathing in his presence, in his creamy voice for an hour or so, watching him gracefully take questions afterwards. He never flinched at hearing the same ones over and over—like, how autobiographical was his work, how did he get his ideas, and did he even *get* any ideas living in Michigan? And afterwards tonight, if we went out with people, we wouldn't end up having drinks with writers, as we did when Stefan read in New York, Los Angeles, or any other big city. I admit I enjoyed listening to all the uproarious gossip writers inevitably dragged out to entertain each other, but eventually a darker tide would wash over the conversation. People started complaining—about editors who didn't return calls, agents who flubbed negotiations, publishers who didn't advertise enough or support tours enough or do *something* enough.

"Are any of you guys satisfied?" I once asked in a Boston restaurant. And there was an awkward silence.

"It's easier being satisfied in Michigan," Stefan said afterwards. "I get all that stuff, but on the phone, in letters. It's not so immediate."

It wasn't that Stefan was a big frog in a little pond, but more that we were surrounded by a different atmosphere. Living in Michigan, neither one of us felt bombarded by anxieties, hungers, demands. The air itself was not electric with the fear of failure as it was in New York or anywhere else where reputations sprouted as quickly as mushrooms after a heavy rain, and just as quickly could go bad, be gobbled up or crushed.

When I got out of the bathroom, my answering machine was beeping, and tightening my towel, I rushed into the study.

Of course it was Stefan who had left a message. "Nick? Nick? Are you out? Hello? Hello? Okay, maybe you're taking a nap and your phone's off in the bedroom. I got your message late, but the secretary didn't say if it was important. I'll see you in a little while, at the reading. Love you."

I was dripping onto my desk, onto the phone. The end-of-messages beep sounded, and I dragged myself off to get dressed.

I PARKED IN the lot behind Ferguson's, which was planted in the middle of Michiganapolis's tiny downtown. At 7:15 P.M., there was already a crowd of several dozen students from writing classes, faculty members, and people from Michiganapolis who were either Stefan's fans or just regularly turned out for readings at Ferguson's. Ranks of black metal folding chairs filled the middle of the store from the counter almost to the back wall, where there was a table and an enormous old dictionary stand turned away from the audience. People were sitting, standing, browsing. I took a spot near the display counter, which held volumes of Americana and first editions. I waited.

I was surprised to see Priscilla Davidoff there, talking to some students in the Women's Studies Program. I couldn't imagine why Priscilla had come if she thought so little of Stefan's work. She saw me and gave me a cool nod.

Chuck Bayer walked in, reeking of Scope and what I thought I recognized as British Sterling. He slapped me on the back as if we were old friends.

"Why are you being so nice to me?" I asked. "What do you want?"

He chuckled. Even rudeness didn't work on him. But then he launched into another pitch for his Didion bibliography, and I cringed.

"Chuck," I said, keeping my voice low. I spaced the words the way parents do when they're mad at their children in public: "I don't—want—to—work—with you."

He shook his head as if I were someone missing the opportunity for "the investment of a lifetime," then sauntered off trying to look casual. He just came off as dopey—but that was his height and build working against any attempt at ease or dignity.

Claire, the chair's secretary, slid into a seat midway back, turning to smile at me. Even off-duty she looked elegant and refined, tonight in a brown suede skirt and cashmere sweater. I wondered where she'd go after the reading, what her home was like. Then it struck me that I had never seen her at a reading before—why was *she* here at all?

Stefan knew the store and had read there last year, so he wouldn't need to be there early to check out the arrangements, and besides, I'd always told him that readings couldn't start until he got there, so succumbing to time pressure was silly. Tonight, though, I wished he *had* come early, wished we could have a few minutes alone before I had to share him with a crowd. Perry's note, the lawyer's letter, all that was like an injury partly dulled by painkillers. Though I felt the damage and the ache only through a sort of fog, it was still waiting.

Automatically, I was counting the audience. It had reached about sixty, with more people still coming in.

"You look peaked," Serena Fisch said behind me. I whirled around like a shoplifter.

She peered at me, obviously taken aback, and held a hand to her neck as if fingering pearls. "Nerves?" she asked.

I nodded, registering how outlandish she looked with her hair pulled back, and wearing a maroon sweater set, tartan skirt, and what I guessed you'd call sensible shoes. She could have been masquerading as somebody's idea of a dowdy English aunt.

"Is Stefan reading from something new?" she asked.

I nodded again.

"What's it about? Lost love?" She smiled, but when I didn't respond, she drifted away with the downcast bored face of a little child who's poked a stick into an anthill with no result.

I saw Betty and Bill Malatesta find seats near the back among other graduate students who possibly felt that closer seats were not their due. Or were they trying to be inconspicuous?

I nodded, thinking Bill had seen me, but he plunged into conversation with some other graduate students. Lynn Broadshaw burst in, followed by his wife, and they noisily settled into a row near the front, spinning off smiles and hellos around them like sparks. Mrs. Broadshaw was all in purple—from her wool dress and shawl down to her eye shadow, nails, and lipstick. The effect was somewhat alarming.

Lynn Broadshaw would be introducing Stefan, as if he were somehow responsible for Stefan's success. But where was Stefan?

At 7:25, I saw him outside, in a cluster of laughing young students, who seemed honestly entertained and relaxed. As the English say, there was no "side" to Stefan with his students; he did not think of them as lesser creatures who had to be browbeaten or even coaxed into some semblance of literacy. I had sat in on some of his classes, and I know other professors might consider him a little dull or disorganized, but I thought he was just right, because he was himself. He didn't adopt a manner in class; he wasn't out to intimidate students with his talent or success, nor was he intent on wheedling their affection and respect (which I think I tended to do a bit).

The happy crowd entered and Stefan headed right for me, kissed me. "Sorry we didn't connect. What's up?"

I wanted to pull him into a corner and blurt it all out, but especially share my anxiety, my frustration, my anger.

I couldn't do any of that right before a reading. "Nothing," I said.

"You sitting in front?" he asked, smiling. I nodded and he headed up to his seat. I followed, counting again. There were eighty-two people there, some standing at the back. Quite a crowd. I slid into the seat next to Stefan. From the corner of my eye I saw something red—it was Rose Waterman hurrying in, slipping into a seat at the back.

"We'll begin," Lynn Broadshaw said, rising with what I suppose he thought was dignity. He just seemed ponderous and stiff to me. He read his introduction from a typed sheet, and I tuned out, feeling like I was at another boring department meeting where nothing got done, but tempers were lost about the wording of this or that minor document or statement.

There was lots of applause, and Stefan walked up to the podium, laid a black binder down along with copies of his books. I knew he would decide what to read as he went along, sensing what might work or not, ready to experiment. I watched him as he adjusted himself, poured some water, chatted about his work. He was wearing black jeans and boots, a black and white Liz Claiborne polo shirt, and a black cardigan. He looked studious and sexy, but when he began reading, I tensed up.

Something was wrong. Nothing major, but he was slightly off. I could feel it in his pauses. He smiled, and word followed word, but at the end of a sentence he'd be left unprotected. For a moment, there was nothing to hide behind. I closed my eyes, which he would think was my usual sinking into enjoyment, and I listened as carefully as I could, as if in those pauses I would hear a different voice.

But that was a mistake, because I imagined Perry there like the Phantom of the Opera, his voice ringing out through the bookstore, majestic and threatening.

I glanced around me. Everyone seemed rapt. It was what I'd often told Stefan: even his middling performance was better than most authors' best. Only I could truly judge the quality of a reading.

I missed the rest of the evening, lost as I was in worrying about how he'd react when I told him about Perry's letter from beyond the grave.

When it was done, and the applause over, Stefan was as usual swarmed by students and faculty wanting autographs or just to talk about him—and sometimes themselves. I nodded at him, gave him a thumbs up, and sidled away.

"Great job! Great job!" Broadshaw was proclaiming to anyone who'd listen, as if he were Stefan's agent, no, Stefan's *coach*.

Serena came over to where I stood near the doorway, glad of the fresh air when it was opened and closed.

"He's damned good," she snapped out. "You're lucky. Stefan's handsome *and* talented."

I thought she was going to give me a macho slap on the shoulder, as if I'd just made a basket at the gym, but she just shook her head up and down in some kind of punctuation and headed out.

The Malatestas were definitely avoiding me, at least Bill was. He was furtively engrossed in front of the Biography section.

Before I expected it, Stefan broke away from the crowd and headed to me. "I need to talk to you," he said.

"Aren't we going out for drinks with—?" I gestured. Surely someone wanted to extend the evening in Stefan's company.

"Not tonight." He took my arm and steered me outside.

"Whose car? Doesn't matter? Then we'll take mine and I'll drive you in tomorrow morning."

He nodded.

I was surprised that he didn't ask me a single thing about the reading, or even seem puzzled by my not mentioning it.

We were quickly seated in my car and making the short drive home.

"What's the rush?" I asked, suddenly reluctant to tell him what had come in the mail for him.

"When I got to campus, there was a message from some lawyer. I called between classes after I tried calling you back."

"And?"

"It was about Perry's will. There's no next of kin. I'm his executor. And I have to make the arrangements for his burial."

We were at a red light a block from our house. There was no one behind us or stopped at any corner. I wanted to rush out of the car and run somewhere, anywhere, but I just put the car in park and buried my head in my arms on the wheel.

# -12-

Stefan asked if I wanted him to drive, but I managed to say no and pull myself together enough to get us down the street and into our driveway.

Inside, stunned, I had several shots of Chivas in the living room while Stefan sat opposite me—calm, but determined. I showed him the letter from Perry, but he didn't react the way I expected him to. I was astonished that he *wanted* to take care of the funeral arrangements.

"But what about Perry's wife?" I asked. "Ex-wife. *Wives*. Weren't there two?"

Stefan shook his head. "He made all of that up. The lawyer said there's nobody."

"Then maybe Perry's not really dead. Maybe he made *that* up too. It's not like we saw the body ourselves."

Stefan went on, talking about the will, which apparently wouldn't be probated for at least five months, the lawyer said. "That's how long it usually takes around here." Stefan fell silent, and his eyes closed a little.

"You actually feel sorry for him," I said. "I can't believe this! He's *dead*."

"He was so miserable," Stefan said quietly. "So lonely."

I didn't buy that for a minute. For Perry to have forced himself between me and Stefan once again was vengeful and cruel. And canny. How many people know how to cause trouble after they're dead? I shook my head. "He's doing this—he did this to hurt me, to hurt us."

Stefan looked appalled. "No, Nick. He was lonely, there was no one else."

I wanted to throw my glass at Stefan, but my hands were so shaky I could barely pour myself more scotch. I would probably miss and break a lamp. "No one else?" I brought out, trying to keep my teeth from grinding. "You're the only person in the world he could make his executor? He could have picked that lawyer, if he wanted to. Or Ann-Margret!"

Stefan shrugged, and I felt lost in some European complication of manners and obligations that was really beyond me. Perry was his ex-lover, not even his ex-lover, but someone Stefan had slept with many, many years ago. There was no real connection anymore as far as I was concerned. But Stefan seemed to be acting the way he thought his European-born parents would want him to act, as a gentleman.

"You think he was still in love with you," I said. "You do, I can see it."

"I have an appointment for eight-thirty downtown. With the lawyer."

"About what?"

"Reading of the will."

The sound of it was so stiff and archaic. Did people actually read wills? I couldn't picture it. Reading tarot cards, or palms— now that I could see.

"What are you smiling about?" Stefan asked me.

"Wait. I thought they read wills *after* a funeral."

"It can be before. You're coming with me, right?"

"Of course I am. Who knows what else that bastard was up to." I wondered about that taunting line, "Expect something else."

THE LAW FIRM's office was a grand and glowing suite in one of the towers right near the wedding cake state capitol building. The office was so sheathed in marble and brass that even the large potted plants looked hard and metallic. The palette in the waiting room and beyond was gray and mauve, meant to be soothing and understated, I guess, but laid on with such singlemindedness that you might have been in a jumped-up Holiday Inn.

A chilly receptionist took our names. She was in her thirties, sleek, blond, overperfumed, and harmonized with her desk in some odd and disturbing way. Like they'd both been ordered as a matched set from an office supplies catalogue.

We waited on an overstuffed mauve print velvet couch which was a soft and clinging trap. When Perry's lawyer emerged from her sanctum, hand outstretched in welcome, we had to haul each other off the couch. June Baker blinked as if no one ever struggled to stand straight there. She had auburn hair pulled back and tied with an emerald green and black striped scarf that matched a Chanel-type suit. Good legs for an older woman, and clear green eyes behind large horned rim glasses that were almost campy. She wore large fake pearls at her throat, her ears, around her wrists, as if she were selling them on the Home Shopping Network.

We followed her to a small sleek conference room with a view of the bulbous ungainly capitol dome. After a secretary brought us a tray with two china cups of coffee, we got down to business. She seemed trim and brisk, and because of the deep tan, I could see her at a local golf course on the weekends, chicly competitive. Her voice was as competent and unemotional as her handshake. It didn't take long, because Stefan was not just executor, he *inherited* everything.

Surprise, I thought.

"Originally," the lawyer explained, "the estate went to Yale University's alumni fund, but there's a codicil making Stefan Borowski the beneficiary."

"A codicil?" This was like a Victorian novel.

"Yes, that's when—"

I cut her off. "I know the meaning. I wanted to know when it happened."

She handed over the will and I turned to the last page, which was dated and witnessed the morning of his dinner with me and Stefan.

"What do you mean by his estate?" Stefan asked.

She seemed to be doing some mental calculations. "Aside from personal property, etc., there are bank accounts, certificates of deposit, a little stock. Somewhere around one hundred fifty thousand dollars."

Stefan drew a deep pained breath.

I slammed down the will. "What! Where the hell did Perry Cross get that kind of money!"

Perry's lawyer looked as decoratively blank as a chiffonier. If she knew, she wouldn't say.

Stefan was blushing from his neck to his scalp.

"Do we have to accept this?" I asked.

She smiled. "You'd like to challenge the will?"

"That's not what I mean. Couldn't we give it away or something?"

She pointedly looked at Stefan, whose eyes were down. "That's for Mr. Borowski to decide." She glanced discreetly at her watch.

"So we're done here?"

She nodded.

There was nothing in the will specifying the type of funeral arrangements, just that the executor make them. In the too-bright elevator, I announced, "We are not going to have any damned gravestone and plot." I pictured Stefan dutifully bringing flowers there once a year, Perry haunting us for the rest of our lives, or as long as we lived in Michigan.

Stefan shook his head like someone trying to clear his mind of the last song he heard on the radio before leaving home.

Trying to change Stefan's mood, I said, "To economize, we could put him in the backyard, near the gazebo."

It didn't work, he still looked dazed.

The elevator let us out in the building's atrium, teeming with exotic plants and little waterfalls—all it needed were a few apes and squawking gaudy parrots. We passed the handsome Hispanic-looking security guard at his desk. He had a dark, broad, impassive face, but his eyes widened slightly as he checked Stefan out. I glared at him and he looked away.

We headed outside to my car. "Cremation's the only choice," I said. Stefan winced, and I felt embarrassed because I knew the word "cremation" reminded Stefan of the extermination camps.

"What about the ashes?" he asked quietly.

"I don't give a damn about Perry's ashes! Dump them in the river!"

Stefan grimaced. "That's disgusting."

"Poetic justice," I said.

Driving off, I was silent, mortified by my flippancy. Stefan had more than once told me he would never be cremated, and if his parents or uncle specified that in their wills, he would disobey their wishes. "That's what the Germans were going to do to them," he explained.

For me, it was clear. The idea of reducing someone to junk that filled an urn or box was no less repellent than imagining what happened inside a coffin, which wasn't pretty either, but I didn't want what was left of Perry to take up so much damned room.

Now WHY DIDN'T I expect Detective Valley to be waiting at my office door? Why did I assume that what had happened at the lawyer's office would only explode a bomb at Stefan's feet and mine, leaving everyone else undisturbed?

Valley was wearing the same suit, the same manner.

"I'd like to talk to you," he said.

"Sure. I have a class at one-thirty. That gives us time."

I opened the door and waved him inside, turning on the light. The boxes were still there at the side of Perry's desk, and I cursed myself for not having finished the job immediately, when Claire first asked me. It still had to be done, and dropping Stefan off at his car after the lawyer's, when I'd asked Stefan if he was planning to do it, since he was the executor, he said, "Don't you think it's a good way for *you* to finish all this?"

"Finish it! The only way to finish this is to jump out a fucking window. It's never going to be finished! And don't tell me I'm getting emotional."

Valley was staring at me now in my office, as if I'd been speaking some of this aloud, or my face had been replaying the scene in the car.

"Sit," I said. And as if to mock me, he sat in Perry's desk chair.

"You still maintain that you and Stefan Borowski were," he paused, 'occupied' at two in the morning of Perry Cross's death?"

"What is this?" I asked. "Are you reopening the case? I thought the paper said it was an accident."

He blinked but said nothing, waiting with exaggerated patience. He crossed his legs, the masculine way, and folded his hands in his lap.

I tried playing his game, but I couldn't keep quiet. "What's the question?" I asked, giving in.

"Was Stefan Borowski with you that morning from two to four A.M.?"

"Of course he was."

"What if I told you that one of your neighbors, who has insomnia, heard a car drive out of your garage just after two that morning? Your neighbor remembered because of that train coming through." He smiled. "Unless it was *you* going for a drive?"

"Bullshit! Stefan *was* home, he was—"

Valley pounced. "He was what?"

I swallowed hard, shook my head.

And though I should have been prepared, his next question made me feel like a Roman galley rammed at full speed. "Did you know Perry Cross was leaving your lover one hundred and fifty thousand dollars?"

The way he said "lover," the word sounded like something criminal and cheap.

I stood up. "I don't have to answer any questions."

"That's true," he said. "Not now you don't."

"What does that mean? *Has* the case been reopened?"

"Everything looks different," he said, "now that there's a substantial sum of money involved. It's a strong motive for murder."

I sank into my chair. He was right.

"Are you still going to tell me that your lover didn't know Perry Cross very well? Then why did Professor Cross make Stefan his beneficiary? And why did he change his will the morning he was going to have dinner with the two of you? Did he know he wouldn't live much longer?"

I tried to deflect him. "Why would anyone leave money to someone he thought wanted to kill him?"

He smiled broadly. "Use your imagination. It sure points the finger, doesn't it?"

That's right, I thought. Perry was giving us, giving *me* the finger. But then I rebelled. "Wait a minute. That's pretty twisted, isn't it?"

Valley shrugged. Then he leaned forward, eyes and face a little softer. "It'll be a lot easier for you to clear everything up right now, but if you and Stefan insist on not giving me any answers…."

"You've talked to Stefan about this? When?"

"I stopped by your house earlier. He doesn't want to talk about it."

"He doesn't have to!"

"Not yet," Valley said again. "Why won't you tell me what the three of you talked about at dinner? Or what Professor Cross's mood was? Why the secrets? It'll all come out anyway, one way or another. You two were the last people known to have seen him before his body was found."

"Maybe you should ask around to see who else could have wanted him dead."

His face tensed. "Like—?"

"You're the detective. Detect!"

He shook his head. "No one else inherited anything from Professor Cross, so why would anyone else want to kill him?"

I refused to be drawn out any more. I just glared at him, wondering if I needed a lawyer.

Valley shook his head disgustedly at my silence, and he left.

I sank into my chair. Valley had seen the will. Which meant he probably knew that Stefan had lied to him and really did know Perry. Or if he didn't know for sure, he guessed. Was the business about a neighbor a snare, or was it true?

IF I THOUGHT I'd be able to refocus myself and get lost in going over material for my first class, I was wrong. The morning's surprises weren't over.

Serena Fisch came charging in a few minutes later, draped in some kind of mauve dress with shoulder pads and dolman sleeves that looked like a fancy straitjacket.

"What is going on with Stefan?" she said, perching on the edge of my desk as if she were a moll. "Somebody who says he's a detective has been asking questions in the department."

"He *is* a detective," I said glumly.

Serena waved that off. "He was asking me all sorts of things about Stefan and Perry and you." She frowned. "Was Perry some kind of government agent? Why all the interest?"

I groaned. "Serena, it's just the Campus Police, not the CIA."

"It has to start somewhere." She peered at me and seemed disappointed. "We'll talk later," she said, bustling off—no doubt to spread the word that something exciting was going on.

I didn't have the heart to follow her and find out what exactly she'd been asked, and more importantly, what she'd told Valley. And I sure wasn't in any mood to phone Stefan and ask him about Valley's visit this morning, and if he had been out around the time Perry Cross died. Or was killed.

This was a crisis, a time for us to be together, but I felt coldly distant from Stefan, seeing him as an outsider might. He had been painfully involved with Perry, Perry had left him a lot of money. Two good reasons for murder. I picked up my copy of the campus paper, and there it was on the front page, my nightmare: a very short article saying that "new information" had appeared pertaining to Perry Cross's death. This was no joke.

I was desperate, so I called Sharon, like I often had in the past when I was in trouble. My favorite picture of her was from *Glamour,* in which she wore a lilac silk portrait-collared dress that made her look like someone Sargent would have painted: rich, assured, and quite beautiful. Whenever I called her, I thought of that photograph, and it calmed me.

Luckily she was in now and I got right through. "Hi, Nick, need some help with the major exports of Tasmania?"

"Devils," I said. "Tasmanian Devils. I already knew that."

She chuckled. Given her position as archivist in Special Collections at Columbia's library, her ease in six languages, and the fact that she read widely and with voluptuous curiosity, the family seemed to think of her as a hotline. Apparently they asked her anything and everything: about quarks, earth science, genetics—you name it. While I had never called her for help with a crossword puzzle, I knew my mother had.

"Sharon, you *know* I wouldn't call about something stupid. I *am* able to use an encyclopedia."

"Then what's up?"

I came right out with it. "I think Stefan may be a murder suspect."

"You're serious."

I almost said, "Dead serious," but stopped in time.

I filled her in on everything that had happened, and she listened with occasional sympathetic noises, saying "Right" or "Sure" or "I understand."

It sounded like she was jotting down notes.

"So," I summed up. "You know Stefan. Do you think he's capable of murder?"

"He's a very capable man."

I laughed despite myself, and realized how badly I needed it.

"Nick, let me ask you a question: Do *you* think Stefan is capable of murder? That's the first question."

"Well, maybe," I said, sounding defensive.

"Okay, then. If he did murder the guy, then you have to ask yourself if you can live with it. Will it become a habit? And how do you keep this from your parents?"

I knew she was trying to make me laugh, but it wasn't working. "Sharon, what can I do!"

"You have to find out where Stefan was that morning when you woke up, and just what he was doing. If this Perry actually *was* murdered, and Stefan doesn't have a good alibi, then it's up to *you* to find out who did it, and why. From what you told me, the

police, the Campus Police, would love pinning a gay man's murder
on another gay man."

"You're crazy! I'm not a detective, I'm an English professor.
What can I do?"

"It's simple. Do what Hercule Poirot does. *Talk* to people, get
a feel for their psychology."

"But they won't tell me the truth!"

"That's never the point. 'Speech is the deadliest of revealers'—
that's what Poirot says in, hmmm, *Cards on the Table,* the one with
all the bridge playing. And that creepy victim, Santana, Montana,
something like that. Speech," Sharon repeated, "speech is the
deadliest of revealers."

"Huh?"

Now she sounded a little impatient. "Haven't you read Agatha
Christie?"

"Not really. I've seen some of the movies, though. But how's
that going to help me?"

"Honey, make a list of all the possible suspects and talk to
them. Somebody's bound to let something slip."

"But what if they *all* did it?" I cried helplessly.

That didn't throw her. "You mean like in *Murder on the
Orient Express?* Then I guess you're outnumbered, so back off." She
added, "And get a very good lawyer."

She wasn't joking.

Somehow, I made it through my classes, expecting more bad
news, more disruption—but the day continued uneventfully,
except for what I was thinking. I kept imagining Stefan's lies about
Perry exposed in court, Stefan in jail, our lives ruined. And mixed
in with these catastrophic images was a recurrent horrible doubt:
could Stefan have killed Perry? What exactly did that mean? And
how could I possibly be wondering such a thing about the man I
had lived with for ten years?

Did I really know him, though? Maybe that's what was
possessing me—the realization that when it came to Perry, I had
no real idea what Stefan might have felt or done, it was all too
mysterious and out of character. Especially since what he'd said
about Perry reminded me of friends in college and after who'd

gotten involved in doomed, obsessive relationships where they spent as much time on the phone complaining to me as they did with the person they were unhappily in love with. Those phantom relationships struck me as absurdly dramatic, the kind of emotional jump-starting people did when they were afraid they couldn't feel anything at all. But doubting Stefan, doubting my knowledge of him, was worse for me than if Stefan actually had killed Perry.

WHEN I GOT home that evening, I felt as exhausted as if I'd been at the gym for hours after a year away: drained, achy, depressed.

Stefan was making dinner and the kitchen smelled great. The dining-room table had been set with Sharon's china.

I perked up a little. "What's the menu?" I asked, sinking into a kitchen chair.

Stefan turned from the counter. "Veal scallopine *au* vermouth, duchesse potatoes, string beans with garlic."

"And the beverage?"

"A bottle of Haut Brion."

"Why such reckless extravagance in one so comparatively young?"

Stefan beamed as he always did when I quoted from *The Importance of Being Earnest,* his favorite play.

"After this morning, you have to ask?"

I smiled. "Now you sound like me."

In a Yiddish accent, he said, "Who else should I sound like? You want I should sound like a stranger?"

But I stopped laughing as soon as I started. While he was talking, Stefan had laid the veal out on the counter between two sheets of wax paper and was pounding it lightly with our large meat mallet. As it rose and fell, I imagined him striking Perry down, with real force in that arm. I was shocked at how easy it was to *see* it.

I closed my eyes and shuddered.

When I opened them, Stefan was staring at me. "Do you want a drink? You look dead."

I flinched as he came toward me. And when he stopped, I blurted it out: "Valley was there at school. Why didn't you tell me he came by the house and talked to you this morning?"

Stefan shrugged.

"Valley asked me about the night Perry died, and where you were. He said there was a witness...."

"What kind of witness?"

"That you left the house, you were driving, around that time. Did you?"

Stefan nodded. "Actually," he said with an odd smile, "I was out earlier than two A.M."

# -13-

I asked Stefan, "Do I need a full stomach to listen to this?" He nodded. "Dinner's almost ready. Can you wait? I'm just doing the veal."

I waited. The veal was soon sauteed in olive oil and Stefan was cooking it with the butter, vermouth, lemon juice, and parsley. He quickly brought the steaming redolent plates out to the dining room, and I followed with the wine and mineral water. It was a good solid meal, like ballast in a storm.

I ate and drank a little feverishly, particularly enjoying the fancy potatoes, while Stefan told me about the night Perry died. "I woke up around midnight. I tried to write a little, but that didn't work, then I ate some of the leftover cheesecake, but I wasn't really hungry, so I got dressed and went for a drive."

"This isn't Los Angeles, Stefan. This is Michiganapolis. How can you go for a drive around here?"

He bit his lower lip. "Good point. But I did. I ended up cutting through campus on the way home—"

"What time was that?"

He shrugged. "One-thirty?"

This sounded terrible. Driving around by himself, with no sense of the time. Who would believe he wasn't out pushing Perry off a bridge, or doing whatever had led to Perry's death?

"I drove by Parker and I saw the lights on in your office, so I stopped and went upstairs."

"My office lights were on ..." I set down my glass very carefully.

He looked right at me. "Perry was there."

"Redecorating?" I snapped. "Or did he slip you a note when he left after dinner, asking you to meet him there?"

"Oh, Nick."

Why was it more awful to think of the two of them in my office together than imagining Stefan ending Perry's life?

"We talked," Stefan said. "I told him what I told you, that I finally saw he was a phony."

"You had to go to the office in the middle of the night for that? What about a fax, huh?"

"I told you it was coincidence. It felt good to finish things off."

"How long were you there?"

"Fifteen minutes? Ten? I'm not sure."

"Well, what did he say?"

Stefan hesitated. "He wanted to have sex."

"What! Did he *touch* you?"

"He tried." Stefan gave me a weary smile. "It seemed pointless, stupid. I felt sorry for him."

"How sorry?"

"I said, 'No, thanks,' and walked out. He couldn't believe it."

I downed my wine and poured another glass, pushed my plate away. "Neither will Detective Valley, when you tell him."

"I can't."

"You have to."

"Nick. Listen to me, didn't you read the paper this morning? And it was on the local news. They're investigating again, so they must think something's suspicious. It's bad enough Perry left me the money. If I tell anybody I saw Perry an hour or two before he was dead, they'll be sure I did it."

"But you *did* see him. It's the *truth*."

Stefan eyed me as if I were a pitifully naive immigrant who'd just been sworn in as an American citizen, declaiming about the unalloyed goodness of my new land.

Then something came to me. "Wait a minute. Was he drunk? Was Perry drunk when you talked to him?"

"I don't think so. I'm not sure."

"You'll be a great witness. Why didn't you tell me about seeing Perry that night?" Before he could answer, I went on. "Let me guess. Same reason you didn't tell me that you knew Perry, that you helped Perry get the job here. You didn't want to upset me, right?"

He nodded.

"Stefan, I'm not that fragile, you don't have to protect me!"

He looked down, obviously ashamed of himself.

And then I said something I knew was dangerous, but I couldn't help myself. "I can't believe that after the way your parents and your uncle lied to you about being Jewish, you could lie to me about anything this important."

Stefan glared at me.

I went on recklessly. "Haven't you learned anything from all that? That lies come out eventually? You want me to end up hating you like you hate your dad?"

At that moment, if he'd reached across the table to smack the shit out of me, or swept the dishes onto the floor, or crushed his wineglass onto the table, I would not have been surprised.

Stefan did the unexpected. He started to cry, mouth and shoulders trembling, eyes squeezed, without turning his face away or leaning down into his hands. He cried unashamedly, utterly exposed, and there was no barrier whatsoever between us. It was naked, thrilling, weird. I felt awed and transfixed, as if I were watching some natural disaster. There was nothing I could say.

I made Stefan go to bed, and sat there cradling him while he fell asleep. "Say you don't hate me," he murmured, just as he drifted off. I was glad he didn't repeat the request, because I couldn't have told you what I felt for Stefan right then. I gently slid my arm out from behind his head and eased myself up to tiptoe from the room. He had clearly been drinking before I got home, and would probably sleep through the night, but I didn't want to risk waking him up. Hell, it wasn't Stefan I was thinking about as much as myself. I wanted to be alone, I wanted to *think*.

I stalked through the house once or twice, like a restless dog unable to find a comfortable spot to curl up in. Finally, I settled into the large armchair in my study, put my feet up on the ottoman. I went through my conversation with Sharon that morning, looking for some exit, but everything seemed hopeless. I had seen enough mysteries to know that Stefan was sunk: he had the motive, *two* motives, the opportunity, and I guess the means. Though that last point wouldn't matter as much as the other two. I could just see him in court saying he went for a drive, and some lawyer subjecting him to withering questions. A drive at that time of night? And he just happened to end up near the department building? And all he wanted from Perry was to talk? Hadn't he said enough at dinner?

Hell, if all that came to *me* so clearly, a prosecutor aiming for Stefan's conviction would do even more damage. And of course the jury would be homophobic, good simple people from Michiganapolis who supported "family values" and were suspicious of the university anyway—even though it was a major source of income in town.

How was it possible to have been so happy here, so happy with each other, growing more and more fond of living in Michigan, and to suddenly find that happiness proven chimerical?

I reached for the phone, dragged it over, and called my cousin Sharon at home.

"What's wrong, Nick? You sound terrible."

I explained how Stefan had lied to me, that he *had* seen Perry not that long before Perry was found dead.

"This is pretty bad," she said.

I moaned, "Tell me something I don't know!"

Sharon clucked her tongue, but she wasn't being noisily sympathetic, it was something she occasionally did when she was thinking and marking time.

"Sweetie," she said gently. "Are you listening? Nick?"

I muttered something.

"Okay, Nick. This feels crazy to you. The thing to do, then, is to be as systematic as possible. 'Order and method,' that's what Hercule Poirot always says."

"Sharon, I can't balance my checkbook—I can't keep my files alphabetized—I can't remember where I put the shopping list!"

"But Nick," she said. "None of that is a matter of life and death, is it?"

That shocked me out of my self-pity.

"You have to make a list of everybody who might have wanted Perry Cross dead or at least out of the way, and then you have to start digging. Find out everything you can, fast, because it doesn't sound like the police there would be interested in the truth when they have a great suspect like Stefan."

"I can do that," I said, sounding less hesitant than I would have imagined, but apparently not convincing enough for Sharon.

"Listen," she said. "Remember when your adviser at NYU was dying of lung cancer and you were terrified they'd make you work with McCracken, who hated you, and that you wouldn't finish the dissertation on time to get the job in Massachusetts, and Stefan would have to move there without you?"

"How could I forget?"

"If you could get through that, you can get through this. I want you to put the list together and call me right back, okay?"

I hung up, grateful, energized, and unexpectedly filled with the wonderful memories of how Sharon had helped me years before, when I felt doomed. With my thesis adviser given just two months to live, despite the chemotherapy, Sharon had sat me down, helped me organize my research, and had nursed along my dissertation, which I wrote in six weeks staying at her lavish apartment on Sutton Place that was like an Art Deco movie set. Whenever I had panicked, and Sharon wasn't working, she was there with food or entertainment or a neck massage or terrific advice: "Your dissertation doesn't have to be perfect, sweetie, it just has to be *done*. It's just a passport, it's your ticket *out*." When she wasn't there, she left cheerful, stirring notes and freshly baked muffins and breads.

And so I had finished my dissertation in a blur, Sharon had paid for it to be typed far more quickly than I could have imagined, and I passed my dissertation defense just in time, before my adviser eventually succumbed. A day after the defense, Sharon had Stefan and me over for Dom Perignon and beluga, and Stefan announced, "You're like a fairy godmother."

"I'll be the godmother," she had drawled. "You be the fairy."

Feeling refreshed by those memories, I pulled out a pad of paper from my desk drawer and started to make notes. As if guided by Sharon, I felt incredibly clear-minded and resolute. I headed one column SUSPECTS and another MOTIVES, and whole-heartedly entered Stefan's name in the first one. Now was not the time to pretend. I hesitated, then put mine there, too. I didn't have an alibi either, and it was clear enough that I hated Perry. Money was Stefan's motive; jealousy was mine.

But who was next? I wrote down Bill Malatesta's name, then added his wife's, since what happened to one could happen to the other. Fear and secrecy were their motives.

Four suspects. Was that all? Of course not—there was our wonderful chair, Lynn Broadshaw. If the Malatestas had wanted to keep Broadshaw's harassment secret, certainly he would too. He had more to lose than they did. And Serena Fisch was a strong possibility, so I added her name; she had lost a rival when Perry died, and it was clear she had despised him. Now I felt a bit better, though the list was not long enough to be comforting. And then there was Priscilla Davidoff, who seemed so hostile to Perry with no apparent reason.

I called Sharon back. I read out the list, and then started filling in the names. I explained about Bill, the chair's whirlpool, their having shared a hotel room at the conference, all of that.

"Is Bill telling you the truth?"

"What do you mean?"

"Maybe he did sleep with the chair. That raises the stakes."

"Which means *Mrs.* Broadshaw?"

"Exactly!"

I flushed like a little child who's gotten a multiplication problem right with the whole class looking on.

"But why wouldn't the chair's wife kill Bill, or her husband, if she was going to kill someone?"

"Nick, murder doesn't have to make sense to *you*, it has to make sense to the murderer. Someone had to feel angry enough, or threatened enough, or desperate enough to do it."

I suddenly remembered the party a few weeks ago, and Mrs. Broadshaw crying out, and Betty Malatesta hurrying from the kitchen. What had happened between the two women? Now I was wide awake.

"Sharon, I can't believe I feel good thinking about why *somebody else* might have a reason to kill Perry."

"That may be the only way you can feel good for a while, Nick, so enjoy it."

I was about to say something when she went on a little breathlessly, "Has anyone gone through Perry's files, his effects? Maybe there's a clue there."

"*Shit! I* was supposed to clean up his junk at the office."

"What are you waiting for?"

"But it's ten o'clock, won't it look suspicious?"

"It's your office, too, right? What's the problem?"

I was so fired up I agreed, and promised to call her from the office if I found anything suspicious. Of course I hoped I would discover some neat clue or piece of evidence that I could hand over to Detective Valley and end the whole thing with quiet flair. I was relieved to be doing something instead of feeling sunk in misery for myself and fear for Stefan.

I LEFT STEFAN a note just in case he woke up—which I thought unlikely—and got to campus in five minutes. Michiganapolis is pretty quiet at night, at least early in the week, and campus seems like an enormous abandoned Hollywood set. Pulling into the lot behind Parker, I thought I saw Claire driving off, but the light wasn't very good and I must've been mistaken. She was efficient, but not obsessed; I couldn't imagine her working there so late at night.

If Parker Hall was depressing during the day, at night it was truly dismal. It wasn't ruined enough to be romantic and interesting in the gloom, it just seemed more dilapidated. The building was locked as usual after ten, and since I rarely came in this late, I had to fumble with my key ring for a minute before I found the right one. Inside, it smelled bad, a smell you didn't seem to notice during the day: some mix of bug spray, which was constantly deployed against the hordes of cockroaches, stale cardboard, moldy plaster, and damp pipes. I carefully made my way up the worn, uneven stairs to the third floor, turning on lights as I ascended.

The third-floor hallway was quite cool and musty, and even when I flicked the nearest switch, the light from the large globe lamps was too far away to be comforting or helpful. I hurried down to my office, hoping I wouldn't see any bugs or bats. One night last year, working after dinner, I'd heard something slam against my office door, and when I opened it carefully, I saw a twitching stunned bat lying there. I called the Campus Animal Patrol, which was used to dealing with the wildlife that blundered into buildings and scared people, and left, assuming they would come right away. The bat died overnight, and in the morning, with the patrol still not there, the entire third floor reeked.

I got into my office, turned on my two desk lamps and the standing lamp in the corner, left by some previous inhabitant: a bronze gargoyle of a lamp with a pink-fringed shade edged in gold brocade you'd expect to see on someone's epaulets. The office wasn't bright enough, but it would do.

I started with Perry's desk, methodically sifting through the ordinary items, the supplies and department directives, separating every object, every page, waiting for something to leap up at me. It was quiet there except for the noise I made, and the occasional creaks and groans of the building as it cooled and settled in the night air.

Nothing. No phone book or academic calendar. I packed it all away, taped the boxes shut after checking through the box I had packed a few days ago. I wondered why everything in his desk was so unexceptional, so stripped of the personal: there weren't any postcards, letters, notes, no sign that he was ever connected to anyone else.

I imagined Stefan nodding at that, and saying, "See, he *was* lonely." But it seemed less like loneliness and more like the efforts of a man covering his tracks. What did Perry have to hide?

Unless someone had gotten to his desk before me, and edited everything out that might be incriminating. Serena had already gotten the materials related to Perry's classes, the ones she would be teaching. What if that wasn't all she had taken?

I moved the chair over to Perry's file cabinets. Since he'd only been at SUM since the end of the summer, his files were not extensive. No surprise there. I found student evaluation forms from different schools he'd taught at, copies of letters of recommendation written for him or that he had written, and Xerox copies of articles. Lots of copies. I leafed through every single one, hoping that I'd find some note somewhere, something in the margin, something that at first glance looked casual, but was deeply significant. An address, a Swiss bank account number. I wished Sharon were there with me, beautifully methodical. This was too boring, and I couldn't see how it was going to help Stefan in any way.

If I were in a house, there'd certainly be more places to look, like a wall safe, for instance.

I blushed at what I was about to do, but I went ahead anyway. I got up and lifted the Fragonard print, which was quite heavy, off the wall. It was stupid, but I had to check the wall. It was blank and cracked, revealing no secrets. I felt the back of the picture, but it seemed completely sealed and ordinary. I hung the print back on the wall.

I decided to see if there was anything behind the file cabinet drawers or the desk drawers. I pulled each one out and reached back to feel, but there wasn't anything there and I felt a little foolish. I sat down again and leaned back in the desk chair, looking around the office. There was no rug to check under.

I stared at the Fragonard print, at the intense frozen struggle, draped in such shiny elegance. Once again, my eyes went up to that straining hand, and then down. But this time I looked up. I followed the hand up along the wall, above the print and to the edge where it met the ceiling. If there'd been some kind of molding there, I would have tried prying it from the wall just for the hell of it. I felt stumped.

Then my gaze went back to the picture, and I turned sharply to the deep-set dark office door. There was a thick piece of crown molding stretching across the top. I dragged over one of the metal department chairs and stood on it. I could just reach the top of the molding. It was thick with dust, but as I felt around I was sure that it didn't quite meet the wall. I had to get higher.

I jumped down and lugged over my enormous Webster's, plopped it on the seat, and climbed up. Perfect. I was high enough and there was enough light for me to see down into the space between the wall and the molding, which looked like the result of settling. There was something beige-colored in there. I yanked out what I saw was a folded-up 9x12 manila envelope.

I hurried down from my perch, tossing the dirty envelope onto my desk. I replaced the dictionary and chair.

Then I thought I heard a noise out in the hallway. It wasn't the sliding pail of a janitor, but something quieter, furtive. I tensed and looked up at the door. Was there someone out there, somewhere in Parker Hall? Or was I just scaring myself like kids at a campfire telling ghost stories?

Then the lights in the hallway went out. This was no story. Someone had turned them out—I knew they weren't on a timer.

Breathing fast, I could feel the skin on my face go tight and cold. I wanted to say something, to pretend someone was there with me, or just ask if anyone was outside, but I couldn't speak. The window was three flights up, I thought, and it was closed. If someone burst through the door, I'd have no way to get out. I waited, terrified, wishing I had taken that self-defense class Stefan had talked about last year, wishing I weighed less and went to the gym every day, feeling vulnerable, feeling my body would not be able to protect me, but would be a source of danger. I was too clumsy, too out of shape.

I could have sworn somebody tried the handle, it seemed to move a hair. What the hell was I supposed to do now?

# -14-

And then the lights came on outside, and I heard brisk strong footsteps heading my way, headed right down the hall to me. There was a knock and I jumped.

"Nick?" A woman's voice.

I couldn't answer.

"Nick?" It was Priscilla Davidoff.

I leapt up and opened the door, grinning with relief.

Priscilla looked startled, since I'm sure I had never smiled that widely at her before. She had on a heavy black sweater, black jeans, and running shoes; with her hair tied back she looked formidable.

"I came in to look for some journals I forgot to take home," she said. "I didn't see your car downstairs. You working late?"

"Sort of."

Priscilla peered behind me at the boxes on Perry's desk, and the Fragonard print. "I thought you were all done with Perry's stuff."

"It's taken longer than I expected."

She nodded. "Not a great job, huh?"

"Yeah—it's pretty weird."

"It would depress the hell out of me," Priscilla said. "I can't stand cleaning up my *own* mess."

I didn't know what else to say.

Priscilla nodded genially. "See you later, Nick."

As she turned away to head for her office, I blurted out, "Did you see anyone in the building? Out in the hall?"

Priscilla frowned and shook her head. "It's just us here. Do you want the door closed?"

"Thanks."

She shut it behind her and I listened as she walked across to her office and shut the heavy door.

It was quiet enough for me to hear her moving around her office. I snatched the rolled-up envelope and headed out, locking my door and leaving as quickly as I could, trying to be alert and ready.

I hurried down the stairs like a burglar and burst out into the parking lot with relief. Even the dim pole lights were comforting. There was one other car there, Priscilla's battered Honda.

I checked the backseat of my car before I got in, and locked the door before starting up. Edging out of the lot onto Michigan Avenue, I suddenly felt faint, like someone who's escaped an accident reliving the moment when everything could have gone wrong.

What if that was Priscilla who turned off the lights, and not to save the university on its light bill? I had imagined her as trained in karate, confident about walking into Parker alone, at night—but what if that wasn't just confidence? What if it was menace? What if she had wanted to get into my office for some reason, and had thought the light had been left on and no one was inside? I was sure I'd heard something and that someone had tried the doorknob.

And hadn't Priscilla been too specific about why she was in the building at night? Why so much detail? She said she hadn't seen my car—how was that possible, when there were only two in the lot?

"VERY GOOD," SHARON said over the phone when I told her about Priscilla. "Hercule Poirot says, 'You should trust nobody—nobody at all.' I think that's from *Death in the Air.*"

I was feeling quite pleased with myself, reporting back to Sharon about searching through Perry's things, the Fragonard print, the discovery. I was curled up on my favorite chair in my study. The danger, or the thought of danger, was over, and here at home I felt less like I was trapped by circumstances than faced by a puzzle.

"How do you remember all that stuff from those books?"

"Context," she said. "If you were talking about Russian history I'd probably think of lines from *War and Peace*."

"Amazing."

"So, what was in the envelope?" Sharon asked.

"I was so spooked I never opened it. I wanted to calm down. I think I'm ready." I pulled it from my desk and tore slowly along one side. I slipped out several Xeroxed sheets, folded in thirds.

"It's something in German," I said, very disappointed. "Newspaper articles? The copying is pretty bad. You know German, don't you?" I put the papers down; even the look of German repulsed me, made me anxious and uneasy. It was an inescapable doorway into marching, bombs, destruction. Though my family hadn't lost any relatives in the Holocaust, like all modern Jews, we lived in its shadow.

Sharon was saying something: "Fax them to me tomorrow at my office. I'll give you the number. It must be important, if Perry went to all that trouble of hiding it there."

"Why put anything in the door frame? Why not keep stuff at home, or in a safe-deposit box?"

"Maybe so no one could find it, or he was trying to be clever."

I could picture that. I agreed to fax her what I had found, but I couldn't imagine how these sheets of copy paper could be connected to what I was beginning to think of as my case.

"You have to get some sleep," Sharon said. "Do you have anything you could take?"

"I hate pills," I said. "I guess I could take some Nyquil—that usually knocks me out."

"Whatever works. Don't forget the fax tomorrow, okay?"

I assured her I wouldn't forget, hung up, and drifted off to the bathroom and then to bed, wondering if I wasn't just fooling myself and stirring up a lot of dust that would settle and leave me exactly where I'd started: facing Stefan's certain arrest for murder.

SOON AFTER I got up in the morning, I realized I had to lie to Stefan. Checking my date book, I had found a notation that Stefan's father would be back in Ann Arbor from vacation. Mr. Borowski knew German too, and I decided to drive the hour down there and ask him to do the translation instead of faxing Sharon. I felt the need for more help, and help that was both nearby and in the family. I called while Stefan was showering, welcomed his father home, and said I had to see him. Mr. Borowski didn't seem at all surprised. I called Sharon next, but she must have been between home and her office, so I left messages on both her answering machines, letting her know my plan. Then I called Claire at the department, and asked her to cancel my office hours because I wasn't feeling well.

At breakfast, I told Stefan I was leaving early to go shopping before I got to campus. He looked so tired and worn down, I don't think he really heard me, but I drove off feeling ashamed of myself. I wasn't weighing this small lie against Stefan's original partial truths about Perry, or his later silence about seeing Perry on campus. I was judging this lie against my own honesty with Stefan, and I was not pleased. Thankfully, there had been nothing in the newspaper that morning about the murder.

Ann Arbor and Michiganapolis were very different college towns. While the University of Michigan is smaller, urban, and somewhat undistinguished-looking, the town itself is larger than Michiganapolis and more picturesque, its many hills lined with big, well-kept Victorian homes bristling with turrets, porte cochères, elegant long verandas, and confidently fronted by crisp lawns. It was a town where automobile industry money as much as taste had left its mark, and where respect for the past—if not reverence— had left it relatively intact despite the accretion of newer buildings. It was very unlike Michiganapolis, where many of the older homes had been bulldozed for parking lots or mini-malls.

Mr. Borowski's house was up one of Ann Arbor's steeper and prettier hills, planted right in the middle of a circle of other small homes—small for Ann Arbor, that is. It looked charming and almost English to me, with mullioned windows, gabled roof. I remembered lots of polished oak trim inside. Stefan and I had visited only once since moving to Michigan, and not very comfortably, but I was glad to be there again, maybe because I was connecting myself to Stefan's life before Perry.

Stefan's father opened up the door before I knocked. "Nick, you look good."

"I look tired, Mr. Borowski." He had once asked me to call him Max, but it felt too familiar, and it seemed to bother Stefan.

Stefan's father nodded, gracefully accepting my correction. He shook my hand and waved me inside. As always, I found it hard to imagine this short, plump, white-haired old man had been a tyrant to Stefan as a boy. He was wearing a white buttoned-down shirt, large charcoal gray cardigan, black and white plaid pants, and black carpet slippers. In his late sixties now, he was a Jewish version of the actor who played Santa in *Miracle on 34th Street.*

"You'll have lunch?" he said.

It was early, but I readily agreed, sure that we'd feast on goodies from the authentic Jewish deli in town. We did. I was soon reveling in a thick pastrami sandwich on real seeded rye bread, and Max Borowski was eyeing me with the warm indulgence of parents enjoying their children's appetites. I half-expected him to caution me not to eat so fast, but he just smiled and chewed and sipped his coffee. We went on to a chocolate babka that was exquisitely flaky and sweet.

"So," he said when we were full. "You came because of the—" He considered his next word. "The incident at your university." I had never heard him refer to SUM by name; it was an example of the snobbery that infected almost everyone who taught at the University of Michigan or lived nearby.

"You know about Perry Cross's death?"

"Friends filled me in last night when I got home. You see, there were messages on my answering machine, one from a colleague at Michigan who heard from a colleague at your university that Stefan might be involved in some way. Is he?"

I nodded, stunned by the speed and accuracy of gossip.

"Stefan didn't call," he said, with only the slightest stress on "Stefan." And between us then was the story of how Stefan, years ago, had come late to his father's second wedding reception here in Ann Arbor, arriving from New York a little drunk, too. Stefan missed the service completely after first having said he wouldn't come, then changing his mind a few days before the wedding. Everything Stefan did wrong was like another malefaction added to the scales.

I flushed and started to defend Stefan now, but his father cut me off: "Tell me what's going on, please."

I took him through everything from before the dinner party the night Perry died up to the present. He didn't look shocked or even startled, just nodded, drained and refilled his coffee cup, nibbled at a piece of babka, taking it all in.

When I came to the end of my weaving, layered narrative, Mr. Borowski sighed.

"So," he said. "You want me to tell you that Stefan is innocent," he summed up.

I must have goggled at him, because he smiled. "Don't you? Isn't that why you came? You think my son is a murderer."

"*I don't know.*"

"Did you ask him?" Then he smiled. "Forgive me. It's not the sort of thing one does ask." He sounded English then, disinterested, cool. "From what you say, this Cross fellow made people very angry. Angry enough to kill? Very possibly."

"But do *you* think Stefan could have done it?"

"Oh, yes, absolutely. Well, what I mean is this, Nick. I couldn't tell you that Stefan is *not* a murderer, could never do it. Which means anything is possible. I know that. After the war, I know that."

I was silent, humbled a little by everything he didn't say.

"However," he went on. "I don't *believe* that he did it, especially with so many suspects, and so much hatred for that man, if what you say is true."

I wasn't sure I wanted to follow Mr. Borowski's distinction, so I handed him the copies I'd found hidden behind the office door molding.

"What is this? Oh yes, the German documents you mentioned." He fished reading glasses from his shirt pocket and surveyed what I'd brought. "Poor copies," he muttered. "Very poor. I'll have to examine these closely. Can you wait?"

I told him I had to get back to Michiganapolis, there were people I had to talk to.

"Yes," he said. "Your cousin—Sharon, was it?—seems to have inspired you. I'll translate these today and call you at home, later."

"Terrific, Mr. Borowski."

"You're a good man," he said as I was leaving. "I suppose Stefan is very lucky."

I drove straight back to Michiganapolis, without even stopping at any of Ann Arbor's terrific array of bookstores. I was glad Mr. Borowski wasn't my father, but I was glad he was Stefan's father, because we needed dispassionate, insightful help.

The ride back was pleasant at first, because of the music on the radio. Ann Arbor was on the edge of what I thought of as the Radio Zone—you could hear some of the good Detroit stations that played house and rap and solid R&B. Up in Michiganapolis, the stations were fairly bland, and as I got closer to home, Top 40 of today and yesteryear took over.

I was nearing my exit when I heard Olivia Newton-John's song "Physical." I perked up—it was so brainless and cheery. And I was suddenly singing along with the chorus, only I found myself changing the words from "Phy-si-cal, phy-si-cal, I wanna get phy-sical" to "Criminal, criminal! I wanna get criminal." I laughed aloud imagining Stefan staring at me, wondering if I was losing it. When the song ended, I felt flushed and triumphantly silly.

That didn't last. I had told Mr. Borowski there were people I had to talk to, but I wasn't sure where to start, or how. Did I just show up and announce my intention? Was I supposed to act casual and try to surreptitiously draw the truth out of whoever I talked to, and then pounce?

Geography decided for me. Driving into town I realized I'd be passing married student housing, so it made sense to see if the Malatestas were in. I remembered their address from a party Stefan and I had gone to last year, and I was able to park in one of the campus lots closest to Michigan Avenue.

The married-student complex stretched for several blocks: a series of ramshackle two-story buildings with all the heartbreaking

tackiness of a trailer park. Every attempt at humanizing the sterile
cheap buildings—window boxes, colorful curtains, prisms hung
from cord ends—had the opposite effect. You were that much
more aware of the overall shabbiness. And inside, there was an awful
smell of diapers, cat piss, mold, and sweat. It was as if all the anxiety
graduate students lived with hung in the air like a mist.

Wandering down a linoleum-floored corridor, I found the
Malatestas' unevenly painted door and knocked.

Betty Malatesta opened it, looking suspicious but quite pretty
in black jeans and what looked like one of Bill's blue work shirts.

"Hello," she said, frowning at me as if she thought I was an
impostor.

"Could I talk to you? Are you busy?"

She moved back reluctantly, and I walked in, aware that it
would have been hard for her to say no to a professor.

The living room was walled with brick and board shelves
crammed mostly with paperbacks. Two plank desks were squeezed
in with the shelves, and large Indian-print pillows lay about looking
forlorn. I didn't especially want to sit on the floor.

"Come into the kitchen," Betty said, and I squeezed past some
shelves to sit at the tiny table opposite her. "Coffee?" I nodded
and she poured me a cup. The cabinets behind her were worn and
scratched.

Betty waited, as if saying anything was too risky. I was not used
to seeing her so ill-at-ease, and it made me even more uncomfortable.
Unless it was just her embarrassment about my being there. I knew
that many graduate students didn't invite professors to their homes
because they were ashamed of being at such different stages in their
career, and unwilling to be cheerful about their relative poverty. I
had already been here, but that was at night, in a crowd, with the
lights low.

"You probably heard that they're investigating Perry Cross's
death again."

Betty nodded, not giving away a thing. I didn't know how to
proceed, and I wondered if she wasn't enjoying my awkwardness.

"Bill told me something about Broadshaw harassing him—"

It was the worst thing I could have said. Betty's eyes widened, and she practically hissed at me, "I don't believe it! Why doesn't he go on public access TV and tell everybody in *town!* That moron … that asshole … that *wuss!* He's going to ruin us and we'll never get out of this dump! Why can't he shut his god-damned mouth and keep things to himself!" Her mouth and neck were quivering and tight.

She was saying all this in a powerful stage whisper, obviously controlled by the fear of her neighbors overhearing—and it was very strange to see her so flushed and furious, but still conscious of where she was and who might be listening.

This was a woman I had no trouble imagining as a murderer.

"It's *his* fault going to that damned conference and asking Broadshaw if there was anyone who'd want to share a room with him. He knew Broadshaw had the hots for him!"

But that wasn't the way Bill had told me the story.

"And then going over that night when he knew Broadshaw's wife was out of town—to 'talk about a paper.' And he's *surprised* Broadshaw jumped him in the hot tub!"

This was exactly what Sharon had said would happen: let people talk, and they would reveal something. If Betty was right, then Bill had been lying to me. But before I could think of some way to draw her out further, she suddenly stopped, breathed deeply, and sat back in her chair as if she had fulfilled her day's quota of self-expression.

"What do you want from me?" she asked, her voice back at a conversational level.

"Do you know anyone who'd have a reason to kill Perry Cross?"

"Besides me and Bill?" She laughed. "Perry was such a weasel, I bet he wormed secrets out of other people too. But I don't really care who did it, because we have alibis."

"What?"

"We couldn't have done it because we were visiting Bill's parents in Cleveland. We flew out the day before and got back that night." She smiled a little maliciously, I thought. "I told this to that jive detective. You could have saved yourself a visit."

If I were a cop or a private detective I would have given her a phone number or business card, and asked her to call me if she thought of anything significant. As it was, I just thanked her and started to slink off.

But then I stopped. "What happened in the kitchen at Broadshaw's party when his wife burned her hand?"

Betty grinned maliciously. "Oh, that fat bitch made some veiled comment about the sanctity of marriage and how sad it was that good men could sometimes be tempted to do things against their nature. Can you believe it! I told her she was full of shit and she tried to smack me. I slapped her hand and it hit a burner on the stove that was off but still pretty hot. I should have hit her harder."

When I got home, my answering machine showed several messages. The first was from Stefan, telling me he was on campus, and asking me to call. The next was from Sharon and I called her at her office right away.

"How do you have so much free time?" I asked.

"For you I do."

Just hearing her voice I felt more cheerful.

"Will Stefan be angry that you went to see his father?" she asked after I'd filled her in on my day.

"I hope not. It's about time they settled things between them."

"Sweetie, you don't have time to stage-manage heartfelt reconciliations for other people."

I knew she was referring to the fact that I wasn't much closer to my family than Stefan was to his.

Then she said, "But I'm sure you did the right thing."

"Do you think Betty Malatesta is lying about her husband, or the trip to Cleveland? I mean, I can imagine either one of them doing it. There were times as a graduate student I went into a rage about being jerked around by professors on my doctoral committee, or bullied into rewriting work to match a professor's opinions. So much stuff simmers underneath, but you're forced to keep it in.

Betty's much tougher than I ever suspected. And she even said she and Bill had a reason to kill Perry. Isn't that"—I hesitated—"well, couldn't she be trying to mislead me, by being honest?"

"You said she and her husband flew to Cleveland? It's not that far, is it? Why not drive?"

Sharon had a good point. If you figured getting to the airport, waiting there, probably switching at Detroit, getting your bags when you landed, then it would probably be the same as driving, and certainly more expensive.

"What airline would they have taken?"

I thought about that. "I guess the cheapest flights right now are on Northwest. Anyway, they have the best connections out of Michiganapolis."

"I'll check into it, see if they did fly Northwest."

"What do you mean?"

"I know someone who works at Northwest. No, not a ticket agent. A bit higher up. I'll just call."

"Wow."

"It's nothing amazing. I just have lots of friends who have lots of friends. I met people when I was modeling."

"You weren't involved in the Iran-Contra stuff, were you?"

"*Please,* those folks had no *style.*"

I gave her the dates Betty said they'd flown. When I hung up, I took out a new sheet of paper to puzzle over who might have wanted to kill Perry Cross. This time, I decided not to put Stefan at the top. It wasn't loyalty, I just needed to think clearly before I waded into the swamp of what Stefan might have done and why.

Serena Fisch seemed obvious. She had been passed over for the position Perry got. She was still bitter about having lost the chair of her department when it was absorbed by English and American Studies. And now she had Perry's courses. But would someone kill for that kind of jealousy?

Then there were the Malatestas. They were afraid for their futures, afraid that Perry would blab about what had happened—whatever that was—between Bill and Lynn Broadshaw. That fear seemed to me a much more compelling reason than Serena's envy. And I could imagine it would be intensely satisfying to knock off a professor—what a way to strike back at institutionalized powerlessness.

Powerlessness made me think of Chuck Bayer. Why had he been so desperate to get help with his Didion bibliography—and even more important, why was he interested in Perry's stuff? Was that just opportunism, nosiness? But he was such a nebbish, I couldn't see him as having the guts to even punch anyone out.

Lynn Broadshaw—now he was bad-tempered and unpredictable enough to hurt someone accidentally. If he really had been harassing Bill Malatesta, and maybe other students, and he had somehow figured out that Perry Cross knew about him and he could lose his job—well, then, that was a perfect motive for murder.

Stefan wasn't off-base about Priscilla Davidoff—she *did* write about murder, so it was natural to her in a way it wouldn't be to other people. Why had she been in Parker Hall last night? Following me, perhaps? And why did Broadshaw's secretary act so secretive when I asked her about Perry; was Claire just being professionally discreet? If that was her I saw the night I found the envelope, why was she on campus so late?

And what about Chad? He said he'd found the body, but why was he so nervous when he talked to me, and what was he afraid of? Why couldn't he identify himself to the Campus Police when he called them?

I surveyed the list, imagining them all in some fabulous wainscotted English study bristling with old bronzes and family portraits, and me, the intrepid investigator, confronting them with the truth, dragging it out slowly, like they did in the movies, showcasing my own brilliance.

But there was something off with the scene. I wasn't even thinking of Stefan or who else might have wanted Perry dead, or had simply been acting suspiciously. Maybe that was the key—just because motives were obvious didn't mean they were good ones.

I threw down the pad, feeling helpless. None of this was getting me anywhere, and I hadn't made any real progress at all. I was just spinning my wheels, while Stefan was in danger of arrest.

I had saved his name for last because I couldn't help believing he had a far better motive than anyone—money, revenge for being humiliated. I could play detective all I wanted, but how did I know for sure that Stefan had not killed Perry? Gone for a walk with Perry on campus, for instance, and then hit him or tripped him or pushed him.

Stefan had left me a message to call him, but I didn't have the heart to talk to him. How was it possible to suddenly be so uncertain about the man I had loved for ten years? I felt disloyal, hopeless, and trapped.

# -15-

There's no way I could have guessed I'd be saved by the bell. The doorbell. I dragged myself out to answer it, and was shocked to find Detective Valley standing there, looking eager and mean.

"Can I come in?"

I felt like someone in a horror movie, faced with a werewolf or vampire in human form, about to make the terrible mistake of inviting the creature into their home. But what could I do? Shut the door behind me and talk to Valley out on the front steps? I didn't even want to do that.

I stepped aside and followed him as he strolled into the living room with the cockiness of a landlord about to eject a tenant from a valuable property.

He nodded, looking around, nodded some more, as if what he saw proved something he'd suspected. I was sure he was trying to intimidate me.

He said, "How about we sit down?"

"Sure." He sat on the couch and I sat at the other end, not because I wanted to be that close, but because I thought he'd interpret my sitting any further away as furtive behavior. I had a lot to hide, and had to keep from showing it. Nervous, I plunged in:

"Is the investigation still open? *Do* you think that Perry Cross was murdered?"

He chewed that over for a bit. Then he nodded.

"Why? Is there some new medical evidence? What's happened?"

"The will, for one thing. It's pretty clear. And your friend not being honest about how well he knew the deceased."

"If you mean Stefan, he's my *partner.*"

Valley shrugged, crossing his arms and peering down his nose as if about to pass judgment on me. "Partner. That's a funny word. It means business to most people."

I was not about to tell him the reasons why spouse or lover didn't feel appropriate to me.

He smiled. "Maybe you were in business together—and the investment paid off? To the tune of a hundred and fifty thousand."

"You're crazy," I said.

"Stefan strongly recommended Professor Cross for the position here. Did you know that?"

Glumly, I said that I did. "He was trying to be helpful."

"Is that all?"

"Stefan didn't lure him to Michigan to kill him. He's not a killer."

"You don't sound like you believe that."

Stung, I said, "I think you should get out."

"I think you should tell me who else might have wanted Professor Cross dead. No one else has even suggested the possibility."

I couldn't believe it. "You mean people are telling you he was a saint?"

"Not exactly.... Let's just say nobody paints the same portrait of him that you did."

It all came tumbling out because I was so angry and desperate. "That's bullshit! What about Serena Fisch!"

"What about her?"

"She despised him because he humiliated her! Perry Cross got the position she really wanted, the one she deserved and he didn't. He's dead, and she's got it now."

"That doesn't sound like a reason to kill someone," he said calmly, studying my reaction.

"Maybe not to you, but I thought you said professors do stupid things?"

He shrugged, granting me that point. "Who else?" he prodded.

I couldn't stop now, though I felt ashamed of saying all this to a cop about my colleagues. It was one thing to draw up lists, another to accuse people of murder publicly. "Priscilla Davidoff—she didn't like him either, but I don't know why. There's got to be something going on there. She writes mysteries—she plans murders on paper. Maybe she did it for real, maybe she's a psycho!"

Valley sneered and I barreled onward. "Try pushing Lynn Broadshaw and Bill and Betty Malatesta to tell you what they had to hide! Ask Claire, Broadshaw's secretary, why everyone's been in such a hurry to clean up after this mess. I can't believe you haven't found out any of this stuff!"

"It's not much, compared to all that money."

"Listen, Detective Valley, I don't care how long you've been here at SUM. You don't know shit *if* you haven't figured out that this place, like *all* universities, is as cutthroat and vicious as any corporation. Hell, as vicious as the Mob. Only they hide it all behind pretend smiles and puffed-up rhetoric about the civilizing nature of education or whatever lousy cliché is hip that month. People get knifed and strangled and poisoned all the time around here—only nobody discovers a body."

"That's a nice speech," he drawled.

"It's not a speech, it's just the truth. And since we're talking about the truth, hasn't anyone told you there was something very strange about Perry Cross being here at all? How does someone who's only had short-term teaching positions fall into a tenure-stream job with a starting salary twenty thousand dollars higher than it should be?"

Valley looked surprised, and interested. "Really?"

"Yeah! He was getting fifty thousand dollars a year! Only some kind of star would get that as an assistant professor. And how come he beat Serena Fisch for the position? She's got two books, he doesn't have any as far as I know. How was he qualified?"

Valley looked eager to head off and follow this up, but as he walked to the door, he said, "You're not legally married. You can testify against Stefan. Otherwise you may end up being charged as an accessory."

I was so furious I couldn't be tactful. I quoted from *Steel Magnolias:* "What separates us from the lower creatures is our ability to accessorize."

It was a stupid time to pun, but satisfying because Valley didn't get it and I enjoyed his puzzled look.

"I've got to go," he said, with the clear implication that he meant "go for *now.*" He obviously intended to come back. "But remember what I said."

I yanked open the door for him, then tried to calm down. I shut it quietly when I really wanted to slam it as he walked over to his car. I imagined him pulling out of the driveway, his suspicious eyes on our house.

As he drove off down the street, I wondered if Valley really had anything new about Perry's death. Or had he just been fishing, trying to scare me into shooting my mouth off?

Whatever the answers, it was obvious that I had to go on with my battered investigation, even if it seemed pointless. I couldn't let a homo-hating campus cop ruin Stefan's life and mine.

I should talk to Chad, I thought, privately, where he wouldn't be so anxious and he could take me through finding Perry's body much more slowly. I dug out my grade book from last year to look up his last name so I could get his campus phone number. But when I found it, and the campus operator gave me the number, I ended up with a tape telling me it had been disconnected. Great—another student forgetting to pay his phone bill! How was I supposed to track him down?

But that wasn't as important as talking to everyone else. I knew Lynn Broadshaw would be in, he always was, and I was pretty sure today was Serena Fisch's long day of office hours, so maybe I'd get to her too.

CLAIRE WAS VERY cool when I spoke with her twenty minutes later on campus.

"Professor Broadshaw is not in," she said.

"When's he coming back?"

She paused, as if offended that I had asked her a question at all, let alone something so specific.

"Why do you need to know?" she said.

If before, I'd considered Claire gracious, today she struck me as appallingly rude. Was that because of Stefan? Was everyone talking about him and the will? Was I along with him suffering a sharp drop in status, so much so that Claire could afford to be impolite?

I wanted to tell her that she had too much jewelry on and that her hair needed retouching—anything to shake her composure, to strike back.

"It's very important," I brought out, slowly, as if to someone with a weak command of English.

"I'll let him know," was all she would say.

I was tempted to slam the door shut when I left, but I knew it would do more than reverberate in the office, it would be reported, embroidered, made part of a profile, a reputation, something I'd be stuck with in this department.

Serena's office was down the hall, and I found her at her desk with the door open. She glanced up from a pile of papers and smiled me in. I closed the door behind me.

Her office was as featureless as most in the department—at least in its outline. But it was softened in many ways. A vaguely Persian rug covered most of the floor, and all the chairs were upholstered and inviting. Framed portraits of modern Canadian and American authors jostled each other on the walls, and there were at least half a dozen small vases of fresh flowers on shelves, tables, and her desk. Though Serena's harsh perfume in that small office defeated any effort the flowers might have made.

Serena herself looked anything but soft in a grim Joan Crawford-ish dark suit, kohl black eyelashes, too-red cheeks and lips.

I sat in the armchair behind her, so that she had to swivel from her desk to appraise me.

"You don't look so good," she said.

"I'm worried about Stefan."

"You should be," she said. "He's the main suspect—they say he's going to be arrested. So, if you're here to interrogate me about Perry's death, why don't you start?"

"Oh God, is it that obvious?"

She leaned over and patted my hand. "I'm afraid so."

"I'm hopeless."

"Don't worry, I'd do the same thing if I were you. I'd go hunting too. So. Let me tell you what I told that slimy detective. Of course I hated Perry, for all the right reasons, and I'm not sorry he's dead. But I was asleep when he was killed, or when he died, whichever it was." Her eyes widened in sympathy—whether with Perry or with her own lack of an alibi, I couldn't say.

Now she studied me like a photographer framing a shot. "I'll tell you something else. I don't think that Stefan killed Perry, not for a minute."

"You don't?"

She practically snorted. "Why would he? Stefan has everything: his job, you, critical respect—and good sales, so they say. Why on earth would he risk losing all that? Perry wasn't a threat to him. Jealousy? Long-frustrated passion?" She rolled her heavily made-up eyes. "That's so corny!"

"Did you tell that to Valley?"

"I most assuredly did."

"If they think Perry was killed, then who did it?"

She sighed. "I can't believe a man like Perry didn't have enemies all over the country. The *continent*. Why does it have to be someone from around here?"

That question didn't help me. If someone had sneaked into town to kill Perry and then disappeared, Stefan and I were sunk. How would anyone ever find that out?

"Who really got Perry the job?" I asked, not expecting an answer.

"I don't know for sure, but I think it's Rose."

"*Rose Waterman!* Why?"

Serena pursed her lips. "To get back at me. She hates me. Why d'you think I lost the chair of Rhetoric and we all got thrown into this department in the first place? Rose started out in *our* department, and the first time she came up for tenure, I voted no. She got it the next year, because she worked harder, but she never forgave me. Like Stewart Green. Did you ever hear that story? He was the chair of Journalism. They were lovers, but when he dumped Rose she took his department away. Enrollment was down, the budget was in trouble, and she got away with it. He *built* that department, and when it was reduced to just a program he went down the drain. Rose is a truly vicious and vindictive woman. People are right to be afraid of her."

"What else has she done?"

Serena ignored that. "And when Rose got to a position where she could hurt me," she continued quietly, "she did exactly that."

"Does everyone know about this but me?"

"Not at all. There've been retirements and moves, people forget. And then Rose has been powerful for so long, no one remembers she was once just an assistant professor of"—she paused melodramatically—"Rhetoric." Serena squirmed in mockery of all the professors who looked down on anyone who taught freshmen how to write.

"When they cut your department, did you try to move? Why not?"

"Pride," she said. "I didn't want to look like I was running away." Musing a little, she said, "And I like it here, very much. I grew up in Grand Rapids. Michigan is home for me."

I got up to go, but decided to ask her another question.

"Do you think Claire is acting strange today?"

Serena waved it away. "Haven't you noticed she's always edgy around paycheck time? It's a lot of responsibility, and frankly I don't think she's all that bright."

Elated by her confidence in Stefan's innocence, I grabbed her hand to shake it in thanks and sailed off. It wasn't until I was heading downstairs that I wondered if Serena hadn't snookered me, hadn't wanted to deflect suspicion from herself by mentioning Rose Waterman.

Shit! Was this ever going to end? How much longer would I be turning over every single remark anyone made to me as if I were deciphering the silences in a Pinter play? I was not used to seeing the world as steeped in lies. I hated what this business had done to my life.

And what it threatened to do.

On the way out, I picked up a campus paper from a stack near the building door and sure enough, on the front page there was an article about Perry's death: "Rumors of Witness in Prof's Death." The few paragraphs were a combination of hearsay and a rehash of previous articles, mixed in with lots of "no comments" from various sources, but it all pointed to some kind of crescendo. Why else would Detective Valley have come to our house? But then I imagined Sharon being asked that question. Wouldn't she say that Valley had come to scare me, that if he had any real evidence he could have Stefan, or me, or both of us arrested?

Maybe this article was a plant, a ruse to make something happen. If that was the case, then I needed to continue calmly, with "order and method."

Which reminded me that I'd never called Stefan back. Damn! I dashed back inside and upstairs to his office, but it was locked. Breathless now, I made my way downstairs, slowly, aware that I should have eaten less at Mr. Borowski's in Ann Arbor.

I DROVE HOME in what I think of as the heavy rush-hour traffic, but friends from either coast jeer at me because even at its worst, the ride from campus to home takes no more than ten minutes. At home there was another message from that eager Channel 9 reporter which I had no interest in returning.

I wondered what Stefan was doing, where he was. I drank some coffee, had half a melon, and decided to go to the gym because I needed an escape, I needed not to think for a while.

The Club, which was practically down the street from us, was a brand-new and enormous series of connected buildings on several acres of land, so stuffed with gleaming weight machines, free weights, and aerobic equipment, it looked like it had been stocked with the plunder of some athletically minded pirates. The weight room stretches for what feels like the length of a football field (especially if you're out of shape), shading into aerobic studios, and is surrounded by tennis and racquetball courts. You almost need a golf cart to make your way around.

Stefan had signed us up last year, since he didn't want to exercise on campus where he might end up unable to avoid chatting with faculty members. Though he worked out and ran on the indoor track at The Club several times a week, I almost never went because I found it all too intimidating. Somehow I'd always find myself struggling with a pathetically light dumbbell while a burly high school hunk on the next bench over glanced at me with pity and contempt as he lifted obscenely large weights with macho ease.

Today, though, the place was so crowded I felt anonymous and safe, and was soon threading my way through the crowds of students, yuppies, and housewives. I passed Lynn Broadshaw. Stefan, who went regularly, hadn't told me Lynn was a member. Broadshaw didn't notice me. I was amazed to see him doing bench presses, lifting a bar with several hundred pounds on it, grunting, his face bright red. No one was spotting him. I got on a free treadmill at the other end and watched him in the mirror when he stood up, breathing very hard.

I would have expected Broadshaw to look incongruous in a tank top and biking shorts, but he was amazingly well built for a man near sixty, at least. He looked completely different in gym clothes: threatening and strong. He was barrel-chested, which the leather weight belt emphasized, and his thighs, biceps, and butt were powerful and tight. He even moved differently, with that showy step I've seen in other lifters that reminds me of prancing Lippizaners. I lost track of him after a while, gazing periodically in the mirror at closer and choicer specimens. Stefan kept telling me to come work out because the men were beautiful, or that there were enough of those mixed in with the rest, but that still wasn't enough to motivate me. I even resented the perky color scheme of The Club: sky blue and daffodil yellow—it made me feel trapped in a child's fingerpaint sketch.

After a grueling half hour program, I headed for the locker room. I got out of my sweaty gym clothes and into my towel quickly, exposing my less than wonderful body as little as I could manage. That's why I preferred the steam room to the sauna and the whirlpool—it was harder to see in there, and I felt less self-conscious.

I hit the showers at a lull. There was no one around, and I staggered with relief into the steam room, deeply inhaling the eucalyptus-scented hot air.

I carefully made my way to one of the tiled shelves, climbed up and settled back against the wall, feeling the hot tiles all down my neck and back. Glorious.

A voice broke into my relaxation. It was Broadshaw, an invisible gorilla in the mist.

"You've been asking a lot of questions," he said.

"How did you know that?"

Broadshaw chuckled evilly. "Claire knows everything that happens in the department."

How could he see me when I could barely make out his outline? Then I realized it must have been the light coming in at the door when I entered.

"You're a pretty nosey kind of guy, aren't you, Nick?"

The steam was clearing a little, and Broadshaw's hairy bulk seemed ominous and threatening. Wrapped in just a towel, he looked more like a hired thug than an academic.

"I want to find out what happened to Perry Cross. If he was killed, Stefan didn't do it, no matter what things look like."

"You should mind your own business," Broadshaw growled. "You're an assistant professor, not Sherlock Holmes. Stop trying to dig things up and make people look guilty."

"I can't let Stefan get blamed for something he didn't do!"

His voice dropped and he said, "You're not acting like someone who *wants* to get tenure."

That was chilling, but the image of him coming on to Bill in bikini underwear suddenly returned and saved me. Why should I be afraid of this man? If he tried to sabotage my tenure, I'd tell everyone about his harassing Bill Malatesta.

"Why don't you go home and slip into your Jacuzzi?" I snapped. "And wait for the pizza boy to make a delivery."

"Fuck you!" He jumped up, wrenched open the steam-covered glass door, and stormed off to the showers.

As the door swung closed, I realized I had momentarily stopped breathing, shocked by the sudden confrontation. Had Broadshaw been waiting for me? Would he have followed me into the sauna or whirlpool if I hadn't come into the steam room? How bizarre!

It was bad enough before that Broadshaw didn't seem to think much of me as a scholar or teacher or even an individual, but this was awful. He was *pissed;* he had *threatened* me. My chair was going berserk.

And he was scared, right? Somehow whatever I had been doing in my bumbling way had scared him enough to have to threaten me.

Damn! I thought. I *must* be making progress, even if I didn't know it.

On the way out of the shower, I ran into what was practically a tour of jaunty businessmen—they were all in suits, lugging big gym bags and tennis rackets, and shouting hearty abuse at one another.

STEFAN WASN'T HOME when I got back, which worried me. I called his office—no answer. And the department office was closed, so there was nowhere else to try. I looked around for a note, in my study, in his, in the bedroom, but couldn't find anything.

I threw my gym clothes in the wash on a quick cycle, and just as I was trying to decide what to make for dinner, the phone rang.

Stefan, I thought, running into my study. But it was his father.

"Nick," he said, "did you look closely at those Xeroxed sheets you gave me?"

I sat down at my desk. "Not really, Mr. Borowski. I don't know any German, and it's not a language I even like to look at."

"I understand."

He was silent, so I hurried him. "Are they done? Have you translated them?"

"It's been very painful," he said heavily. "Do you remember, a few years ago, the Paul de Man scandal?"

Of course I did. The famous and highly respected Yale professor was revealed to have published anti-Semitic newspaper articles during World War II, in Belgium. It was an international scandal.

"Wait," I said. "The articles are something de Man wrote?" Suddenly I thought of Chuck Bayer prying about Perry's "stuff." If he knew that Perry Cross had managed to get hold of more of de Man's Nazi propaganda, no wonder he was interested. But—

"No, Nick, this isn't de Man's, but it is Nazi writing, from a German newspaper published in Alsace-Lorraine in 1944. The same horrible clichés: Jews as rats undermining pure Aryan culture, *und so weiter,* and so on. Madness."

I realized that the dates I had found at the back of Perry's copy of *The Rise and Fall of the Third Reich* must have referred to these articles. "But why did Perry have them, and who wrote them?"

"The first question I cannot answer, but the second—the name is clear enough. Rosa Wassermann." And he spelled it out for me. "Does that mean anything to you?"

"Oh my God! That could be Rose Waterman! She's SUM's Provost."

"She may also be an ex-Nazi," he said quietly.

"*Wait.* If she was trying to hide her identity, wouldn't she have changed her name to something completely different?"

"Who knows? Maybe she couldn't let go of it completely, let go of her *self,* so she just made it sound more English."

I couldn't believe it. All the times I'd felt weirded out by Rose's accent—I wasn't completely off-base. I did some quick figuring. "She was in her late teens then. How'd she get anything in print?"

"That I don't know. But it's not so amazing. Maybe her father was a Nazi Party official. Shall I bring these up to you or mail them?"

"No. Put them in a safe place, and wait." I was so wound up by this discovery, I almost forgot to thank Stefan's father. I did, and I also apologized: "I'm sorry you had to read that crap."

"I've lived through worse," he said, and wished me luck.

I called Sharon immediately, and thankfully got her at home. She had to urge me to slow down.

"So however he got the stuff," she finally said, "Perry was probably blackmailing Rose. And didn't you say she's about to retire? What a time to have your past exposed."

"You think Rose killed Perry Cross?"

"Of course, Nick. Don't you? Think of the exposure, the public humiliation, the headlines, the news reports. Maybe she even got into the country by lying, what if she's some kind of war criminal?"

I sighed.

"Nick, you told me that Rose works late on campus. She could have been there. Maybe she was even meeting with Perry that night, who knows?"

"But if he was pushed, or tripped or whatever—? She's not a strong woman."

"Physically? You don't know that. You don't know what she'd be like with her reputation at stake."

The *money*. Was that where Perry had gotten so much money? From blackmailing Rose. It was common knowledge at the university—and a cause for envy—that her salary was well over a hundred thousand. Administrators' salaries were published every year in the student newspaper. Could all of his money have come from her?

I asked Sharon what I should do next.

"Gee, Nick, I'm not sure. I didn't think we'd get this far."

"What! Are you joking?"

"Seriously. I didn't."

"So all that business about Agatha Christie and investigating was just to keep me busy?"

"Well, partly. You were so miserable. You needed to be doing something to stop feeling so hopeless."

I had to admit to her that it had worked fairly well. "But what did you think was going to happen with Stefan?"

"I *didn't* think, much. I hoped it would sort itself out. But you've done a great job, Nick, really you have."

"Well, I did find the stuff about Rose." I was still having trouble envisioning Rose as a murderer, or at least Perry's murderer. Why didn't I feel a true sense of triumph and discovery? Something was missing.

"What do I do now, Sharon? Contact the killer?" Despite myself, I started laughing—it sounded so melodramatic and stagy, a weird parlor game: Contact the Killer.

"It's not funny, Nick. You have to be very careful. I think you've done more than enough. You should call the Campus Police, call that detective and tell them what you know, tell him everything."

I heard Stefan's car driving up, told Sharon I had to go, promising that I'd be careful, very careful.

# -16-

I ran to the front door and pulled it open before Stefan could ring or let himself in. I hugged him fiercely.

"I was worried about you! Are you okay?"

Stefan held me for a long time before he said, "I'm fine." And then with a slight laugh, he said, "Can we go inside?"

Stefan hung up his jacket and led me to the kitchen where he made us both two very strong cups of coffee. "Sit down," he said. He was leaning back against the sink. "I think I know who killed Perry Cross."

I burst out with, "You've been sleuthing too?"

Stefan scowled. "What do you mean?"

There was no way I could take it back, so I had to explain everything, or almost everything about my search to find out what happened to Perry Cross the night he died. I didn't tell Stefan I had been shaken by wondering if he was the murderer.

All of that took us through more coffee, a quick dish of spaghetti carbonara, and a slice of cheesecake each. Stefan kept shaking his head at each new turn of my investigation. And he laughed, he did laugh, mostly *with* me, though occasionally *at* me, I have to say. He seemed charmed when I told him I was worried he'd be arrested, and a little annoyed, too, especially that I'd seen his father.

"He was very helpful," I said, not adding that his father had guessed I was worried that Stefan had killed Perry. There was so much to feel guilty for: wishing Perry was dead, hiding information from Valley, not being completely honest with Stefan.

"You and Sharon are amazing," Stefan said more than once, and I beamed, choosing to take it as a compliment.

I wound up with the translation and Sharon's conviction that Rose Waterman had killed Perry.

"But *you* don't seem to think so," he observed.

"No. My money's on Serena. She hated Perry for taking the job she wanted, the job that was rightfully hers. And look how she sort of threw suspicion on Rose, and tried to get me thinking about Rose."

"That feels like a cliché—bitter single woman full of twisted passion, etc., etc." Stefan shook his head, deeply dissatisfied.

We were loading up the dishwasher when I remembered my laundry. I scurried into the laundry room and took the sopping gym togs out of the washer. Stefan followed, stood in the doorway, smiling benevolently as I threw them in the drier. I forgot my laundry loads at least once every few weeks, and I was too sensitive for a joke about it, especially now, so I bristled, feeling very defensive.

Stefan said, "You haven't asked me where I've been. I was talking to Bill Malatesta. He's convinced that Broadshaw did it. And doesn't that fit with the way Broadshaw threatened you in the steam room at the gym?"

I went back into the kitchen and sat down at the table. "Broadshaw," I said, picturing how intimidating he had looked doing his bench presses. He would have had no trouble overpowering Perry, knocking him out, heaving him into the river.

"Because of the harassment?"

Stefan came to sit by me. "If Mrs. Broadshaw knew, she wasn't going to say anything, and Betty and Bill wouldn't either, so Perry was the only threat."

"Blackmail."

"Probably. Bill thinks so."

"God, they should have called him Double Cross."

Stefan checked his watch. "I have to leave soon. I'm doing a guest lecture tonight, for one of the graduate students teaching creative writing."

"But—"

"It's all over. We've done enough. Tomorrow morning we call our lawyer, and then we call Detective Valley and whoever else we have to. Let them figure it out."

"And spill our guts? You're not afraid?"

He stared at me. "Afraid of what? We have all this information— somewhere in there is a killer."

"But you'd have to tell them *everything*."

"So what?"

"Everything, Stefan. Not just your relationship with him, but going out for a drive, being there with him on campus late at night. Add all that up with the inheritance, and it's not pretty." And because his face was so blank, I stumbled on: "It even looked bad to me—"

"No!" Stefan clapped his hands together in discovery. "You really thought I could have done it! I don't believe you."

I flushed and looked away.

But he was standing right in front of me now. "You don't trust me. You think I could have killed him. You think I could be a murderer."

"Well, you lied about Perry all those different times! That's what they do in your family—they lie, they lie about the big things!"

He shook his head, looking completely disgusted with me. "I don't believe what you're saying."

He stalked off to the bedroom. I heard a closet door violently pulled open, some shoes thrown, drawers yanked open and shoved back in. Then water running in the bathroom sink, the bathroom door shut hard, opened a minute later, the pipes working. Stefan soon disappeared out the front door without saying a word. Why did he have to? The whole house vibrated with his rage and betrayal.

But I *didn't* trust him, not entirely; how could I? And that distrust in addition to my fear for him had been enough to propel me into this crazy hunt for a murderer. I couldn't stop just because Stefan or Sharon said I should. And I sure as hell wasn't going to depend on Detective Valley or *any* cop to find out the truth, when Stefan was a sitting duck: no alibi, the opportunity to do it, plenty of reasons, all those stupid lies about how well he knew Perry, and being Perry's only heir.

Hell, we were both in trouble. I was the one who had told Detective Valley that Stefan and I were in bed early that morning. How could a lawyer explain that in court? "Anti-homophobic rage?" What would they call it, The Cappuccino Defense? Puh-leeze.

I stomped into my study, pulled out the faculty directory, and dialed Rose Waterman's home number. Her answering machine message was curt and anonymous—giving just her number, not her name. And tonight that seemed significant to me. I left a message asking her to call me, hung up, but kept staring at the phone.

I checked the listings for the provost's office, and dialed the number listed under her name, but which was probably her secretary's. No answer, no tape. But at the bottom of the page was a handwritten phone number with the same first three digits as Rose's office number, though the rest was different. The number was in Stefan's writing. Could that be a direct unlisted line to Rose's office? Stefan did have occasion to talk to people I would never call.

There was a good chance she was working there tonight as usual. I dialed. Someone picked up at the first ring, as if they'd been waiting.

"Yes?" The woman's voice was low, suspicious.

"Rose?" I asked.

"Who is this?"

"It's Nick Hoffman."

"How did you get this number!"

"It was in our book, Stefan had it—" I shook myself, shook off the fearful explanations that I had no need to give. "I wanted to talk to you," I said, my voice steadier.

There was a painfully long pause. At last: "Why?"

"It's …" How was I supposed to do this? Plunge right in, or hint, or toy with her?

She sounded sharper, angrier, when she went on. "What is this about? Why are you calling me here at night?" She made me sound like a crank caller.

"It's about Perry Cross," I said carefully. But before I could think of how to proceed, I heard some kind of crash, as if something fell or was broken, and the phone fell, bouncing and thudding.

Then the line went dead.

My first thought was that she'd slammed down the phone, but when I went into the kitchen to try calling on Stefan's line I got a busy signal, and the operator said there was trouble on the line.

Trouble. Rose was seventy. What if she'd collapsed because of my call? Now what? Think, Nick, *think.* Call 911? But I didn't know if something had actually happened or not. Why wasn't Stefan here? I had to decide on my own. I looked down to see that I had somehow brought the faculty directory with me as I roamed through the house, so agitated I hadn't realized I was twisting it like a towel. I let it drop to the floor in the hallway and raced to the phone to call the Campus Police. I gave them the location on campus where I thought something might have happened, my name, and then I grabbed a jacket from the front closet. So what if I was wrong? So what if it was a false alarm and I got bitched at by the cops, or wound up in the newspaper?

Five minutes. At night, with no traffic, I could get there in under five minutes. I jumped into my Cutlass, screeched out of the driveway, and tore off down the empty street, imagining the neighbors complaining to each other about "all those damned teenagers." I heard sirens but didn't see anyone behind me. The light changed just as I got to Michigan Avenue and I made a gut-wrenching left turn and headed for the closest campus entrance. But I had to slow down as soon as I entered campus—the roads were too twisting, and there wasn't enough light. When I made the right onto Jackson Drive, which led straight to the Administration Building, I could see flashing lights and a small crowd, with more people running across the Administration bridge.

I parked as close as I could get and then ran over the dry lawn to a scene as eerie as a UFO landing in a movie. There was too much light here—strange light from the flashing campus police cars and ambulance. People's clothes flashed and changed colors as if they had their own weird life and meaning. It was breezy, and dead leaves hissed along the concrete paths radiating out from the spot where there was already some kind of cordon.

I drew closer, and heard someone say, "Look!" I looked up and saw a broken window in the top floor of the Administration Building, the jagged bright hole like the aftermath of a rocket attack on that temple like ornate structure. I thought of Ceausescu's overthrow, and the ravaged buildings of Bucharest. A short dark girl being hugged by a girl almost twice her height was sobbing quietly, "I saw her fall, I saw her fall."

And when I got nearer, where three policemen stood holding back the growing crowd of students, I saw the evening's centerpiece: Rose Waterman lay there, limbs sprawled as widely as if she'd been trying to form a swastika. There was blood under her head, her back, her legs and arms. So much dark blood on the light-washed concrete that I wavered, and thought I might faint.

"Nick!" Stefan was breaking away from a knot of stunned-looking students. I grabbed him, suddenly exhausted. I felt wrenched out of my own life, completely disconnected, except where my body touched Stefan's. People milled about us, talking loudly now, telling each other what they knew or thought they knew.

"I was across the river," Stefan said, breaking away gently so he could point. "Over in Fisher doing my lecture." That was where most of the EAR night classes were held; the building was almost directly opposite the Administration Building. "A woman in the class screamed, and we rushed to the window. I didn't see anything, but she did. They all ran out, and I called 911 in the hallway."

"I was talking to Rose," I said quietly, so no one else could hear. "I was on the phone with her at her office."

Stefan looked incredulous. "What the hell for?"

"It's not my fault!" I hissed, moving further from the crowd that had swelled to several dozen. "I couldn't let it go, I wanted to talk to her."

The police were busy getting statements now, pulling students aside, taking things down, and when one approached me, I said

I had been on the phone with—I couldn't say her name, I had to point.

"I called the Campus Police when the line went dead, and came over."

The campus cop was lanky and blond, dark-eyed, and looked so uncomfortable in his crisp uniform that he might have been doing all this on a dare. He dutifully took my name, my phone number and address, but thankfully didn't make a big deal out of what little I had to say. "We'll contact you," he said, moving on with his pad.

"What now?" I asked Stefan, who started to lead me away from the lights and noise and horror. Halfway across the bridge, I turned back, and Stefan did too. I gasped and pointed up at the building. Why hadn't I noticed this before?

"Nick, what's wrong?"

"Look! If she didn't do it, she must have seen who did," I said, pointing up to Rose's office window. "She's here every night. Her window has a perfect view of the bridge. If the night was clear and you were there, you could see whoever killed Perry."

Stefan glanced up and then back down to where we stood. He moved to the railing, turned, and leaned back, eyeing the Administration Building whose massive pillars were bathed in light as if they were part of some holiday celebration. Absurdly, I remembered a Bastille Day we'd spent in Paris, and historic images projected on some building near the Place de la Concorde.

"You're right, but wouldn't the police have asked her if she saw anything?"

"Maybe she didn't want to tell." I felt cold, jammed my hands into my jacket pockets, and started to walk off.

"Wait." Stefan caught up with me, slipped his arm into mine, and we got to the other side of the river like that. "I don't have any notes in that classroom," he said. "We can head home. I'm sure class is over tonight. My car's behind Parker. How about you get yours tomorrow?"

"Maybe she didn't want to tell," I said again, as we neared the oldest and darkest part of campus. This area was slightly elevated, as if these crumbling nineteenth-century buildings had been constructed on the ruins of some demolished fortress. It was somewhat picturesque and intimate during the day, walking surrounded by century-old maples and elms. At night it could be a little gloomy; the infrequent lampposts marking the paths were copies of the original Victorian poles and more decorative than helpful. "Maybe she was glad someone killed Perry, if she didn't do it herself."

"So it was suicide?" Stefan said. "You called her, she figured out somebody knew, and she jumped. Or it was some kind of accident, or...."

"Oh, God, here we go again!"

Those words floated around us, unreal, cold, disconnected from the smashed body lying on the other side of the river. It was like being in a nightmare where everything you think clearly comes out as babble. No, it was as if the last week hadn't happened, as if we had just heard Perry Cross was dead, and Stefan and I were sitting in my office, trying out different possibilities. We had gotten nowhere, it had all been a terrible waste of time and emotion.

"Well, you have an alibi, and so do I," Stefan said, as we headed down the sloping path that led to Parker Hall.

I didn't say anything, silenced by shame. How could I have thought of Stefan as a murderer? It was a delusion, like some crazy story little kids tell each other with such excitement that they believe it's true.

"If she didn't fall," Stefan said, stopping me, turning me around to face him on that poorly lit and empty path, "if she didn't fall, then someone pushed her. Someone who pushed Perry too."

His grim silence said the next line: that someone was still out there.

"Serena," I said firmly. "Who else? She hated Perry, she hated Rose. Perry got her job, Rose took away her department." But the words disgusted me. Who was I to impute a crime or even motives to anyone? What arrogance. We would just tell everything to the police tomorrow and let them take care of the whole mess.

"You're right," I said to Stefan. "It really is over. And you were right from the beginning. It's none of my business. We're out of it completely."

Stefan beamed at me as if I were an alcoholic finally confessing my addiction.

"Let's go somewhere to eat," he said. "Pizza?"

"*Terrific.*" We headed down to Parker Hall as if each step were taking us out of a nightmare. I felt hungry, not just for pizza, but to plunge back into a normal life free of suspicion and planning and second-guessing. Somewhere off behind us, I heard someone whiz by on one of the bike paths.

"Can we stop a minute?" Stefan asked. "I want to run upstairs to my office and get some essays."

"I'll go up too, and see if there're any notes from students." Even though I told my students not to slip notes or papers under my door but put everything in my mailbox, they did so anyway. I suppose it was less intimidating for some of them than braving the department office.

We climbed the worn-down sandstone stairs of Parker Hall and Stefan unlocked the scarred wooden door. The shabby main hall seemed cavernous, but there was some light filtering in from outside. He headed for the stairs without bothering to turn on any lights, since the stairwell had windows all down its length, and I stumbled after him. I called out, "Come get me when you're done."

"Okay," he shouted, taking the steps quickly as he headed to the second floor. I slowed down as I trudged up to the third floor, and when I got to the stairwell door, whose upper half was glass, I stopped, remembering my fearfulness a few nights before, when I'd thought someone was trying my office door.

I blushed a little. I had done that to myself, made myself afraid. Thank God Stefan and I didn't live in an old and isolated house with any kind of history! Then I'd never be able to sleep and I'd probably haunt the house myself, trying every door and window to make sure it was secure.

Heading jauntily down the hall, I thought I heard something fall but decided it was only the echo of my own footsteps. When I turned the corner to head to my office, I saw the light was on, the door open. Having just thought about ghosts, I had to tell myself what I was seeing was real.

"Shit!" I heard, and something was flung to the floor. I couldn't see anyone, and wondered if I could make it back to the stairs quickly enough to shout for Stefan. But before I could get any further, Chuck Bayer was standing there, looking straight out the doorway.

"What are you doing in my office?" I advanced on him, taking in the mess. Desk drawers gaped, and everything had been tumbled out of Perry's boxes, the ones I had so carefully and self-satisfyingly filled.

Now I was really shouting. "*What are you doing in here?*"

Chuck backed away from the door as I crossed the threshold. "Don't tell me you got confused in the dark, or you found the door open. I'm not buying any of that."

Chuck nodded. "Okay," he said. "It's pretty simple. Perry had something of mine, and I want it back." He shrugged. "No big deal."

"Why didn't you ask me?"

He licked his lips, eyes down, cringing like a disobedient puppy. Well, a tall, skinny, badly dressed puppy.

"What did Perry have of yours?"

Chuck wouldn't look at me.

"How did you get in?" I turned to check the lock, and that's when Chuck sprang at me, knocking me into one of the file cabinets. I felt the jolt from my shoulders down to my legs, and when my head snapped back, he was grabbing at my throat. I kicked at him but his arms were so long I couldn't connect. I couldn't believe how much strength there was in that gangly physique.

*He killed them, he's the one*, I thought, as Chuck punched me in the chest and I staggered. His eyes were terrifying—there was no anger there, no emotion at all, just calculation, as if I were a problem in logic he was solving. He hit me again and I fell backwards onto my desk. I heard some kind of crack and suddenly couldn't see anything. My lungs felt empty of air. I was whirling in darkness and agony. He's going to kill me too, I thought, starting to cry as his hands found my neck and he began to squeeze.

There was a roar, the hands were ripped from my throat, and I heard an enormous crash. Through my pain I could make out Stefan slamming Chuck against the wall between the windows, blood spattered on Chuck's forehead and shirt.

Coughing, I tried to tell Stefan to stop, but when Chuck slid to the floor, Stefan backed off, staring down at him red-faced, panting, as if he wanted to kick him.

I gasped out, "No. Leave him alone."

Stefan turned, still so caught in his rage that I was almost afraid for myself. He didn't move toward me. "You okay?"

"And I thought department meetings were bad...."

Stefan grinned wildly, shaking his head as he came to peel me from the desk. "He's woozy. Let me check you out."

"Am I bleeding?" I pointed to the back of my head.

Stefan leaned over, parting my hair gently, feeling for an injury. "No. Does anything feel broken or fractured?"

I cautiously stretched my arms and legs. Though I was dizzy, and would probably be covered with bruises in the morning, I was still more stunned than in pain.

Stefan held me gently, stroking my hair. Then he said, "Give me your belt," and I slipped it off without even asking what he needed it for. He dragged a chair over to Chuck, yanked him up onto it, his head lolling, pulled his arms around and behind, and wove the belt through the slats, fastening it so Chuck couldn't break free. Then he took off his own belt and tied Chuck's legs together.

"Stay clear of his legs," Stefan warned. "He could kick."

"Don't worry. If I was in one of those monster movies where someone always walks closer to the monster to see if it's *really* dead, I'd be the guy out booking a long cruise."

"How can you make jokes? He could have killed you."

I nodded. "And probably figured out how to make it look like *you* did it."

Stefan grimaced. "A lovers' quarrel?" He sat on the edge of Perry's desk, well back from Chuck, who seemed to be coming around. "What happened?"

"I came up here and he was tearing through Perry's stuff, and mine too. He said he wanted something back, something of his that Perry had. But he didn't tell me what it was, and when I was looking over at the door to see if he'd broken in, he jumped me." The words sounded flat and empty to me.

Stefan reached over for the phone, dialed 911 to report an assault, gave the address and our names. When he hung up, Chuck said:

"It's attempted murder, really."

We stared at him.

"Could I have some water?"

Stefan motioned for me to stay put. He grabbed a mug, went out to the fountain and brought it back, carefully standing to the side of Chuck's chair, so Chuck couldn't use his feet. He held the cup up and Chuck drank from it very calmly, as if he weren't tied to a chair, as if we were all having a civil and even friendly little meeting.

"Is she dead?" Chuck asked when Stefan moved back to his perch on Perry's desk.

"Rose? Yes," I said. She must have been, there had been no doctor or nurse hovering over Rose, trying to revive her.

"It's true," Chuck said, not looking at either one of us. "Murder's a trap. You can't end with one, it leads to another. You have to keep covering your tracks."

"What were you looking for?" I asked again.

Chuck cleared his throat. "A letter from a professor of mine back in grad school."

Stefan and I exchanged incredulous looks. Both of us seemed to be wondering if he was delusional.

"Everybody is curious why I never got anywhere after I found the Wharton letter and published that article. That's because I didn't find the letter, and the article wasn't really *mine*."

Plagiarism is a crime that for academics is a combination of slander, rape, and drug smuggling. I was wide awake, thrilled, oblivious to any pain or the fact that I was listening to someone who had been strangling me a few minutes ago.

Chuck was smiling a little. "You know the story. The letter was in a Wharton book that Walter Berry owned, and like most of his library, it ended up scattered in Paris. I was there when it was found, but I didn't find it."

"Then who did?"

Chuck was clearly enjoying himself. He looked cocky. "My graduate adviser, Marilyn Fellowes."

Stefan whistled. Somehow I had forgotten that Chuck worked at Yale with the famous feminist author of three major books on women novelists of the nineteenth and early twentieth centuries, books that were scholarly but accessible, and brought her a great deal of money, critical acclaim, and popular notice. She had died some years back, I recalled.

"We were in Paris, on vacation. She wanted my first time there to be terrific, so we stayed at the Meurice."

Stefan gave me a warm smile. The Hotel Meurice was opposite the Tuileries and we had often walked past it on our long strolls through Paris.

It felt indelicate, but I asked, "You were lovers?"

Chuck sneered at me. "Of course!"

He went on. "When we got back to New York, she asked me if I'd proofread the article she was doing, and she'd put my name on it as second author. She wanted me to get a good start when it came to job hunting. Just when the proofs came, her cousin in Atlanta called her and she had to go down there because of an illness." He shrugged, and I finished the story for him.

"You made sure *you* were listed as the first author." I understood how tricky that was. He couldn't have taken Marilyn Fellowes's name off the article since the editors had already seen it there when the article was submitted. But he could reverse the names, and then everyone would assume (as I had) that her name was on the article just for prestige, just to give the article an extra push.

Chuck smiled. "I did something even better. I sold the Wharton letter to a private collector in New York for twenty thousand dollars."

"It wasn't yours to sell," Stefan said a little primly, then shook his head as if wondering why he was lecturing a killer about professional ethics.

"What did Fellowes do?"

Chuck looked uneasy for the first time since he'd been talking. "She wrote me a letter from Atlanta—don't ask me how she heard about it so fast. I shouldn't have kept it. Perry found out about it. It was when we were both grad students at Yale. I ran into him in town one night, we were both pretty bombed, and—" Then he frowned, as if not quite sure how something so valuable had slipped out.

"Perry was good at worming out people's secrets," I said.

"I was wasted, and he came right out and asked me if I had really found the Wharton letter. And then I was bragging about what happened. He said he didn't believe me, and there we were at my dorm room and I was showing him the letter from Marilyn as proof. Next thing I know, I wake up hours later on my bed, can't find the letter."

I thought Chuck was lucky Perry hadn't raped him while he was unconscious, or at least stolen his wallet.

"Perry was the only person alive who knew about the letter, so you had to kill him, and Rose must've seen you do it," I said.

"You could say that." He looked right at me, as if daring me to say it mattered. He shrugged, as much as he could tied up.

"I met Perry by the river, on the terrace that night. It was his idea. A joke. But he wasn't joking when he said he needed more money. He'd been blackmailing me for years. He reminded me that I was a complete fraud and that if it ever came out about the letter, not only wouldn't I get tenure here, but I'd never teach anywhere in the country. And he was right. He was also drunk. And when we walked back across the bridge, he stopped to throw up. He was leaning way over the rail, pretty unsteady. He lost his balance—"

"And you pushed him."

"But I had to. It was one thing when he was on the East Coast, but when he was here, in the department! Then I waited."

I shuddered. I knew Chuck meant that he waited to see if Perry was really dead.

"I was fine until I read the article in today's paper about a witness, and I put that together with Rose. She works nights and her office is right there with a view, so she must've seen me. That's why she acted so strangely when I ran into her yesterday in town. When I called her, she asked me to come to her office tonight because she didn't want to talk on the phone. She promised me she wouldn't tell anyone, but how could I trust her? And why should she keep it quiet?"

Stefan and I looked at each other. *We* knew. Perry must have been blackmailing her too about her Nazi past. Rose really *would* have kept silent; killing her was unnecessary.

We heard a siren approaching, and Stefan said, "I'll go down and open the door, otherwise they'll have to break in. Be careful."

Down the hall, he turned on the lights.

"You got a lot of mileage out of that Wharton letter," I said.

"Oh, yeah. A fellowship, a postdoctoral fellowship. But everyone was waiting for what I'd do next. There wasn't anything I could do! I'd never equal a find like that, and have anything to say as good as Marilyn had."

"Why didn't Marilyn Fellowes expose you? She could have."

Chuck shook his head. "She was married, she had a family. Too much to lose. And besides, don't you remember what Ben Franklin said about choosing old women for lovers—they're so grateful."

Disgusted, I turned away, to see Stefan and two campus policemen heading toward us. Valley was right behind them. The office seemed unbearably crowded now.

"I explained what happened," Stefan said, "but we'll have to come along to the station anyway."

"Busy night," I said, recognizing one of the cops from across the river. I nodded at Valley, too. "You were right," I told him.

Valley looked puzzled.

I said, "Professors around here do some pretty stupid things."

Valley smiled. "Do you need a doctor?" he asked.

"No, I'm okay." His whole manner toward me had changed, and I took that to mean he believed Stefan and I were innocent.

"I'm okay," I repeated. "But I'm really disappointed. It's not like this in the movies."

The cops, Valley, Stefan, and even Chuck stared at me.

"In the movies, the criminal traps you and makes you listen to his long and detailed confession first, *then* he tries to kill you."

# -17-

The phones were unplugged because even though it was the weekend, we were getting so many messages our tapes were filling up faster than we could return the calls, or decide not to. Stefan and I had separately and together done eight interviews already, and that was just for Midwestern TV stations and newspapers. Stefan had arranged for the cremation of Perry Cross's remains, and we had stayed away, fearful of it turning into a freak show. Unable to reach us by phone, Sharon had wired us two dozen roses and sent a first edition of Agatha Christie's *Appointment with Death* in which she'd simply written "Bravo!"

With the phones off, the quiet was blissful. Stefan had made a fire and we'd established ourselves in front of it with bed trays and an ample supply of treats. Stefan had bought two bottles of Veuve Cliquot rosé champagne, and I had driven down to a bakery in Southfield just to bring back my favorite dessert in the world: an ambrosial seven-layer chocolate cake. Usually we just bought a small section since the cake was so rich, but this time I bought an entire two-foot log, and I decorated the length with white rosebuds, laid it out on a silver platter. I did not tell Stefan that the tiny old woman behind the counter had recognized me. "You're that crime fighter, right?" I had wanted to say, "Yes, I'm Batman," but couldn't, because she seemed so pleased I thought she was going to scoot around the counter and pinch both my cheeks in delight.

Tonight I was wearing the black silk lounging pants and velvet smoking jacket Stefan had given me last Hanukkah, and I had convinced him to put on the black and white Henley step-ins I'd ordered for him from an *International Male* catalogue. I hoped all the black made me look slimmer. Stefan looked tousled and sexy.

"What about Perry's money?" I asked, breaking one of the long companionable silences.

"We should give it all away, whatever comes to us. It's poisoned."

"Good." I was glad he agreed. "He left you the money to cause trouble. Between us, and for you. I bet he figured it would make you a suspect."

Stefan nodded.

We had no idea how much money would be traced to Rose or Chuck or someone else. All that would eventually come out through investigation and Chuck's trial, I supposed. The police would be going through all of Perry's belongings, including what they'd carted away from his office. Following my suggestions, they had already found the letter from Chuck's adviser; it was simply folded in half and used as a bookmark in a Wharton first edition: *The Reef.* Hiding in plain sight.

There was more excitement in the EAR Department. When Stefan went in the morning after Chuck attacked me, he found a policeman posted at Claire's office to make sure that nothing was removed. She had apparently been arrested and charged with embezzlement. A College of Humanities audit had revealed years of scholarship checks written to people who didn't exist—which explained her monied air and her odd behavior at times. Even better, I thought, whatever had happened between Lynn Broadshaw and Bill was already leaking out in the department. Serena had told this to Stefan.

As for Chad, it turned out he had nothing to do with the murder. The Campus Police arrested him the morning after Rose Waterman's death for dealing steroids to other athletes at SUM—that was why he'd been so edgy and afraid of giving them his name.

Stefan sighed now in front of the fire.

"Tired?" I asked.

"No," he said. "I can't stop thinking that Perry's dead because of me. I helped him get the job here."

"You felt sorry for him—it wasn't your fault. He was a creep. Somebody was going to kill him sooner or later. Who knows how many other people he was blackmailing?"

"Even if that's true, it was sooner, not later. And then what about Rose?"

"I can't feel bad about the death of an ex-Nazi, or whatever she was, can *you*, really?"

He reluctantly shook his head, looking very much like his father when he'd driven up to see if I was okay. Both had agreed that a thorough airing of Rose's past would have been preferable, educating people and punishing her. "She escaped," Mr. Borowski had said simply. "Escaped all those years, and then finally." Stefan had nodded and then stopped, turning a little red. It was an awkward moment for him to feel even that close to his father. But he didn't draw back. And Mr. Borowski stayed for coffee and a complete recounting of my adventures. I did not, however, tell him how strongly I'd suspected Stefan.

"Hey," I said now, pouring more champagne. "Remember how Rose was worried about bad PR for the university? Look at it now: two murders, blackmail, sexual harassment, academic theft, embezzlement, plus one ex-Nazi. And student drug dealing, too." I looked at Stefan eagerly. "This would make a great novel!"

"Not for me," Stefan said a little haughtily. "I do not write mysteries."

"Just an idea, hon. It was just an idea."

I sliced myself another piece of cake.

# Acknowledgements

My thanks for their valuable assistance to Dr. Dean Sienko, Chief Medical Examiner of the Ingham County Health Department; Captain Mike Rice of Michigan State University's Department of Police and Public Safety; and Carol Seaman of the Ingham County Prosecutor's Office.

I'm grateful to my wise and witty editor at St. Martin's, Keith Kahla, for his good advice.

I owe special thanks to two people whose help was both general and specific. My best friend, Kris Lauer, warmly shared her encyclopedic knowledge of mysteries with me, pointing me to writers and books I needed to know or reread. Our frequent talks about those books and about various aspects of writing and reading mysteries gave me energy, confidence, and insight.

I began work on *Let's Get Criminal* while touring with *Dancing on Tisha B'Av*, and my lifepartner, Gersh Kaufman, deserves a medal for coming on so much of the tour with me. He also went on a different voyage while I wrote this book, sharing his own love of mysteries. He never got tired of helping me, and his spirited assistance and enjoyment encouraged me to test my own limits.

Many years ago, my mother's love for Agatha Christie, Phoebe Atwood Taylor, and John Creasey opened up a whole new world of reading for me. I wish she could read this book.

## About the Author

Lev Raphael grew up in New York but got over it. He's lived half his life in Michigan where he found his partner of twenty-five years, and a certain small fame. He escaped academia in 1988 to write full-time and has never looked back, except for material. The author of nineteen books in many genres, and hundreds of reviews, stories and articles, he's seen his work discussed in journals, books, conference papers, and assigned in college and university classrooms. Which means he's become homework. Who knew?

Lev's books have been translated into close to a dozen languages, some of which he can't identify, and he's done hundreds of readings and talks across the U.S. and Canada, and in France, England, Scotland, Austria, Germany and Israel. Lev has reviewed for the *Washington Post*, *Boston Review*, NPR, the *Ft. Worth Star-Telegram*, *Jerusalem Report* and the *Detroit Free Press* where he had a mystery column for almost a decade. He also hosted his own public radio book show and currently reviews for bibliobuffet.com. He can be found on the web at http://www.levraphael.com.

9 781590 212042